A Very Au

About the Stories

v me. 4·13

Her Christmas Gift

Elizabeth Bennet finds herself snowbound at Rosings with two rejected, but highly eligible, suitors. Does either man have a chance? Will her childhood friend, Meryton's golden boy, win her affection, or will she accept the master of Pemberley? Perhaps she will refuse them both a second time. *Her Christmas Gift* deftly combines tension and emotion with humor and romance.

The Matchmaker's Christmas

It's raining; it's pouring – and what could be better than a little Christmas matchmaking? So says Emma Woodhouse who is unexpectedly stranded at Netherfield Park. Mr. Darcy disagrees, for she has someone else in mind for adorable Elizabeth Bennet. Amid meddling, misunderstanding, and an unwelcome proposal or two, will True Love find a way?

No Better Gift

On his way to Derbyshire to spend Christmas with his family, Mr. Fitzwilliam Darcy plans to retrieve an item he left behind during his rushed escape from Netherfield—and the country miss who touched his heart. Finding Meryton practically deserted, he fears the worst. What fate could have fallen upon this once-thriving village in only three weeks? More importantly, was Miss Elizabeth Bennet in danger?

Mistletoe at Thornton Lacey

When Edmund Bertram realizes that Fanny is the perfect wife for him, he wants to propose without delay. What better time than at Christmas? Ah, but the course of true love never does run smooth ...

A Very Austen Christmas

HER CHRISTMAS GIFT

THE MATCHMAKER'S CHRISTMAS

NO BETTER GIFT

MISTLETOE AT THORNTON LACEY

A Very Austen Christmas

ISBN-13: 978-1979275026

ISBN-10: 1979275025

Cover design by Damonza
Formatting by Wendi Sotis and Robin Helm

HER CHRISTMAS GIFT

Robin M. Helm

HER CHRISTMAS GIFT

Editing suggestions by Gayle Mills and Wendi Sotis.

Chapter One

Elizabeth glanced out the window of the coach, remembering the first and only time she had made the long journey to Kent, nearly nine months before. *Last March, all these gardens were in flower and the trees were clothed in various shades of green. It was so beautiful.*

The second week of December, however, displayed a severely altered landscape.

My heart is changed as well, and not for the better. In fact, I fear it is broken beyond repair.

The lady shivered in the cold. She sighed and stared at her gloved hands folded primly in her lap.

Feeling a soft touch on her arm, Elizabeth looked up to see her young friend gazing at her with open curiosity.

I must remember people are watching me. I should not burden them with my despondent mood.

"Yes, Maria?"

Maria's blue eyes were filled with concern. "Are you unwell? You seem to be in low spirits. I thought you would be eager to see my sister again."

Elizabeth forced a smile, patting her companion's hand. "I am most content, dear, for I long to see our dear Charlotte."

And very pleased to be away from Longbourn for Christmas, she thought. Listening to her mother's constant laments regarding her unmarried state was not conducive to a peaceful mind.

Elizabeth, the second eldest of the five Bennet sisters, had refused marriage proposals from more than one eligible bachelor in the past year, and her obstinance regarding the issue had driven Mrs. Bennet to distraction. Fortunately, the eldest daughter, Jane, had married the previous day, giving Elizabeth a short reprieve.

Very short.

Nearly as soon as the marriage breakfast had ended and Jane was on her way to London with her handsome Mr. Bingley, Mrs. Bennet turned on her once more, berating her for her failure to secure a comfortable life for them all by marrying.

Had her mother known of a third gentleman's offer for her hand during her previous visit to Kent, Elizabeth would never have known a moment's peace. Her life, already quite bleak without her dearest Jane, would have been considerably worse.

Yes, she was most pleased to be on her way to the comfortable parsonage abutting the grand estate of Rosings Park, even if she would again be obliged to see one of her rejected suitors – Charlotte's husband and her own cousin, the proud parson of Hunsford, Mr. William Collins.

The thought that she might be of assistance to her friend gave her a purpose which far outweighed her discomfort at seeing her cousin, and she dearly needed to be useful.

It was her fond wish that in travelling fifty miles from her home to help Charlotte through the last month before the arrival of her baby, she would find a measure of comfort.

The time had come to accept her error in judgment and create a meaningful life for herself, for her blind prejudice had led her to refuse the only man who could have made her happy in matrimony. When that gentleman and Mr. Bingley had visited Longbourn in September, he had quit Hertfordshire within a few days and not returned until his friend's wedding, leaving again immediately after the wedding breakfast.

She sighed quietly as she remembered, recalling his solemn, handsome face at Longbourn's dinner table.

He barely spoke to me, though we sat side by side when the gentlemen dined with us. How he must despise me now, especially since the unfortunate episode with Lydia. I wish I had never confided in him at Pemberley. How he must congratulate himself on his escape, for who would want to sully his family name with such a scandal? I cannot blame him for seeking to protect his sister from an association of that sort.

Elizabeth shook her head, her heart wrenching within her. She had made up her mind. Her course was decided. He would not offer again, and she would marry no other.

Squaring her jaw, she turned her face to gaze at the scenery.

I must learn to be of use, she thought, *for one day soon I shall have to earn my living.*

~~oo~~

Elizabeth was pleased to see a radiant Charlotte waiting for them when they pulled up at the door. As a footman unloaded their luggage, she and Maria followed the lady of the house into the parsonage hallway where a maidservant waited to help them out of their pelisses and bonnets.

"It is so good to see you both," said Charlotte, smiling broadly. "Betsy will take your things. I have put you in the same rooms you occupied on your last visit. Come into the house. I have ordered tea with your favourite sandwiches, Lizzy, and there are biscuits for you, Maria."

Elizabeth embraced her friend. "You look well. I am pleased to see you in such blooming good health."

Charlotte placed her hand on her stomach. "I anticipate greeting our child in a month or so. With you and Maria here, the time will pass much more pleasantly."

She led them to the parlour and served tea before continuing the conversation.

After taking a sip, Charlotte groaned quietly.

Elizabeth leaned forward. "Are you in pain?"

She grimaced. "No, my dear. However, I am uncomfortable. My feet are beginning to swell. Tomorrow, if you are in agreement, I should like to visit Rosings. Soon, I shall be unable to go anywhere, and I would like a visit with Lady Catherine and Miss de Bourgh before my confinement. They have been most solicitous of me, and when I told them you were coming to Hunsford, they were quite anxious to reacquaint themselves with you and Maria."

Though Elizabeth rather doubted that Lady Catherine would wish to visit with her, she kept her thoughts to herself. She had visited Rosings several times during her visit in March, and the lady had glared at her on more than one occasion.

I must try not to be so outspoken.

Elizabeth nodded her acceptance of the plan. She would do whatever Charlotte wished. "I seem to remember your writing to me that Lady Catherine had been ill. Is she well now?"

"She is better than she was in October, though she has never fully recovered the vigour she enjoyed previously. Lady Catherine is almost entirely housebound now. Very sad in such an active person. I cannot remember whether or not I told you of her plan to visit Hertfordshire on her way to London."

Elizabeth raised her eyebrows. "No, I never heard of anything like that. Why would she visit Hertfordshire?"

"Mr. Collins told Lady Catherine of Jane's engagement to Mr. Bingley, and she wished to convey her congratulations in person. She was quite adamant about it."

Elizabeth remembered a letter her father had received from Mr. Collins around that time, congratulating him on Jane's betrothal and hinting at a coming engagement between her and Mr. Darcy, Lady Catherine's nephew.

She had put no stock in it, for she never thought the gentleman would renew his addresses to her. Her father had been most amused, but Elizabeth could take no joy in it. Perhaps Lady Catherine had believed the tale and wished to come in person to forbid it?

"I am all astonishment. I cannot imagine that she would travel so far for a person she has never before met."

Charlotte smiled. "Lady Catherine has never met Jane, but she is acquainted with you, and you are both cousins to her parson. She was on her way to London to meet the Darcys, and Hertfordshire is between here and London. She did not mean to stay – only to stop at Longbourn to offer her best wishes, though I thought at the time she did not seem very pleased at the news of Jane's engagement. It is of no import, for she was not able to make the trip as the pain came upon her quite suddenly."

Elizabeth knit her brows. "The pain?"

"Yes, my dear. She was wholly incapacitated by some malady in her chest. Her physician came all the way from London, as the local apothecary feared it was beyond his capabilities."

"And what did the physician say?"

"Mr. Hough said it was a problem with her heart and told her to rest. He also adjusted her diet somewhat, though she said quite plainly that his suggestions were balderdash. She still eats whatever she likes."

Elizabeth smiled. "Yes, that sounds just like her."

Charlotte laughed and nodded.

It was agreed to everyone's satisfaction that the party would call on Lady Catherine the following morning, and with that settled, the few hours remaining in the day were spent most pleasantly.

Chapter Two

Elizabeth carefully assumed a pleasant expression as she, Mrs. Collins, and Maria curtseyed before Lady Catherine de Bourgh, her daughter Anne, and Mrs. Jenkinson, Anne's companion.

There was a reason for her forced smile.

Lady Catherine had been most put out with Elizabeth during her previous visit to Kent, for the young lady had insisted upon returning to Hertfordshire, though Lady Catherine had expressed a wish for her to stay.

Her ladyship was not one to suffer in silence.

Lady Catherine narrowed her eyes and raised her eyebrows in a show of displeasure as she looked at the assembled party.

Her imperious tones resonated through the room. "Where is Mr. Collins? I specifically asked him to come with you, Mrs. Collins. You should not be without your husband when you visit in your – delicate condition. Why, you might require his assistance in walking or climbing stairs. He should be more considerate of you. Your health is of paramount importance. I am quite put out. I shall speak to him concerning this breach of manners."

Elizabeth lowered her eyes, struggling to keep a cheerful attitude. *I must remember she has been quite ill. It would not do to upset her and risk throwing her into another episode.*

The grand lady gestured towards the chairs, and the visitors took their seats.

Charlotte smiled. "Thank you for your solicitude, your ladyship, but Mr. Collins remains at the parsonage this morning. He was feeling unwell and was forced to retire to his room. My husband sends his most sincere apologies and bade me to assure you he will come as soon as he feels there is no possibility of contagion. In fact, he sent his man to inform me rather than telling me himself, for he would not chance being in my presence if there were any possibility he is truly ill."

Lady Catherine's expression thawed a bit, and she moderated her voice.

"Well, I suppose he should have stayed away if that be the case. His actions display a very correct concern for the well-being of the inhabitants of Rosings Park, though it is most inconvenient."

The grand lady nodded sagely before continuing her soliloquy. "Perhaps he can send me his sermon notes this week rather than come to go over them with me himself. Yes, that will do very well."

She resumed her glare, focusing on Elizabeth. "Miss Elizabeth Bennet, I was told that your sister was most advantageously married to a close friend of my nephew just a few days past. At first, I thought it must be a scandalous falsehood, but then I remembered the degree of acquaintance between you and both my nephews here last Easter. How amazed I was to see them dancing attendance on you as you played the piano so badly. It seems that you and your sister must be equals in using your arts and allurements to draw men in. In fact, when I first heard of your sister's planned union, I intended to travel to Hertfordshire and confront you myself, but it was not to be."

Elizabeth raised her eyebrows. *My arts and allurements?* "Yes, your ladyship, my sister married Mr. Bingley two days ago, though I cannot fathom your objection to the match. I beg your pardon, but I must ask why you would travel so far to confront me when it had nothing to do with you?"

Lady Catherine narrowed her eyes. "Some part of the news had a great deal to do with a close relative of mine; therefore, it was my express concern. I was also told that you, Miss Elizabeth Bennet, would, in all likelihood, be soon afterwards united to my nephew, Mr. Darcy. I determined to make my sentiments known to you and have such an alarming report universally contradicted with all haste."

Elizabeth tilted her head, feeling the blush on her cheeks. *I must speak with moderation. She has been seriously unwell.* "Your coming so far to deny the rumour, if indeed it exists, would not have served your purpose well, your ladyship, for your visit would have been seen as a confirmation of the report."

The elder lady's voice rose. "My character has ever been celebrated for its sincerity and frankness. I shall certainly not depart from it. I would know this. Has my nephew made you an offer of marriage?"

The young lady raised her chin, fighting to keep her voice from betraying her agitation.

"I do not pretend to possess equal frankness with your ladyship. You may ask questions which I shall choose not to answer."

Lady Catherine leaned toward her, eyes flashing. "This is not to be bourne! I insist on being satisfied. He has been engaged to *my* daughter from their infancy. Had you not heard me say it myself? Did you not know that it was the favourite wish of his mother, as well as of hers?"

Elizabeth nodded, struggling against her emotions. "Yes, but what is that to me? I shall certainly not be kept from marrying your nephew simply by knowing that his mother and aunt wished him to marry his cousin. Indeed, does your daughter not have any say in the matter either?"

Miss de Bourgh cleared her throat, fluttering her delicate hands. "Mama, I – "

Lady Catherine stood to her feet, her colour rising, glaring at her guest. She grasped her left arm as she ranted. "Obstinate, headstrong girl! I am ashamed of you! I have not been in the habit of brooking disappointment. Is this to be endured? It shall not be. If you were sensible of your own good, you would not wish to quit the sphere in which you have been brought up."

Outrageous!

Elizabeth rose from her chair, facing the lady, her words clipped. "In marrying your nephew, I should not consider myself as quitting that sphere. He is a gentleman; I am a gentleman's daughter. So far we are equal."

The elder lady's pitch rose higher still as her face reddened alarmingly. "But who was your mother? Who are your aunts and uncles? I am no stranger to your youngest sister's infamous elopement. I know it all! Are the shades of Pemberley to be thus polluted?"

Elizabeth lowered her head as she held back tears. *Poor Lydia. My foolish, thoughtless sister. She will pay for that error in judgment all her life, and all of us will continue to suffer by association with her. The scandal she caused was the end to Mr. Darcy's addresses to me, though he was kind enough to help our family. I have never had an opportunity to thank him properly. He flees at the very sight of me.*

Her heart broke again.

She looked up and turned to leave. Her voice held a note of flat finality. "You can now have nothing further to say. You have insulted me by every possible method. I must beg to return to the parsonage."

Her ladyship was highly incensed. She gripped the handle of her walking stick with both hands, leaning on it with her full weight.

"You have no regard, then, for the honour and credit of my nephew! Unfeeling, selfish girl! Do you not consider that a connection with you must disgrace him in the eyes of everybody? You – are resolved – to have him – and make him – the contempt – of the world."

Elizabeth whirled back to face the lady, her agitation clear, her control in tatters. "I have said nothing of the sort. I am only resolved to act in that manner which will constitute my happiness, without reference to you, or to any other person so wholly connected with me."

Lady Catherine's face contorted in pain as she dropped her walking stick, grasped her chest with both hands, and dropped heavily into her chair, eyes shut tightly.

Faith! What have I done?

Utter confusion followed, as Elizabeth quickly ran to kneel before her, holding her cold, unconscious form in the chair.

My fault. All my fault. I should have held my tongue. What if I have killed her with my temper?

The ladies of Rosings Park rose from their chairs, wringing their hands and sobbing. Maria looked as if she might be ill.

Charlotte called for the footmen. "Send for Mr. Sims posthaste. There must be no delay. Bring him here immediately."

~~oo~~

Mr. Sims, the apothecary, entered the parlour at a run and conducted a hurried examination of Lady Catherine. He then directed the footmen to fetch the litter he had left at Rosings when she had suffered her earlier illness.

Before half an hour had passed, the lady was in her bed, as comfortable as it was possible to make her. She had not yet fully awakened, and her skin was cold and clammy, though she sweated profusely.

Elizabeth and Charlotte stood by her bed with Mr. Sims and Miss de Bourgh.

Anne de Bourgh grasped her hands together tightly as she looked at Mr. Sims. "How is she?"

His eyes were solemn. "I fear she has suffered another episode with her heart. The next several hours are crucial, so I will remain here by her side."

Charlotte nodded. "I shall collect Maria from the parlour, and Elizabeth and I will return to the parsonage with her. If you have need of us, do not hesitate to send word, Miss de Bourgh."

Mr. Sims shook his head. "No, Mrs. Collins. You and your party must remain here. I have just come from the parsonage, and your husband appears to have scarlet fever. I understand he has been out in the wind very often of late, working in his garden through all types of weather, and I believe that may be the cause of his illness."

"If the wind is the cause of my husband's disease, I cannot understand why we are not allowed to return home. I should be there to care for him."

The apothecary sighed. "I must be entirely honest. While the prevailing opinion holds that scarlet fever is caused by intemperate weather, I have also read the work of Mr. Plenciz. He postulated that the disease is caused by animalcules. He believed that scarlet fever is as contagious as mumps or measles. We must not take that chance with you and your infant."

Elizabeth spoke quickly. "Then I shall return to the parsonage to do what I can."

Mr. Sims looked at her with kindness. "While I appreciate your willingness to expose yourself to the parson's illness, I must caution you against it. You are here to care for Mrs. Collins upon the birth of her child, I understand."

Elizabeth nodded.

The apothecary continued. "You shall not be of much use to her if you contract scarlet fever yourself, my dear. Both you and Mrs. Collins's sister must remain here at Rosings with her. I do not wish for her to help lift or turn her ladyship. I think it would be unwise for her to attempt anything so strenuous before her accouchement. As Miss de Bourgh is unsuitable for the sick room, perhaps you and Miss Lucas could help in Lady Catherine's care."

"I very much doubt her ladyship would want me to help her," Elizabeth replied in a low voice, looking at the lady's expressionless face.

I caused this. She was angry with me, and I could not stop myself from replying in kind.

Mr. Sims smiled. "Until she is herself again, she likely will not know who is caring for her. Do you not want to help? You seem a most capable person to me."

I must help her if I can. I must be of use. The guilt is mine; so must the remedy be.

"Will you tell me what I should do?" she asked quietly.

"Most certainly, my dear. I shall be between here and the parsonage quite often, though I must suggest that we send to London for Lady Catherine's physician. He may know more than I about the best treatment for her condition. In the meantime, try to keep her as comfortable as possible."

Charlotte touched his arm. "What of my husband? Who will care for him?"

"I hope you will not think me impertinent, but I have already instructed his manservant and your housekeeper, Mrs. Collins. Perhaps Lady Catherine's physician would condescend to see your husband as a patient, as well. For now, I have already told Mrs. Bailey to pack your trunks, as well as Miss Elizabeth's and Miss Maria's, and bring them here as soon as ever may be. You may be here some weeks. Miss de Bourgh, would you speak with your housekeeper about rooms for the ladies?"

Miss de Bourgh's voice trembled as she spoke. "Of course. There are several empty bedchambers on this hallway, where they may remain close to my mother."

She glanced at each young lady, worry plain on her face. "I so appreciate your willingness to see to my mother."

Elizabeth inclined her head. "It is the least that I can do."

Miss de Bourgh then returned her unhappy gaze to Charlotte. "I shall dispatch a footman to assist in the care of Mr. Collins, if that pleases you."

Charlotte nodded her agreement to the plan, and Miss de Bourgh turned to leave. She paused at the door and looked back. "I must go send an express to London for our doctor and make arrangements for the rooms for you ladies. Please excuse me."

Mr. Sims sat in the chair by the bed. "I shall be with her for several hours. Both of you should have something to eat and settle yourselves in your chambers. Miss Elizabeth, you and Miss Lucas must rest as much as you can. We are facing a long day and a longer night, and neither of you should neglect your own health."

Elizabeth knitted her brows. *It is not yet noon, and this has already been an interminably drawn-out day. If Lady Catherine wakes to see me by her bed, will she be so angry that she suffers another attack and does not survive it?*

Chapter Three

Elizabeth had been sitting by Lady Catherine's bed for several hours, reading Wordsworth's poetry aloud to her. Though the lady had not yet spoken, she appeared to be conscious as she stared at the ceiling.

The sun was just dipping below the horizon, and the room was in shadows, for the maid had not yet come to light the lamps.

Hearing a slight sound, Elizabeth glanced at her charge and noticed her eyes moving, turning in her direction. The young woman laid the book on the table by her chair, stood, and walked to the side of the bed.

"Lady Catherine, can you hear me?" Her voice was soft and melodic.

The lady focused her alarmed eyes on Elizabeth's face.

I see fear of her condition, but no anger towards me.

"Ah, very good. You do hear me. Your ladyship, you have suffered an illness, and you are in your own room at Rosings. Mr. Sims has been to see you and stayed most of the day. Miss de Bourgh sent for your doctor in London. We hope he shall be here by the morning."

I would apologize for my temper, but if she has forgotten it, I would not wish to remind her.

Lady Catherine blinked her eyes. She cleared her throat and moved a hand towards Elizabeth.

"Things I – must do. Help me."

The lady tried to raise her head, but gave up after one attempt. "Fatigued."

She is frustrated. I would not have her work herself into a fit.

"Is there something you require, your ladyship? Do not distress yourself by trying to rise. Simply tell me what you want, and I shall get it for you."

The lady simply looked at her.

"Are you thirsty?"

"No."

"Would you like for me to read to you?"

"No."

"Shall I bathe your face with cool water?"

"No."

"Is there someone you wish to see?"

"Yes. I – wish – to – see ..." She stopped.

"Mr. Sims?"

Lady Catherine knit her brows in apparent frustration. She took a breath and spoke slowly. "No. Soon enough."

"Miss de Bourgh?"

"Yes. Summon her. Now."

Elizabeth smiled. "I shall have her fetched immediately, your ladyship."

She stepped to the door and opened it, addressing the maidservant who was seated by the door.

"Her ladyship wishes to speak with her daughter. Please bring her here immediately."

The maid nodded and hurried away.

~~oo~~

When Miss de Bourgh arrived at her mother's bedchamber, Elizabeth hurried to the door and stepped into the hall with her. Once there with the door closed, Elizabeth quickly informed her of her mother's progress, but cautioned her not to expect her mother to be her normal self. After Miss de Bourgh nodded her understanding, the two young women returned to the invalid's bedchamber and stood by her bed.

Elizabeth spoke first. "Lady Catherine, Miss de Bourgh is here."

The lady shifted her gaze to her daughter.

"Anne."

Elizabeth continued. "Shall I stay with you, your ladyship?"

The answer was swift. "No. Leave. Shut the door."

Miss de Bourgh looked at Elizabeth, pleading with her eyes. "Do not go far."

"I shan't. I shall just go below to see to Charlotte, and then return. Your mother wants something, and she does not wish for me to know what it is."

"What shall I do if she needs assistance?"

Elizabeth smiled. "You will be fine, Miss de Bourgh. I shall be back in an hour, and there is a maidservant by the door. Send for me if you require my help."

"Very well. Have a footman direct you to the drawing room. I believe Mrs. Collins and Miss Lucas are there."

~~oo~~

A scant half hour later, Anne de Bourgh rejoined her company, seating herself across from Elizabeth and Charlotte.

Her voice was kind as she leaned towards Elizabeth. "Have you eaten?"

"No, thank you, I have not."

"Oh, my. I am quite useless as a hostess."

She fluttered her hands and called for the butler. "Please inform Mrs. Robinson that we shall dine in the small dining room as soon as possible."

The man bowed slightly and hurried away.

Elizabeth stood. "I must return to Lady Catherine."

Miss de Bourgh shook her head. "My mother has decreed that you will no longer sit with her. I am sorry for her rudeness, Miss Bennet. I am very grateful for your willingness to care for her, but she prefers that Miss Lucas read to her in your stead."

Elizabeth lowered her gaze to her hands and sat down. "I cannot blame her ladyship for feeling that way, though I am most sorry for it."

Maria rose and turned towards the door, but Miss de Bourgh's voice stopped her.

"You will not go now, Miss Lucas. My mother's maid shall read to her while you have your dinner. If Mama insists on being stubborn concerning Miss Elizabeth, she shall have to concede to whatever arrangements I can make, and I will not overburden you. You and Miss Elizabeth are guests here, along with Mrs. Collins."

Maria returned to her seat without a word.

Elizabeth's face betrayed her astonishment. "I must be useful or return to Longbourn."

Miss de Bourgh surveyed her with gravity. "You will be of great use to me and Mrs. Collins. Please do not think of leaving us in this condition."

"Of course, I shall not go if you wish me to stay, but I am more of a burden than a help. Surely her ladyship will relent if I apologize to her for my behaviour. I cannot see my responsibilities shifted to Maria when she already has her share."

The lady took a deep breath, and spoke softly. "My companion and I are both able to read to my mother for an hour or two a day. Mrs. Jenkinson will make a schedule for us. A maidservant can sleep in her room at night, and we shall hire a woman, one of our tenants who is somewhat skilled in nursing, to attend her several times a day. Mrs. Smith does not read, but she is strong and able to lift and turn her."

Mrs. Jenkinson nodded.

Miss de Bourgh continued, quietly but with resolution in her tone. "And when Mama is left alone with a servant from time to time, it shall be no one's fault but her own. If she complains, I shall know how to answer her."

Elizabeth's eyes filled with unshed tears. "Please do not be harsh with her on my account. I would not have you quarrel with your mother. I am far too outspoken."

Miss de Bourgh's eyes flashed though her voice was low. "You speak your mind, true, but so does she. Even knowing how I feel about any understanding she imagines between me and my cousin, she persists in trying to control us. We have told her; however, she will not listen."

"Surely your mother is merely looking out for your best interests. After all, she dearly loves both you and her nephew."

Miss de Bourgh's mouth settled into a firm line. "She dearly loves to interfere, Miss Bennet. He does not wish to marry me, and I do not intend to marry anyone. He and I have talked, and we are in agreement. She cannot force us to marry, after all. We have settled the matter between us."

Elizabeth raised her brows in surprise but was saved from the necessity of reply by the entrance of a footman announcing that dinner was served.

Notwithstanding, she left the room thinking, *There is some of her strong-willed mother in her, after all. She is most certainly not the timid creature I imagined her to be. She simply keeps her thoughts to herself in front of her mother. Perhaps I should follow her example.*

~~oo~~

After dinner, Mr. Sims arrived to see Lady Catherine, and once he had completed his examination, he pronounced her to be doing better than he had expected.

When the apothecary took his leave, Mrs. Smith remained in Lady Catherine's chambers to watch over her through the night.

The ladies parted for their rooms, all citing fatigue from the events of the day.

Elizabeth had not been in her room for more than a few minutes before she heard a soft knock at the door.

She crossed the room to see who it was and was pleased to see her friend, Charlotte.

"Come in, for you are a most welcome sight. We have hardly had a moment to visit since I arrived."

Elizabeth took her hand and led her to the sitting area, settling in a comfortable chair and gesturing to Charlotte to do the same.

"This is a lovely room," said Charlotte, smiling. "I do believe Miss de Bourgh likes you and wishes for you to feel welcome at Rosings."

"I must admit that I have been quite mistaken in my understanding of her. Though her health is not robust, she is not a retiring sort of person. I quite like her. She is not fearful of her mother, and she has decided opinions of her own."

Charlotte smiled. "I thought you might have to change your mind about her. I have seen this side of her before. Did you not think it was interesting that she does not intend to marry?"

Odd that she feels as I do. I will not marry rather than marry a man I do not love. We have more in common than anyone would suspect. "Perhaps, though it does not affect me."

"Mr. Darcy has always looked at you a great deal."

"Charlotte, you must know that much of what Lady Catherine said, though offensive and unfair, was true."

Charlotte tilted her head. "Did you not enjoy your visit to Pemberley?"

"Very much, until I received a distressing letter from Jane."

"Ah, I wondered if you were there when you received the news of Lydia's elopement."

"Mr. Darcy was with me when I read Jane's letter. I was so upset that he insisted on knowing what was wrong, so I confided the whole, sordid business to him."

"And what did he do?"

"He left immediately, and before an hour passed, the Gardiners and I departed for Longbourn."

"I have always wondered how Lydia and Wickham were discovered and made to marry."

Elizabeth looked away. "Aunt Gardiner told me Mr. Darcy found them in London. I imagined he put out a good bit of money to force Wickham into matrimony with my sister."

Charlotte leaned forward to put her hand on Elizabeth's arm. "And why do you think he did that?"

Elizabeth sighed. "He seemed to think it was his fault, though it most certainly was not."

"I think he did it for you."

Elizabeth shook her head. "No, Charlotte. When Mr. Bingley returned to Netherfield in September, Mr. Darcy came with him. My mother sent an invitation for the gentlemen to dine with us, and he sat by my side, hardly uttering a word, never offering a smile. He left very soon after that and did not come back to Hertfordshire until the wedding two days ago. As soon as the ceremony ended, he climbed into his carriage and never looked back."

"Did you never speak to him about his assistance with Lydia's situation?"

She lowered her eyes. "I certainly wished to. I wanted to thank him on behalf of all my family, for they do not know to whom they are indebted. However, the opportunity did not present itself. There was no time when we were alone. In any event, I imagine the subject would have been distasteful to him."

"Perhaps you shall have another chance."

"What do you mean?" Elizabeth asked, looking up at her friend.

"These things have a way of working themselves out, my dear. Friday, the twenty-ninth of November a little more than a year ago, I had no prospects for marriage, and before the day was out, I was engaged. We married in January, and soon we shall have a child. I had no idea of what this past year would hold. You cannot know what is in your future, Lizzy."

She pursed her lips. "I assure you, there is no one out there for me. I have no intentions of marrying." She smiled, though it pained her to do so. "So, I will be an old maid governess. Shall you have me come and teach your ten children to play their instruments very ill?"

Charlotte smiled and rose from her chair. "My little one is jumping about at the prospect. I think I shall go to my chambers. You and I both need to rest, for neither of us knows what tomorrow holds."

Elizabeth walked with her friend to the door, closing it behind her after she left.

I know what it will not hold. I know that I shall start the day alone, and I shall end it in the same state. And every day after that will be the same.

Chapter Four

Elizabeth rose with the sun the following day, as was her habit. She dressed quickly and left the house for her usual morning walk, looking forward to enjoying the brisk air.

After half an hour of wandering, she looked at the sky and decided to return to Rosings.

I think we might have snow for Christmas, if those clouds are any indication. I hope Lady Catherine's doctor arrives soon, for I would not wish him to be stranded.

She hastened her steps.

The first flakes were drifting down as she arrived at the front door of the manse, shivering.

Charlotte met her at the door, wringing her hands, waiting as a maid helped Elizabeth out of her coat and bonnet.

"Lizzy, where have you been? I cannot believe you left the house alone in this weather. I have been so worried about you."

"Why would you worry? You know I must have some time outside, dear, but I am not foolish. As soon as I noticed the gathering snow clouds, I turned back towards Rosings. You should not worry on my account, as you well know I can take care of myself."

Charlotte shook her head. "You must not do this while we are all so concerned with Lady Catherine. I thought you might have fallen and were lying somewhere, unable to make your way back."

Elizabeth took her friend's hands between hers. "I promise to let you know before I go for a walk from now on. If it will make you more comfortable, a stable boy can accompany me. Am I forgiven?"

The lady smiled. "Yes, of course. Come. Maria is in the breakfast room and would have us join her."

"Excellent idea. I am famished after my exercise, and the meals here never disappoint."

~~oo~~

Once they were seated and served, Elizabeth turned to Charlotte. "Has the doctor arrived from London?"

"No, but the housekeeper said Miss de Bourgh had an express this morning. He informed her he would be here by noon."

Elizabeth frowned. "By then, the roads may be impassable."

"I thought the same, but Mrs. Robinson assured me that the roads between here and London are excellent. She said 'tis very unlikely that the snow will be so deep a good carriage cannot travel. It would be different if he were coming during the darkness, but he planned to start out last night and should be in daylight most of the time."

"You probably have the right of it. The snow just started falling, after all, and it may not be more than a few inches. We have no way of knowing."

Maria glanced between the ladies. "I heard Mrs. Robinson call the doctor Mr. Jones. I wonder if he could be related to our own Mr. Jones in Meryton?"

Elizabeth coloured. "I think Mr. Thomas Jones, the son of our apothecary, is a physician in London, but I have no idea whether or not Lady Catherine's physician is our Mr. Thomas Jones."

Surely, they are not the same man. If they are, I absolutely must return to Longbourn.

Charlotte observed her Elizabeth with interest, her eyes sparkling. "Would it not be wonderful if it were your Thomas, Lizzy? You and he were inseparable as children. Quite the best of friends, even though he was several years older than you were. He had such patience with you. The two of you were forever being caught climbing trees together or hiding from your sisters and his brothers."

Elizabeth stared at her plate. "Yes, I followed him around then, and he was always quite kind about it, but we are both grown up now. He is not *my* Thomas."

Charlotte's lips twitched. "When did you last see him?"

Elizabeth took a deep breath and looked up. "The gentleman is Mr. Jones now, and I saw him this past May. He visited his father in Meryton, so he came to Longbourn."

She forced a light laugh and continued. "We refrained from tree climbing, though it was very tempting."

"Is he married?" Charlotte asked.

Elizabeth blinked before she answered. "He was not married in May, but it is possible that he is now."

"Was he in good looks?"

"Charlotte!"

"Yes, Lizzy, I am quite impertinent. However, I would know, is he handsome?"

Elizabeth made a sound of exasperation. "He was a nice-looking boy, and he has grown into a fine young man. Why are you so interested in Thomas Jones?"

"Do not upset yourself, Lizzy. Thomas was my friend as well as yours, though I never climbed trees with him. I have not seen him in several years, and I wondered how he has turned out."

Elizabeth raised a fine brow. "He is a handsome man. At least six feet tall or perhaps a few inches taller. Blue eyes and fair, wavy hair. Well dressed. He is a man who gives the appearance of having an important, successful profession, and along with all of that, he maintains the demeanour of a gentleman. From what I apprehended, Thomas Jones has done very well for himself. What else would you know?"

Charlotte chuckled. "Did you find him attractive?"

Elizabeth stared at her. "I refuse to answer any more questions concerning Mr. Thomas Jones. You shall soon see him for yourself, if Lady Catherine's physician is the same Thomas Jones we knew growing up."

"How interesting. 'The lady doth protest too much, methinks.'"

"And now you quote Shakespeare in everyday conversation?"

"Do you not remember how we endeavoured to stage The Bard's plays when we were little more than children?"

Elizabeth smiled in spite of herself. "Who could forget you in the role of Queen Gertrude?"

"You were far more memorable than I. After all, you carried the lead very well, indeed."

"You played the part of Hamlet?" Maria's astonishment was evident.

Elizabeth rose, lifted her chin, and extended her hand in a dramatic pose. Her voice was sonorous. "To be, or not to be. That is the question. Whether 'tis nobler in the mind to suffer the slings and arrows of outrageous fortune, or to take arms against a sea of troubles, and by opposing end them.'"

Anne de Bourgh and Mrs. Jenkinson entered the room at that inopportune moment, and Elizabeth reddened as she quickly sat down.

Miss de Bourgh and her companion settled in comfortable chairs.

After a moment, the younger lady fixed her gaze upon Elizabeth. "Pray, do not let us interrupt you. *Hamlet*, I believe?"

Elizabeth swallowed painfully. "I am so sorry, Miss de Bourgh. Please do not think we were making light of the situation."

"I would never think such a thing of you, Mrs. Collins, or Miss Lucas. After all, the next line is, 'To die. To sleep no more.' There is nothing humourous in Prince Hamlet's speech."

Charlotte took up the thread of the conversation. "We were reminiscing about our childhood, Miss de Bourgh. Elizabeth and I were always great friends, and we often compelled our siblings to act out plays with us."

"I had no childhood friends, and my mother would never have allowed me to participate in a play," said Miss de Bourgh quietly.

Elizabeth's voice was gentle and kind. "Our mothers encouraged it in the name of education, and no one outside our families was ever in attendance, except the apothecary's youngest son. Our attempt at staging *Hamlet* was particularly memorable, but Maria was too young at the time. I believe we may have shocked her with the idea just now. I hope we have not offended you."

"Indeed not. I must admit I am rather jealous," replied Miss de Bourgh. "It sounds as if you had very happy times together as children. I was usually solitary. Mrs. Jenkinson was my governess during my entire childhood. She became my companion when I was sixteen."

Elizabeth smiled at her. "You had many cousins, did you not?"

Miss de Bourgh nodded slowly. "I still do, but I have rarely seen any of them more than once or twice a year. They are such a lively group of people, and I never was."

I was hardly ever alone. Though my younger sisters often exasperated me, we always loved one another. We did nearly everything together. How sad it would have been to be the only child with no near neighbours. Though Miss de Bourgh had fortune as well as connections, I believe I was the wealthy one.

~~oo~~

After breakfast, the ladies, with the exception of Elizabeth, took turns sitting with Lady Catherine. Even Charlotte spent a half hour with the lady, after sensibly pointing out that she could call for help if she need it. As the patient slept much of the time, there was no need to read aloud to her. The ladies did needlework or read a favourite book instead.

Elizabeth occupied her time in practicing the piano and perusing the library. She found several books which caught her interest and took them to the parlour to occupy her time until the doctor arrived.

Maria brought her sewing and settled on the settee beside her.

"How was Lady Catherine when you left her?" asked Elizabeth.

"I cannot say. She slept all the time I was with her. Does that mean she is better?"

Elizabeth shrugged. "I have no way of knowing. We can only hope that her sleep is healing, I suppose."

Silence reigned until Charlotte joined them, coming directly from the sickroom.

"Come sit by the window with me, Lizzy. The snow is so beautiful."

Elizabeth moved to be by her friend, watching the steady accumulation of the snow. *Is Thomas caught in this storm somewhere between London and Rosings Park? Is he well? Has he been in a carriage accident? We parted on less than friendly terms. What if I never have another chance to speak with him?*

She shuddered.

Time crawled by, and her apprehension grew.

Surely he should be here by now.

Just before noon, they heard a commotion at the front entrance.

Charlotte and Maria stood to smooth their skirts, but Elizabeth could not wait.

She hurried into the hall to see if it was indeed Thomas, but he was not the first gentleman she saw.

Elizabeth came to a full stop. "Mr. Darcy!"

His surprise matched her own. "Miss Bennet!"

Thomas Jones stepped forward and grasped both of her hands. "Elizabeth! What an unexpected pleasure! 'Tis so good to see you again. I have missed you most dreadfully."

She blushed crimson. "Thomas! You are Lady Catherine's physician?"

How shall I extract my hands from his without being rude?

"I am Mr. Darcy's physician and a partner to Lady Catherine's. Mr. Hough was unable to come, for he is ill, so Mr. Darcy brought me in his place," he replied, dropping her hands and stepping back to look at her.

He smiled. "You are even lovelier than when I saw you last May. I have been meaning to return to Longbourn to speak with you again. Had I known you were here, I would have insisted the coachman drive faster."

Speak with me again? So, he is no longer angry with me. She blanched. *Does he mean to renew his addresses?*

Darcy, meanwhile, had divested himself of his coat and hat. He turned to face her.

"Miss Bennet, please forgive me for not greeting you properly just now."

He extended his hand, and she took it. Without smiling, Darcy bowed his head in acknowledgement, then released her.

Elizabeth's heart sank. *'Tis as if he hardly knows me.*

Thomas watched them speculatively. "You are acquainted?"

She nodded. "We met several times in Meryton, at Netherfield, and again this past summer when my Aunt and Uncle Gardiner and I visited Pemberley. A few days ago, Jane married Mr. Bingley, Mr. Darcy's friend, who let Netherfield. He stood up for his friend, and I for my sister."

I am babbling. It seems I have been overtaken by Lydia's predilection. Silent. I will be silent. He that refraineth his lips is wise.

Darcy's expression was solemn. "I had no idea you were so well known to my physician, Miss Bennet."

She swallowed, choosing her words before she spoke. "Thomas's father is the Meryton apothecary. He and I are of an age, Mr. Darcy. We played together as children."

Thomas smiled, his eyes never leaving her face. "We were always very close, even though she is four years younger than I. Elizabeth taught me to dance. In fact, I was privileged to be the first man with whom she ever danced at an Assembly. That was six years ago when she was but fifteen, and I fear her toes have likely not yet recovered from the experience."

Anne de Bourgh spoke from behind Elizabeth. "How very interesting. And detailed. Since my mother is resting comfortably, shall we all go into the small dining room to continue the conversation where it is warm? You gentlemen must be cold and hungry, so I directed Mrs. Robinson to have a hot meal served before you go to your chambers and then to my mother's rooms. I ordered your favourite soup, Fitzwilliam, and a roaring fire awaits us. Mrs. Collins, Miss Lucas, and Mrs. Jenkinson are already there."

She turned immediately and led the party from the hall.

Elizabeth followed her without hesitation, pleased that Miss de Bourgh put the comfort of her guests above the established protocol.

To her surprise, she found a gentleman on either side of her.

Each man offered her the crook of his arm, and Elizabeth did the only thing she could think of at the moment which would offend neither gentleman. She gave one her right hand and the other her left.

Mama would be quite pleased.

It was not altogether unpleasant.

Chapter Five

Without quite understanding how it had been arranged, Elizabeth found herself seated between the two gentlemen, across from Charlotte who smiled at her entirely too much, and Maria who kept her eyes lowered. Mrs. Jenkinson sat beside Maria.

Miss de Bourgh took her rightful place at the head of the table with Darcy to her right.

Elizabeth found herself at an uncomfortably quiet table full of people. The pointed glances and sounds of soup being sipped were far too obvious for her lively disposition to bear.

This will not do.

She took it upon herself to begin a conversation.

"Thomas, how came you to arrive with Mr. Darcy?"

The young doctor gave her his most handsome, confident smile.

Unfair! He is well aware I like his dimples. I wonder if he realizes he did not use them to his best advantage last May? A smiling gentleman is so much more appealing than an angry one. Nonetheless, I am not inclined to change my mind.

"Mr. Darcy sent a note to me at my office last evening requesting my presence here at Rosings. I was happy to oblige him and come to care for Lady Catherine since Mr. Hough was quite ill and in no condition to travel. When I agreed, he very generously suggested that we travel together rather than bring two carriages."

Thomas chuckled. "As you must know, his carriage is far superior to mine. Consequently, I was delighted to accept his magnanimous offer."

Elizabeth, puzzled, turned to Mr. Darcy. "I understood that an express was being sent to Lady Catherine's physician. How did you come to know of her illness?"

Miss de Bourgh quickly replied in his stead. "There is no mystery. I sent an express to Fitzwilliam at my mother's request. We knew he was staying in London for Christmas, and she wished to see him, so I charged him with bringing the doctor."

Elizabeth took a spoonful of her soup as she gathered her thoughts. *Lady Catherine did not ask for Colonel Fitzwilliam, though he is also her nephew. In fact, she did not wish to see any of her numerous relatives except Mr. Darcy. I think the lady has a scheme in mind, and I would wager I know what it is, for she is not the sort to allow a crisis to go unused. It would be wasteful.*

A small noise of mirth escaped her, and she looked up to see Darcy's intelligent green eyes regarding her as if he could read her mind. His lips looked as if he fought amusement, and he brought his napkin to his mouth.

She felt the heat rise up her neck. *Is he hiding a smile? I cannot remember ever seeing him wearing that particular expression. In fact, I do not recall ever seeing him smile before, and I find that I am quite eager to observe him thus.*

"My cousin did not tell me she had company," he said, lifting his glass. *Would you have come if she had?*

Elizabeth looked at him, careful to keep her expression guarded. "Charlotte, Maria, and I are not guests, strictly speaking. We were visiting Rosings when Lady Catherine became ill. Mr. Collins now suffers from scarlet fever; therefore, Mr. Sims, the apothecary, would not allow us to return to the parsonage."

I am responsible for your aunt's attack. 'Tis my fault she nearly died.

She dropped her gaze to her plate.

Miss de Bourgh's gentle voice cut into her thoughts. "You are most certainly my guests, and I am extremely happy to have you here. Though my mother is much better now, last night I did not think she would survive. Having you, Mrs. Collins, and Miss Lucas here was a source of great solace for me. I knew that I could ask anything of you, and it would be done."

Elizabeth lifted her head. "You sound quite encouraged. I am glad to hear it."

Charlotte smiled. "Mr. Sims came early this morning while you were walking. I was so upset thinking you might be injured and in a snowbank somewhere that I entirely forgot to tell you. Lady Catherine is greatly improved; Mr. Sims feels she will live, though she may be bedridden."

Both gentlemen turned their attention to Elizabeth, and she stole a quick glance at each. Neither was happy. In fact, one seemed overly concerned while the other appeared to be fighting his temper.

The physician's ire gained the upper hand.

"Elizabeth! How like you to tramp about the woods in a snow storm. You could have frozen to death. What do you mean?"

He makes me feel like a child.

"Thomas, I had no idea it was going to snow, and I do not tramp. I walk briskly. As soon as I saw the gathering clouds, I returned to the house. Pray, refrain from scolding me in company. You are neither my father nor my brother."

She heard a low voice from her right.

"Miss Bennet, I feel certain that Mr. Jones is merely worried for your welfare. To confess it myself, I am also apprehensive. I know that you enjoy your morning walks, but I had no idea you continued the practice in the dead of winter. Could you, perhaps, walk the long halls of Rosings instead?"

"I so enjoy taking my exercise in the outdoors." She clasped her hands in her lap. "When I stay inside too long, I do not feel well. My walks soothe my mind."

He put his spoon on the edge of his bowl, and the motion attracted her attention. The expression of unease in his eyes held her.

"My aunt's estate boasts the largest orangeries and botanical gardens in the south of England. Indeed, the structures rival those of Chatsworth and Versailles. Could you not walk in those instead? They are quite beautiful."

Her eyes lit with delight. "I had no idea."

Miss de Bourgh's amiable voice broke into the conversation. "I am not at all surprised, for the buildings are behind the house, and you have never been shown those grounds. If you would enjoy it, I can send a footman to lead you there while the gentlemen are occupied with my mother."

"I would very much appreciate it."

Mr. Darcy cleared his throat. "As it was my idea, and I feel certain you would not mind, Cousin, I would prefer that Miss Bennet wait and allow me to guide her through the gardens after I visit my aunt. The design is quite large and varied. It is my favourite thing about Rosings Park; 'tis even more beautiful than the grounds in spring."

"What a capital idea," said Mr. Jones. "I will join you, if you do not mind, for I am most curious about the medicinal properties of plants. I should be glad of the opportunity to learn from an enthusiast."

"I do not profess to know a great deal concerning the essence of plants in that regard," replied Mr. Darcy, "though I have studied the varieties of flowers, shrubs, vegetables, and herbs in an effort to improve the yields, as well as the beauty, of my estate. I believe that most of creation can be useful as well as ornamental, and there is something peaceful in meditating upon what is both lovely and constructive. If you wish to be enlightened concerning the uses of the plants to your profession, perhaps the head gardener would be a better guide for you than I."

He retrieved his spoon and turned back to his soup.

Thomas smiled. "I am certain you are an exemplary docent in whatever you study, Mr. Darcy. I think it would be advantageous to hear your thoughts in addition to those of the head gardener."

"Then, by all means, join us." Darcy's voice was flat, without its earlier hint of excitement.

The atmosphere in the room grew decidedly chilly.

This is more awkward than the earlier silence. I suppose the burden of congenial conversation falls to me.

"Mr. Darcy, I am most curious and would learn more. Upon what lovely, constructive things do you ponder to bring yourself to a peaceful state?"

He turned his face deliberately to hers, as if in challenge, green eyes sparkling with intelligence and a hint of mischief.

"For the past year or so, from time to time my mind has been agreeably engaged in reflecting on the very great pleasure which a pair of fine eyes in the face of a pretty woman can bestow. Such musings formerly made me uneasy, but now I find the opposite is true."

Then he smiled at her, and the world fell away.

Her mind went completely blank.

Charlotte's chuckle broke through Elizabeth's reverie, jolting her back to the present.

"May one inquire as to the owner of the eyes?" asked Charlotte.

The room was hushed for a moment, then Thomas's voice broke the silence.

"Mr. Darcy was likely not referring to a specific lady, Mrs. Collins, for to make such a declaration in a public setting would not be entirely proper."

Darcy stared at his plate. "And heaven knows, I am nothing if not entirely proper."

Miss de Bourgh sighed, her eyes fixed on the far wall. "Oh, yes. Both of us are always conventional, orthodox, and acceptable in every aspect of our lives."

She glanced around the table before she continued. "Is there any doubt that our family embodies all that is correct? Shall we then agree that Fitzwilliam has been enjoying a variety of fine eyes in the faces of several lovely women? Or would that make him a rake? How many women is a proper gentleman allowed to admire? What number is neither too small nor too large?"

Elizabeth's mouth fell open. She quickly recovered and closed it.

Within a moment, her smile was back in place. "I think a proper gentleman may admire as many women as he pleases until he is wed."

Thomas laughed. "You cannot mean it. I well know that you do not esteem men who ogle ladies. Are they not rakes? Have you not said so yourself more than once?"

She tilted her head. "So long as a man does not act on the admiration, he cannot be justly accused of being a rake. I have known Mr. Darcy more than a year and have observed his behaviour in varied circumstances, and I have no doubt that he has always acted honourably. Additionally, I have never observed him ogling anyone. He is inordinately discrete."

Darcy's tone was dry. "While I thank you for your spirited defense of my character, Miss Bennet, I think I would prefer a change of subject. I have never sought the notoriety that comes with being scrutinized by my acquaintances, friends, and relations. It is inevitable, I suppose, but perhaps it would be better to engage in the exercise when I am absent."

She bowed her head. "Pardon me, sir. You are, of course, correct. Please accept my apologies, for I meant no harm. My mother has often lamented that I have been allowed far too much latitude in the things I say."

Miss de Bourgh gestured to the butler to bring the next course. "Of course, you were being flippant, my dear. That much was obvious. Pray, do not distress yourself. There has been such a lack of merriment around this table as to make us unable to recognize benign humour."

Elizabeth was amazed to feel a light touch on her wrist, not visible to the rest of the party. She lifted her face to the gentleman and saw him shake his head very slightly.

Mr. Darcy appeared to be frustrated. Perhaps sad?

She drew her brows together. *I do not understand.*

As the footmen collected one course and replaced it with another, taking the attention of the rest of the party, he leaned over to speak to her.

She inclined her head towards his. She barely caught his whispered words.

"You are void of reproach. You are completely innocent."

Charlotte cleared her throat. She looked pointedly first at Elizabeth, and then at Thomas.

Elizabeth followed her friend's gaze and saw that he was watching them, much interested in what Mr. Darcy was saying to her.

She sat up straight and took her hand from her lap, using it to lift her glass for a sip of water.

A change of subject is in order.

"I see that it still snows heavily. Will that affect our plans to explore the botanical gardens and orangeries?"

"Not at all, for they connect to the main house and each other. Though the buildings are heated with Franklin stoves, the hallways may be a bit cold, so wear warm clothing."

Mr. Darcy glanced around the table. "Everyone is invited who wishes to go. Mrs. Collins, there are benches scattered throughout if you become fatigued."

She smiled. "I confess I was hoping to see the plants. I have admired the flowers spread throughout the rooms of Rosings at all times of the year, and I wondered how it was possible. Will you come with me, Maria?"

Her sister's face brightened as she nodded with enthusiasm.

"Then you shall all go as soon as Darcy and Mr. Thomas visit my mother," said Miss de Bourgh. "Mrs. Jenkinson and I will sit with her while the rest of you enjoy the outing. I shall send a servant for you, Mr. Thomas, if you are needed.

"We offer little in the way of entertainment here, and I am vastly pleased to give you all a respite from the sickroom."

The remainder of the meal was uneventful, as topics were limited to the weather and the various Christmas customs of the four families represented by the assembled group.

It appeared as if they might have to plan their own holiday festivities, as the snow showed no signs of letting up.

Chapter Six

Elizabeth ascended the stairs to her chambers with the intention of fetching her warmest pelisse before they toured the indoor gardens. She had sewn it herself for Jane's wedding as well as the trip to Kent, and it was beautifully quilted for winter.

As she entered the hallway, the sight of her childhood friend pulled her up short.

Why is Thomas standing in the hallway outside Lady's Catherine's rooms?

He was eavesdropping at the door! He held his finger to his lips when he saw her.

"What are you doing?" she whispered, appalled.

"What do you think I am doing?" he whispered back, raising an eyebrow. "I should think 'tis fairly obvious."

"Listeners never hear any good of themselves."

His blue eyes danced with mischief. "Ah, but Lady Catherine is not upbraiding her nephew concerning *his* relationship with *me*."

Elizabeth's eyes grew round, and Lady Catherine's voice rose enough for her to hear the lady's words clearly, without putting her own ear to the door.

"Fitzwilliam, you must do your duty and marry Anne! I cannot die in peace if you continue to refuse to take your place as master of this estate and secure the future of your cousin as well as yourself. Rosings Park and Pemberley would be joined by your marriage, as they should be. The two of you would be one of the wealthiest couples in all of England."

Darcy's reply was too muffled to understand.

Lady Catherine's volume increased. "If your intention is to marry Elizabeth Bennet, you must reconsider. Somehow, she has drawn you in! How could you even consider a union so far beneath you? How could you forget the claims of honour, family, fortune, connections, and society?"

Elizabeth gasped and put her hand over her mouth.

Again, Darcy's answer to Lady Catherine was unintelligible.

The lady continued to rage. "I have already spoken with her, and her rudeness is the cause of my illness! She told me to my face that she cared not at all for my opinion, and she would marry where she chose. Even when I pressed her, she would not give me her promise she would never marry you. Such a lack of gentility! She does not know her place. The hussy claimed to be equal with you, saying she is a gentleman's daughter and you are a gentleman! She did not recognize that she is beneath our family in every way and cares not how she would be ostracized by all of us. I told her we could not receive her."

Thomas's shoulders shook with suppressed laughter. Elizabeth glared at him. He smirked in return.

Darcy's voice was even quieter.

"And what of the infamous elopement of her youngest sister? Surely you would not align your sister with such people! You cannot put Georgianna in the company of the Bennet family with its wild girls! You must see that! It would be a disgrace! What would your dear mother say? How would your father advise you on this matter? I stand in their place as head of your family. You *will* marry Anne within the week!"

Hearing Darcy's abrupt tones followed by rapid footsteps, Thomas moved away from the door, quickly placing himself a few steps down the hallway.

Elizabeth turned to face her own chamber, reaching for the door knob.

As the door to Lady Catherine's room slammed, Elizabeth looked back.

Darcy's red face and pronounced frown spoke of his anger. He took a deep breath and glanced at Thomas, his expression grim. "My aunt needs your assistance now, I fear. She has worked herself into a state, as you no doubt heard."

The physician nodded and opened the door to the lady's room. Before he closed it again, he smiled and winked at Elizabeth behind Darcy's back.

Darcy quickly inclined his head to her and strode down the hallway to his own chambers.

He will never renew his addresses to me. Lady Catherine has now made certain of it.
The little hope she had gained since his arrival shattered around her.

As tears ran down her face, she went into her room and closed the door.

~~oo~~

Two hours later, a much-subdued Elizabeth heard a knock and went to the door.

"Charlotte. Come in."

Charlotte shook her head. "We must hurry. Come downstairs with me. The party has assembled, and we only await Thomas's return from the parsonage before we go. He has very graciously gone to see to my husband but should be back quite soon."

"I think I shall remain in my rooms. Please give my apologies to everyone."

"Are you ill, my dear?" Charlotte's concern was evident. "This is most unlike you. I have never known you to give up a chance to walk. The flowers should be very beautiful, and I would love to see them; however, I will not go without you."

"I am well," replied Elizabeth.

"Then I shall stay with you."

Unable to think of an excuse good enough to send her friend away without distressing her, Elizabeth relented and forced herself to be cheerful. "Allow me to fetch my pelisse and bonnet. I was going to read, but I can do that this evening."

"Are you certain? For I could sit with you and forego the outing."

"No, I have decided that I would rather walk among the plants. I should like to know the way so I can go there alone whenever I choose."

Charlotte nodded. "I shall get my warmest pelisse and bonnet as well, and we can stop at Maria's room to collect hers."

Elizabeth's mind wandered as they hurried to complete their tasks.

And there is something else I must do, for I may never have another opportunity after today.

~~oo~~

Thomas entered the front door just as Elizabeth and Charlotte reached the bottom of the stairs. He was covered in snow, bundled from head to foot in scarves and a woolen cap. As they waited, he allowed a footman to help him remove the layers that covered him. A second footman stepped forward to help him out of his great coat, cap, and thick gloves.

He adjusted his waist coat and jacket before he hurried to meet the ladies.

Elizabeth noticed his grim expression. "Was Mr. Collins no better?"

"Since it was my first time to examine the gentleman, I have nothing with which to compare his present health."

He avoided her eyes, focusing instead on her eyebrows.

She knew that trick very well, for he always employed it when he wished to dodge the truth.

Charlotte's sharp intake of breath told Elizabeth that she was aware of Thomas's evasion as well.

"Tell me plainly," she said, placing her hands on her burgeoning stomach. "How is my husband?"

Thomas adjusted his cravat. "Not as well as I would like, though I have given instructions to Mr. Sims and your staff which should put him to rights soon enough."

"What sort of instructions?" asked Charlotte.

"They are to burn his clothes and personal belongings, and he is to eat nothing but boiled vegetables and bread. He is to have no animal food, liquor, or anything spicy, but I shall see him again tonight to decide what else is to be done. I may have to purge him, but I do not hold with blood-letting."

Elizabeth looked out the windows, troubled. "But 'tis still snowing. How shall you travel in this weather?"

"The same way I travelled just now. Mr. Darcy had the head groomsman retrieve a sleigh which was stored in the stables. Two fine horses pulled it as a coachman drove, and I was covered in blankets with a footwarmer for my feet. The men were most considerate. Everything possible was done for my safety and comfort."

Elizabeth frowned. "But it will be night soon. Would you not be in danger if you went out in the darkness in this storm? Can you not wait until the morning?"

Thomas took her hand in both of his. "Your concern warms my heart, but it is unfounded. You know the parsonage is not far away, and, as I will be alone in the sleigh, there is plenty of room for two groomsmen to join me and hold lanterns." He blew out a breath. "I fear Mr. Collins will need me more tonight more than he did today."

Charlotte touched his arm. "I so much appreciate this, Thomas, but should you leave Lady Catherine? Perhaps Mr. Sims would stay the night with my husband. You have told him what to do, and he is an able man."

"I shall certainly check on her ladyship before I go, but I think she is out of danger for now. Your husband is in a precarious state."

Elizabeth glimpsed the weariness in the young doctor's eyes. He caught her glance and smiled before he continued.

"Shall we walk an hour in the gardens before I must return to the parsonage? I am in great need of exercise. I confess I returned expressly for that purpose."

Thomas looked down at Elizabeth, uncharacteristically serious as he bent his head towards hers. His voice dropped nearly to a whisper. "Once I leave, I shall not see you again until tomorrow, if then."

Darcy's voice sounded behind the ladies. "I confess I heard all you said. My cousin will order a substantial meal for you to have before you leave Rosings. Vegetables and bread are not enough for you to maintain your own health."

Elizabeth quickly pulled her hand from Thomas's grasp as he straightened himself, sighing.

The physician locked eyes with Darcy. "Mr. Darcy. I did not see you standing there."

Darcy's smile was benign. "I heard a commotion and came to investigate, hoping you had returned with a report on the parson's condition."

The gentleman took a few steps and stopped beside Elizabeth.

"Eavesdropping is discourteous and dishonourable, I know," Darcy continued, looking at Thomas, "but you were not speaking of me. Under those circumstances, and knowing you had just returned from Hunsford parsonage, I thought it better to remain where I was and listen rather than interrupt or have you repeat yourself. Had it been a personal matter, I either would have shown myself or left the area, just as any man of honour would have done."

Elizabeth blushed deeply and lowered her eyes. *He is right. We violated his privacy.*

She turned to Darcy and fixed a smile on her face. "Shall we go tour the gardens before Thomas must leave again?"

Darcy stepped closer to her and offered his arm. "Certainly. We should go immediately so Mr. Jones may enjoy as much of the flora as possible. We are all indebted to him for taking such exemplary care of my aunt and Mr. Collins."

She took his arm, and Thomas escorted Charlotte.

They stopped at the parlour door just long enough for Darcy to speak to Miss de Bough and to collect Miss Lucas before they continued to the back of the house.

~~oo~~

Elizabeth hardly blinked, she was so fascinated with the beauty around her. The snow on the glass sparkled in the late afternoon sun, casting prisms throughout the structure. Though she knew Thomas wanted to walk, she was continually distracted by unexpected delights around every bend in the path.

Darcy remained by her side, answering her multitudes of questions with great patience.

"How did you conceive of such a structure?"

"Very few of my ideas are original, Miss Bennet. I visited Versailles just before Napoleon rose to power. I was astounded, so I studied drawings of the buildings and adapted them. Nôtre and Hardouin-Mansart were geniuses of design and symmetry, and though Rosings is quite limited in space compared to the palace grounds, I sought to incorporate as many of their ideas as possible into the outdoor gardens as well as the orangeries. These glass buildings housing the flowers and fragile plants are based on the construction of the Versailles orangeries, though I added the Franklin stoves myself."

"Truly amazing and wonderful," she murmured.

"There is still much more to do," he continued. "Until the prohibitive glass taxes are lifted, I shall have to be content with improving the existing buildings rather than expanding them. I doubt the work will be finished during my lifetime. After all, the Versailles orangeries have been under construction for more than one hundred fifty years."

Thomas strode up beside them, looking at his pocket watch. "I must leave if I hope to get to the parsonage at a reasonable time." He shut the lid and released the fob. "Please do not feel you must cut short your walk on my account, for I have seen how much you are enjoying yourself, Elizabeth, and it does me good."

She looked up at Mr. Darcy. "Could we not continue our explorations tomorrow after Thomas returns? I should like to dine with him before he sets out for the parsonage."

The gentleman nodded his agreement. "I am at your disposal. Perhaps we should all join Mr. Jones. An early supper in this cold weather would be quite pleasant. At any rate, it is quickly becoming too dark to see well, in spite of the lanterns."

Charlotte and Maria, who had walked behind Elizabeth and Darcy on either side of Thomas, agreed to the plan, and they all made their way back to the house, their order reversed.

Darcy, still escorting Elizabeth, walked a bit more slowly than those in front of them, and shortly they could see their friends in the distance, but could not make out their conversation.

He stopped and turned to her, apparently intending to speak, but she stepped away from him and rushed to say what she had been harbouring in her heart since he had arrived at Rosings.

"Mr. Darcy, I beg you would allow me to say what I must, as I may never have the liberty to do so again. Please accept my thanks for your unexampled kindness to my poor sister. I realize you never intended for anyone to know what you did, but Lydia betrayed that you had been concerned in the matter. I could not rest until I wrote to my aunt and pressed her to tell me everything. Let me thank you on behalf of my entire family, for they know not to whom they are indebted."

"I am exceedingly sorry," he replied with surprise, "that you have been informed of what may, in a mistaken light, have given you uneasiness."

She was breathless, wringing her hands. "Oh, no! Let me thank you again and again for that generous compassion which induced you to take so much trouble and bear so many mortifications for the sake of discovering my sister and Mr. Wickham."

"If you will thank me," he replied gravely, "let it be for yourself alone. I believe I thought only of you at the time."

Her face fell. *And I have ruined it.* "That is very kindhearted, sir, particularly knowing how badly you must think of me. I must apologize for listening to your conversation with your aunt today. I was entirely in the wrong, but I beg your forgiveness. She spoke the truth, and I know we cannot be friends in the face of such obstacles, but please, try to think of me as a person who will always desire the best for you and your family."

She stepped away from him and ran to catch up with the others, wiping the tears from her face. *He must not see me cry.*

He stood in shocked silence for several moments until he realized she had run away.

"Miss Bennet – Elizabeth!"

But she had disappeared from his view.

Chapter Seven

The meal began as a sombre affair.

Everyone sat in the same arrangement as the previous day, but there was no conversation, no liveliness, no smiles or laughter.

Miss de Bough watched Elizabeth from the head of the table. At length, she said, "You seem very out of spirits, Miss Bennet."

"Not at all," she answered, looking with disinterest at her food.

"You have scarce spoken a word, and you have eaten nothing, my dear. Are you ill? If you are, please say so at once, before Mr. Jones removes to the parsonage."

Elizabeth swallowed past the lump in her throat. "I am quite well, thank you."

"Is the meal not to your liking? What would you rather have?" asked Miss de Bourgh.

She picked up her spoon and began to eat her soup. "This is very good. Please, do not trouble yourself or your cook."

Thomas glanced from one lady to the other. "Elizabeth is likely worried for her cousin, Miss de Bourgh. While Mr. Collins is not as well as I would like, I have confidence that he will fully recover within a month."

Another silence ensued.

"Your father's estate is entailed upon Mr. Collins," said Miss de Bourgh. "Is it not so, Miss Bennet?"

Elizabeth glanced at Charlotte and forced herself to smile. "It is, and I could not imagine a better keeper of my childhood home than my friend and her husband, though I hope they will not take possession of Longbourn for a great many years. The death of my father predicates their ownership, and he and I are very close."

"I, too, pray for a long life for your father," Charlotte replied. "I am very fond of him, you know, having spent so much time with your family."

A low, masculine voice spoke from Elizabeth's right. "Mr. Bennet is a great wit. I enjoy sparring verbally with him, though he usually wins the match."

Thomas tilted his head quickly to look at Darcy. "When have you joked with Elizabeth's father? He and I are great friends, as we have been acquaintances all my life, but I had no idea you knew him so well."

Darcy smiled. "I saw Bennet many times when I was in Hertfordshire. I have been a guest in his home on several occasions, and we spent many hours together in London a few months ago. Though I was in Hertfordshire only a short time for my friend Bingley's wedding to Miss Bennet's sister recently, I made certain to converse with him again, for I consider him to be a good friend of mine."

She bit her lower lip. *He called my father 'Bennet.' He views him as a friend and an equal.*

Thomas narrowed his eyes. "And are you fond of Mrs. Bennet as well? I adore her, and she quite dotes on me. I practically grew up at Longbourn, and I make it a point to visit her every time I am in Hertfordshire."

Elizabeth looked from one gentleman to the other. *Whatever are they about?*

Darcy touched his napkin to either side of his mouth before he replied. "Mrs. Bennet and I may have had a difficult beginning, but we understand one another much better now. I believe I have improved her opinion of me, and I very much admire her abilities as a mother and a hostess. When last I saw her at Longbourn, she accepted my compliments very prettily."

Elizabeth raised a brow as she glanced between them. *He must have visited Longbourn while I was gone, for she did not receive him very well in September. When?*

She felt truly buoyant for the first time all day.

Perhaps all is not lost.

~~oo~~

Elizabeth came down the stairs to see Thomas standing in the great hall, allowing the footmen to again swath him in his great coat, scarves, woolen cap, and heavy gloves.

The young physician looked behind him at the sound of her footsteps, and a heart-stopping smile lit his handsome face. He turned to face her, removing his cap and handing it to a servant, then running his hands through his curls.

"I wondered if you would come to bid me *adieu*. Sometimes, I think you forget what you mean to me."

Thomas had grown into a tall, handsome, well-framed gentleman. As the candlelight caught the blond strands of his hair, every angle of his face was shown to perfection.

He truly is the most beautiful man I have ever seen.

She noticed the way his dark lashes and brows framed his light blue eyes and sighed. "Of course, I could not let you go without telling you goodbye. Silly man."

He took a step closer to her and waved at the footmen to move back. "Elizabeth, you must not make any momentous decisions until I see you again."

She looked up at him, astounded. "What nonsense you talk! You shall see me again tomorrow. What could happen between now and then?"

"I may not be able to come back to Rosings that soon. Any number of things could take place."

He lowered his voice nearly to a whisper. "You love me. I know you do. We were meant for each other. 'Tis the favourite wish of my mother as well as yours."

He put his gloved hands on either side of her face as she laughed quietly.

"I cannot even give you a proper goodbye hug," he complained, dropping his arms to his sides, fists clenched. "What a foolish figure I must cut, and this shall be the last memory of me you carry until I return."

She grinned indulgently. "I have years of memories of you, and the ridiculous ones are the best. One of my favourites involves the day you tried to teach me to fish and fell in the lake yourself. You were so angry!"

"You laughed at me!"

She chuckled. "Had you laughed at yourself, we would have been merry together."

"I cannot bear to be a simpleton in your eyes." His eyes flashed. "You must never again laugh at me."

"I dearly love a laugh, Thomas." She put her hand on his arm to calm him. "I hope I never ridicule what is wise or good. Follies and nonsense, whims and inconsistencies do divert me, I own, and I laugh at them whenever I can."

"I can jest with you concerning the stupidity and frailties of others, but I cannot be happy when I am made to feel foolish." He frowned; his voice was resentful. "It has always been thus. You have never apprehended how I despise being made a joke in your eyes."

"I must beg your pardon, then." She looked away from the irate expression in his eyes, her joy gone. "I shall try to bear that in mind in the future so as not to give offense."

"Good." His lips formed a smile. "I knew you would agree to do as I ask."

He bent to kiss her cheek, and she felt his perfect lips hard against her face.

"You are the ideal wife for me – beautiful, loving, intelligent, malleable." His face was the sun. "I shall see you tomorrow, I hope. Will you give me your promise?"

Her smile did not reach her eyes as she took a small step back. "I promise I shall be as I am now when next I see you."

"Excellent!" Thomas replied, his pique forgotten as he motioned impatiently to the footmen to give him his cap and open the door. "Think only of me until then. Remember."

The hall was cold and empty after he left.

All these years we have been the very best of friends, yet he does not understand me in the least. He cannot love me as I am.

She took a deep breath. *Perhaps it is my fault. After all, any other woman would be beyond happy to be his wife. He is handsome, strong, successful, intelligent, and loving. The failing surely is mine.*

I must be unlovable.

She walked slowly to join the others in the drawing room.

~~oo~~

Elizabeth sat by Charlotte and watched the fire.

"Miss Bennet," said Miss de Bourgh. "If you truly are feeling well as you said before, I have a request to make of you."

"I am rarely ill," answered Elizabeth, turning to look at her hostess. "Please, set me a task, for I fear I must have an occupation. I have never enjoyed being idle."

The lady smiled her approval. "My mother has expressed a wish for Rosings to be decorated for the season, and I should like to indulge her. She hopes to be carried downstairs for Christmas dinner, and I know festive seasonal trimmings would greatly cheer her. Mr. Jones said a sanguine state of mind is crucial to her recovery."

Thomas. Even when he is gone he tells me what I must do.

"Certainly, but I shall need help gathering the greenery and hanging it. A stable boy or footman will do nicely."

Miss de Bourgh smiled. "I have already thought of that, my dear. Mrs. Collins, Miss Lucas, Mrs. Jenkinson, and I are much engaged in reading to my mother, so we cannot be of use to you. I understand Mr. Jones has departed for the parsonage and may not return for some time; therefore, he is unable to help you. There is only one acceptable solution to the problem. As her ladyship has no desire to see you or Darcy, he has agreed to assist you. Have you not, Cousin?"

Elizabeth spoke before the gentleman could. "I am sure Mr. Darcy has much better ways to employ his time. A stable boy will do."

He cleared his throat. "I have nothing else of import to occupy my time, and I would greatly enjoy being of assistance to you, Miss Bennet. It appears that neither of us takes pleasure in being useless."

"Then it is settled," said Miss de Bourgh. "Darcy knows where the holly, cedar, and other decorative plants grow, Miss Bennet. He will see to everything the two of you need. You may begin in the morning, as it is too late this evening."

Elizabeth nodded. "Very well." She picked up a book.

"Miss Bennet?"

She raised a brow and turned to her hostess once more.

Miss de Bourgh smiled. "Would you play for us? I think all of us would welcome such a lovely diversion, for we are a very dull party. You must cheer us and distract us from unhappy circumstances we cannot change."

Why did I ever think she was weak? I am full of error.

"Of course." She stood up and walked to the piano.

Elizabeth needed no music, for the piece she wanted to perform, she knew by heart. She sat and began to play, pouring out her pain, expressing through her music everything she could not put into words.

When she finished, no one spoke for a few moments. She started to stand and had every intention of excusing herself to the company, but a voice spoke softly behind her.

"That was lovely, but so sad. I cannot place the piece. Who is the composer?"

She did not look at him. "Mr. Beethoven. 'Twas a selection from his *'Quasi una fantasia.'*"

"I thought I recognized the master, but I have never before heard it."

"It has not been published long. That was the Adagio Sostenuto movement. 'Tis not technically difficult. The second movement, the Allegretto, is not so mournful, and the third, the Presto Agitato is quite fast and challenging."

Mr. Darcy moved so that he could see her face. She kept her eyes on the ivories.

"Why did you choose a piece in a minor key?" he asked. "If questioned, I would have speculated that your musical preferences would be light and cheerful. Are you unhappy that your friend is gone?"

Elizabeth looked up at him, surprised at his question but determined to answer him truthfully. "Thomas? I enjoy his company, but I am not melancholy because of his absence. In fact, more and more I find he is not absolutely necessary to my happiness."

She searched his expression for a reaction. "Now I have shocked you."

"I admit I am surprised," he answered, smiling, "but not shocked. I think you take delight in expressing opinions which are not your own."

"I assure you, I meant exactly what I said."

He continued. "But you do not always say everything you think. Was your original statement meant to astonish me? Should I be appalled? Tell me what I should think, and I shall endeavour to do it in order to gratify you, for you are a woman worthy of being pleased."

Elizabeth considered his words. *A woman worthy of being pleased.*

She found she quite cherished his opinion. Furthermore, she was surprised to note that she wanted to please him in return. It reminded her of Aesop's fable of the wind and the sun, learned at her father's knee.

What the wind could not achieve by force, the sun accomplished using the persuasion of its gentle warmth.

"Mr. Darcy," she replied, "I am content with you just as you are, and I would never presume to tell you what to do or think."

She stood, and he offered his arm. Together they crossed the room to join the others.

As Elizabeth settled herself again by Charlotte, and as she watched Mr. Darcy return to his chair, she was quite looking forward to the next morning.

Lord, I do not wish Mr. Collins to be seriously ill — only enough to keep Thomas at the parsonage tomorrow. Amen.

Chapter Eight

Elizabeth rose with the sun, planning to walk in the glass buildings before breakfast, for she knew that the remainder of her time would be spent decorating Rosings for the Christmas season with Mr. Darcy. She could not deny that she was cheerfully anticipating spending the day with the gentleman.

As she reached the bottom of the stairs, she was surprised to see the man himself, already hard at work preparing for their day in the snowy outdoors.

He looked up at her, his face alight with pleasure. "Miss Bennet! I had hoped to have everything in order before you awoke, but I see you have caught me checking off my lists."

"I had no idea such a fuss was necessary in order to gather greenery. I wish you had told me, sir, and I would have joined you earlier," she replied, looking at the piles of blankets, tools, baskets, sheets, gloves, and caps.

"No need, for I have done this sort of thing many times," he said, waving his hand. "I am quite good at the organization of such an enterprise, but I fear I sorely lack in the artistry necessary to place the decorations in a pleasing manner."

She crossed the hall to stand by him. "Ah, but that is my strength. I shall likely tax you greatly with my demands in that area."

He chuckled and stood to face the lady. "And shall you select the foliage which pleases you? For only you will know what you require, and you may have whatever you wish. I was quite the tree climber in my youth. High branches were a welcome challenge."

Elizabeth was delighted with his teasing and clasped her hands in front of her. "Shall we have a Christmas tree? We had one last year at Longbourn, and it was beautiful. It was quite my favourite part of the decorations."

"My sister has insisted upon a Christmas tree at Pemberley for several years, ever since Queen Charlotte began the tradition."

A shadow crossed his face, tugging at her heart.

"You must miss your sister."

"Indeed, I do," he answered with a sigh. "This will be the first Christmas we have spent apart since she was born, sixteen years ago."

"Where is she?"

"We were both at our house in London, preparing to return to Pemberley, when I was summoned by my cousin to come here with all haste. Georgiana remained in Town, though she removed from Darcy House to my uncle's residence there. I would not have her endanger her health by travelling so far through the country in the cold and snow."

But you would risk your own.

"She will be with Colonel Fitzwilliam and his family?" she asked.

"Yes. In fact, she joined them the day after I left. And you, Miss Elizabeth? Will you miss your family?"

"Yes, but I would not have been home in any case as I planned to be in Kent to help Mrs. Collins." She looked at her hands. "I confess this has been no great inconvenience for me. Jane will be with her husband and his family in London, and my other sisters shall be merry together with my mother. 'Tis unlikely they will suffer very much due to my absence, though my father shall feel the loss, I think."

He stepped to her side, offering her his arm. "Shall we break our fast together before we venture into the wilds of Rosings Park?" he asked gently. "I admit I am eager to be on our way. I have not helped with hanging greenery for several years – not since I was twenty-two, I believe."

"Why not?"

"I had so many more responsibilities after my father died that I had to choose where I spent my time. I went with Georgiana to gather what she wanted, but I allowed servants to take my place in the decoration of the estate."

His smile faded. "Perhaps I should have spent the time with her instead."

Elizabeth looked up at him. "I am certain you did what you thought was best for everyone at the time. 'Tis always easy to see a better path after the fact. Hindsight is better than foresight, you know."

He nodded, and they made their way to the small dining room for breakfast.

~~oo~~

Near the end of their meal, Darcy cleared his throat.

"Miss Bennet, please do not take offense, but I have a suggestion. Of course, you always have the power of refusal. You must do what you think right."

"You have piqued my curiosity, Mr. Darcy. Please, speak your mind."

He took a deep breath. "Georgiana was extremely cold the first time she went with me on an excursion similar to the one we undertake today, so I proposed a remedy. She agreed, and the next year did as I recommended. My sister was happy to tell me it was a splendid idea, as she was much more comfortable. Since this is the coldest Christmas I have known for many years, I would share my recommendation with you. I sincerely hope you will not be too shocked at the impropriety."

She chuckled. "Mr. Darcy, you are, without a doubt, the most proper gentleman I have ever met. If *you* think your scheme is not improper, I doubt *I* shall think it is."

Darcy coloured. "This is a bit embarrassing, but please remember, I am thinking only of your health and comfort."

He rushed through the rest of his speech. "You will freeze in the clothes you are wearing. I spoke with the head groom, and he gave me an older boy's trousers and heavy coat. For you."

"You think I should dress like a boy today?" she asked, her eyes open wide. "Would that not scandalize the neighborhood?"

He shook his head. "I have considered that. There will be no one there but the two of us and a few trusted servants."

Elizabeth swallowed hard. "I do not object on my part, but perhaps I should not expose myself to the censure of others. It may reflect badly on you, as we will be together."

"Pray, do not worry for my reputation. I have no misgivings, for my concern your wellbeing far outweighs any reservations I might have otherwise," he replied, eyes twinkling.

"Besides," he continued, "you could simply wear a dress over the trousers. Your pelisse coats are all too fine to subject to a day of tromping about the woods, and they are much too thin to keep you warm. I would loan you one of my own great coats, but anything of mine would be far too large for you."

Elizabeth bit her lower lip. "That is all very true. You have put a great deal of thought into this." She was quiet for a moment. "You are right, and I shall do as you advise, but I ask a favour."

He raised a brow. "Ask whatever you will."

"It must be a secret, for both of our sakes. I doubt your aunt would approve of either of us," she said, laughing quietly. "You would be condemned for thinking of me in such a way, and I would be excoriated for exposing myself to the disapproval of the world."

Darcy nodded, smiling. "I have already thought of that. No one else shall know. You can trust me."

"I trust you implicitly, Mr. Darcy."

"I shall always strive to deserve your confidence in me, Miss Bennet."

I have never before seen him smile so much.

She basked in the glow of his warmth.

He has gone to a great deal of trouble to please everyone. He thinks of others before himself. That is what makes a man truly handsome.

~~oo~~

Elizabeth nearly skipped down the stairs after she donned her thickest dress. Seeing Mr. Darcy awaiting her at the front door, she tried to contain her enthusiasm and walk more sedately.

He walked forward to meet her. "Was everything to your liking?"

She chuckled, placing her hand in the crook of his elbow. "If you refer to the trousers, yes," she whispered. "Most warm and pleasing."

"Do you have proper shoes for the snow?"

She pointed her toe so that it showed beneath the hem of her dress. "I walk every day, sir. As you see, I have sturdy, leather walking boots, to my mother's great distress."

"Excellent. I was wondering if I should send you a pair of Hessians," he said, knitting his brows. "The snow is quite deep and still coming down. I fear it may come above the top of your boots. Your feet will be cold and wet – you may catch a chill."

"I truly appreciate your concern," she said, patting his arm lightly as she looked up at him. "However, my father worries for me even more than you do. He had these boots made for my Christmas present last year. As you see, the toe is rounded. They are in the style of Hessians, but made to fit me. I doubt even you could find fault with them."

A smile danced on his lips. "But did he think of long socks?"

"Of course. Woolen ones. In fact, I am over-warm while we remain indoors. Shall we go?"

He motioned to the footmen, and soon they were swathed in coats, caps, scarves, and gloves.

Darcy looked at her and laughed. "Have no fear that you will be talked of, for I doubt anyone would know who is hiding under that mound of clothing."

His laughter is wonderful. A truly glorious sound, worth any amount of my mortification.

"Sir," she replied, striking a gloved hand to her chest. "You wound me."

He tilted his head. "I did not dare to hope that I had the ability to wound you. I thought you did not care at all for my good opinion. Has that changed?"

Her muffled voice was merry. "Can you not tell?"

"All I see is your eyes, and they appear to be mocking me."

"I should like to get to know you better, and that is definitely different from the way I felt in April. I think I misjudged you badly, and I am sorry for it."

He closed his eyes for a moment, and then opened them to look at her. "You did not. I am not the same as I was then."

A horse whinnied just beyond the door.

"Shall we go?" she asked. "The men and horses await us in the cold."

He shook his head, as if to clear it, then held out his arm to her. "Of course. Come."

~~oo~~

They had been hard at work for several hours when Darcy ordered the men to return to Rosings with the loaded sleds and horses.

"You must be cold and tired. We should go back for tea and hot soup," he said to Elizabeth. "I asked Mrs. Robinson to have it ready for us."

She resisted the urge to stretch and ease her cramped shoulders. "I confess I am frozen and weary, but a little rest and something to eat and drink will soon put me to rights."

They began to walk towards Rosings.

"Do you think we have enough greenery?"

"Nearly," she replied. "I have a few more ideas, but it should not take long to gather what I need."

"I have a scheme as well."

She turned her head to look up at him and tripped over a root, sending her sprawling in the snow.

Darcy knelt beside her. "Are you injured?"

"No, I think not, though I am a bit humiliated. Will you help me up?" She extended her hand to him.

Darcy tried to help her to her feet, but she cried out as soon as she put weight on her foot.

Without a word, he picked her up as if he were cradling a child.

"Mr. Darcy, you must put me down."

"You cannot so much as stand, and the sleds are much too far ahead for me to catch them. I see no other solution."

He began to walk towards Rosings.

"Miss Bennet, 'twould help if you put your arms about my neck. You are dead weight otherwise, and we have over a mile before we reach the house."

She blushed furiously but did as he asked. "Will you agree to put me down when we are in sight of Rosings?"

"If you are able to walk by leaning on me, I will. Otherwise, I shall carry you the entire way."

Elizabeth began to chuckle.

Darcy glanced down at her. "You are amused?"

"I am. You are covered in snow and look like a snow beast of some sort."

"And what are you? My prey?"

She feigned shock. "Do you mean I am in mortal danger? I thought gentlemen protected young ladies."

"You said I was a snow beast. I suppose that means I am not a gentleman."

In the midst of their banter, Darcy and Elizabeth had failed to notice the man directly in front of them.

"You will unhand my future wife this instant!"

Thomas had returned; he was very angry.

Chapter Nine

Elizabeth jerked her head around to see him. "Thomas?"

Darcy's response was immediate. "You forget yourself, sir!"

Thomas took a step towards them, pulling the scarf from his face. "I repeat: put her down. Now."

Elizabeth heard the menace in his voice, but in Darcy's arms, she was not afraid. "Calm yourself. This is not what it seems. I tripped, injuring my ankle, and Mr. Darcy is kindly carrying me to the house."

"Then I shall take you, as is my right." He looked at Darcy. "Give her to me, sir."

Darcy's eyes shifted to Elizabeth. "Is it true? Are you engaged to him?" he whispered.

She shook her head, and the gentleman adjusted his weight subtly. Elizabeth could tell he had planted both feet firmly, pulling her closer to his chest.

He has no intention of yielding.

"Enough, man! Miss Bennet is freezing as we argue. I shall take her to Rosings, and we can continue this discussion there where it is warm. Perhaps you will agree to accompany us so that you can ascertain the extent of the damage and treat her, or would you rather stay out here until she is ill as well?"

Without another word, Thomas turned abruptly and stalked in the direction of the manse, pulling his scarf back over his mouth and nose as he went.

In due time, Rosings was in view.

Darcy lowered his face to whisper. "Do you still wish to attempt walking?"

"If you are not afraid of damage to your own reputation and I am not too heavy for you, I am inclined to continue as we are." Her eyes met his. "I have no wish to encourage Thomas in thinking he has any sort of claim which entitles him to speak for me. He is my friend, but that is all."

She could see the relief in his eyes.

"You are no burden to me."

Thomas was standing at the entrance when Darcy walked up the steps to Rosings. He gestured for them to enter as the footman opened the door.

Darcy carried Elizabeth to the empty drawing room, issuing orders for tea and soup to be brought for them as he walked.

He placed her in a chair close to the fire.

A maidservant hurried to help the lady remove her outer garments, and a footman came forward to receive the clothing as she removed it.

Darcy and Thomas removed their snow-covered outerwear and tossed it into a pile on the floor. A second footman immediately retrieved it.

"You there. Bring a footstool," Darcy said. "Build up the fire."

Within a few moments, Elizabeth's foot was resting on the cushioned stool as Thomas knelt beside it.

He frowned when he saw her boots.

"Wherever did you get these Hessians, Elizabeth?" he thundered. "They are fit for a man, not a lady, and they shall be the very devil to remove without hurting you."

"My father gave them to me last year," she replied in a clipped voice. "He knows how I love to walk in all weather, and I suppose he was more concerned with my health than he was for convention."

She winced and stifled a grunt as Thomas tugged the boot from her foot.

He gasped. "What is this? What the dickens are you wearing?"

"Trousers, Thomas," she said tiredly. "Surely you know what trousers are? I knew I would be outside for several hours in the snow, so I chose to wear warm clothing."

"Elizabeth, this sort of behaviour was excusable when you were a child," he scolded, brows drawn together. "But you are a grown woman now. This is most unbecoming! Is your father responsible for this as well?"

Darcy stepped forward and put his hand on the back of Elizabeth's wing chair. His mouth was set in a grim line.

"He is not," said the gentleman. "I both suggested the trousers and procured them for her. She would have been amenable to dressing 'properly' to please those around her, but I wished for her to be protected from the cold. Can you not examine her without a constant diatribe criticizing her for her actions?"

Thomas stood, scowling. "So, you forced her to do this? Knowing how it could damage her standing in society? I knew I should not have left her with you."

"Mr. Darcy has never tried to force me to do anything," answered Elizabeth, glaring at him. "He does not order me about as you do."

"You mistake his courtesy for interest, Elizabeth. He is of a different sphere than you and I inhabit," Thomas replied angrily. "We two are alike. Do not deceive yourself. A wealthy, powerful man like Mr. Darcy will never propose marriage to you as I have. He will never offer you his name."

Elizabeth, astonished at his audacity, put her hand over her open mouth as the oppressive silence grew.

Finally, Darcy's deep, steady voice echoed in the stillness. "I already have."

Thomas looked from one to the other, settling on Elizabeth. "So, am I to understand that you have engaged yourself to him? You have broken your promise to me?"

She lifted her chin. "I have broken no promises."

The physician narrowed his eyes.

"Do you intend to stand there all day?" asked Darcy impatiently. "Shall I send for Mr. Sims to care for her, or will you stop talking and get to the task at hand?"

"*I* will do it. 'Tis not necessary to send for the apothecary," he replied tersely, kneeling and roughly pulling the sock from her foot. "This conversation is not over, Elizabeth. We shall finish this discussion later."

Elizabeth closed her eyes tightly against the pain, trying to make no noise. A small cry escaped her.

Darcy moved to stand to the left of her chair. "You are hurting her unnecessarily. Be gentle."

"Am I the physician, or are you?" asked Thomas through clenched jaws.

"I am no physician, but I am capable of removing her sock without causing her pain," replied Darcy, enunciating each word.

"You will not touch her," replied Thomas, glowering.

Anne de Bough's calm voice came from behind them.

"Ah, there you all are. I confess I was confused to hear that you were in this room." She clucked her tongue. "Darcy, you know we sit here in the evening."

She walked sedately around the chair to stand beside Thomas in front of Elizabeth, looking down at her foot.

"My dear, you are hurt. I am so sorry. It looks quite swollen and discoloured to me, but I know nothing of these things. Mr. Jones, are you capable of seeing to my guest, or should I send to London for Mr. Hough?"

The young man took a deep breath and exhaled it slowly.

"There is no need to send for anyone else. I think 'tis sprained, but not broken. I am quite fit to treat her injury."

"Excellent. You may continue, Mr. Jones, if you are able to do so without causing Miss Bennet undue discomfort," answered the lady.

The butler entered, followed by several footmen bearing trays which they placed on a table.

"Wonderful!" Miss de Bourgh clasped her hands. "There is the tea and soup you ordered, Darcy. Mrs. Robinson has her spies everywhere, and she keeps me abreast of what is happening in my house. Such a jewel. What would I do without her?"

She moved with dignity to sit in the chair to Elizabeth's right, leaning forward to pat her hand for a moment.

"Smythe, please inform Mrs. Collins and Miss Lucas that we shall have tea and soup in here today, along with the sandwiches and biscuits I ordered. I believe the ladies are in the morning parlour. And tell Sally I should like for her to serve, for Mrs. Jenkinson is with Mama, and I am quite fatigued from all the activity."

The butler nodded and quickly left the room.

"Now, Mr. Jones. Tell me what you shall do to help my friend. Do you need anything?"

Elizabeth hid her surprise. *Her friend?*

"I require a bowl of snow or ice and some clean cloths," answered the physician, standing to face Miss de Bourgh. "Her foot is growing larger as it gets warmer, so I shall apply ice wrapped in the cloths to reduce both the swelling and the pain."

Charlotte and Maria entered the room, followed by Sally and Smythe.

As the ladies seated themselves, Sally began to pour the tea and serve the soup.

Miss de Bourgh smiled. "Smythe, Mr. Jones has expressed a wish for ice or snow as well as clean cloths. Please have them fetched immediately, along with a pillow to be placed under Miss Bennet's foot, and a warm blanket."

He turned and left the room.

Miss de Bourgh sipped her tea with delicacy and sighed. "There is nothing which gives me more satisfaction than to see everything at Rosings done efficiently. Everyone is content when there is no confusion or animus. Do you not agree, Mrs. Collins?"

"I do, Miss de Bourgh. I feel the same about the parsonage."

"Miss Bennet, I noticed your trousers, socks, and boots. I must say that I appreciate how sensible you are. Many people are far too shallow, placing the importance of society's foolish constraints above their own health, as well as the health of others. If I were going outside," she shivered slightly, "which of course, I am not, I would follow your wise example."

Elizabeth nearly choked on her tea.

Miss de Bourgh raised a fine eyebrow. "My dear, are you quite well?"

She tilted her head. "Darcy, you must learn to take better care of our guest. First, you allowed her to suffer injury and agony under your watch, and now you have neglected her to the point that she may actually expire in my drawing room. I trusted you with her welfare, and you have been quite careless. I am shocked, indeed. Can you not help her?"

She waved her hand languidly. "Pat her back or hold her cup. Surely you are able to do something to relieve her present distress. A great, tall fellow like you should be more useful as you are too large to be ornamental."

Darcy's mouth twitched, eyes sparkling. "You are right, Cousin, as you usually are. People mistakenly underestimate your strength because you are so calm and unassuming, yet you direct this house with the crook of your little finger."

"You know I saw you from the parlour window when you were walking back to the house." Her eyes gleamed.

"I was quite sure you were watching, my dear," he replied, "for nothing which happens at Rosings Park escapes your notice. Aunt Catherine would be quite lost without you."

Elizabeth sipped her soup as she glanced from Darcy to Miss de Bourgh.

How curious. I have never before seen this side of Miss de Bourgh. 'Tis clear that she and Mr. Darcy are a great deal more than friends or relatives, yet he made an offer to me. Has he changed his mind because of my folly? Should I be jealous?

Smythe entered the room with white cloths, a pillow, and a blanket, followed by a footman carrying a large bowl of snow and ice. They placed the items by Thomas's feet.

The young man placed his cup on a table and knelt before his patient.

He lifted Elizabeth's foot carefully and tucked the pillow beneath it, and then busied himself in making a loose pack of ice within several cloths folded neatly.

Elizabeth shifted in the chair as Thomas placed his handiwork on her ankle, leaning towards her to whisper, "I am sorry I hurt you. This will make it better quickly."

"Thank you."

He stood and bent over her, putting his mouth to her ear. "I cannot bear to see you with him. It makes me angry and foolish."

So, it is my own fault when he acts in this manner?

She turned her head and bit her lip as Thomas straightened, nodding to Miss de Bourgh. "Elizabeth should be able to walk a little tomorrow, as long as she remains indoors and does not overdo. I must go to her ladyship and make certain she is well enough for me to return to the parsonage. I dare not leave Mr. Collins alone with servants for too long, and Mr. Sims is on his rounds."

The lady gazed at him. "No, indeed. Do not neglect our parson. You most definitely should go back to Hunsford and make certain he recovers as soon as is possible. My mother seems to be doing well, and we shall all be sure to encourage Miss Bennet to stay off her foot. There are many of us who care deeply for her. You are needed more at the parsonage than you are at Rosings."

He nodded. "Someone must replace the ice when it melts and keep checking her ankle. Remove the towels from time to time so that the cold does not freeze her skin."

He touched Elizabeth's shoulder before he bowed and hurried from the room. She flinched and averted her face.

"Miss Bennet," said Darcy, asking for her attention. "Christmas is but three days away. I can begin hanging the greenery this afternoon if you will sit and give me directions."

He picked up the blanket and draped it over her legs and feet.

She looked into his kind, emerald eyes and smiled. "I shall be happy to tell you what to do, sir, but first, you must finish your soup and eat some sandwiches and biscuits. You will certainly need your strength."

He bowed. "I am yours to command."

Because you allow it.

She knew in that moment her heart would always belong to Mr. Darcy.

I will enjoy this time with him and remember it for the remainder of my life. If he marries another, I shall always have these days to cherish.

Chapter Ten

After Darcy finished his meal, he excused himself, saying he would return shortly.

He was as good as his word and soon appeared, pulling a large, cushioned chair on three wheels.

"Miss Bennet, I thought perhaps you would be more comfortable in this Bath chair than being lifted and carried from place to place."

"Surely, this is too much trouble for you, sir," she replied.

He chuckled. "I assure you, I am well able to move this contraption quite easily. I procured this for my aunt when she was recuperating in October. When I was unable to be here, the footmen assisted her. She said it was most agreeable."

Elizabeth smiled. "Then I shall accept your kind offer for today, and hope that I am able to walk from chair to chair tomorrow."

"Darcy, you appear to have everything in hand," said Miss de Bourgh, standing. "As I am no longer needed, I shall take my other guests with me to the parlour I prefer in the morning and early afternoon. Come, Mrs. Collins and Miss Lucas. Let us allow Miss Bennet and my cousin to put their minds to making Rosings beautiful for the season. I so look forward to seeing what the two of them have planned for our enjoyment."

Elizabeth nodded. "Mr. Darcy and I shall do our best to please you, Miss de Bourgh."

"Is there anything I could do to help you, Lizzy?" asked Charlotte.

"Perhaps you and Maria could provide some ornaments for the tree. I plan to decorate with apples, ribbons, sweetmeats, and toys. It would be wonderful if you could make some paper or silk flowers to add more colour. You could also wrap small packages of raisins and nuts."

"A tree?" Miss de Bourgh smiled. "I have wanted a Christmas tree for several years, but Mama felt that a custom begun by our German-born queen would not endure among the aristocracy."

"The royal family has a Christmas tree every year," said Darcy, "so I think we may safely assume that the idea will continue. After all, people in Germany and other countries have displayed decorated trees for over a century. It appears we are late to the party."

"Then we shall present it to Mama as a grand surprise for her," replied the lady, laughing.

Elizabeth's eyes sparkled as she looked up at her hostess. "And we could allow the children of the estate and the town of Hunsford to come see it. On Boxing Day at Longbourn, my sister and I gave our tenants' children all the decorations from the tree as presents. I encouraged my younger sisters to continue the tradition in my absence."

"We do the same at Pemberley," said Darcy. "Georgiana plans a celebration for them, as well as the children of Lambton, and they all come for an hour or two to have refreshments while she and I hand out the gifts. For some, 'tis all they receive for Christmas."

He turned to look at his cousin. "Anne, could you procure some small toys?"

"Most certainly," she answered. "I shall have the fruits, nuts, ribbons, and paper gathered and brought to the parlour, as well."

"Excellent idea, Miss de Bourgh," said Charlotte. "Maria and I will begin our work at once. We have much to do."

Maria clapped her hands. "What fun! A Christmas party for the children! Elizabeth, you must play some lively music at the piano. I would be most pleased to turn your pages for you."

"If you wish it, my dear," she answered with a bright smile, and then turned to her hostess. "Miss de Bourgh, would you please have red ribbon, scissors, and apples sent to me in the main hallway?"

"Of course, my dear. What is greenery without festive ribbon and fruit? I believe we have pears, too."

And with that, the ladies quit the room, laughing and talking of their plans.

Elizabeth glanced up at her companion. "Now, Mr. Darcy, you must take me to the front entryway, for we shall begin there."

She began to lift herself from her chair, but the gentleman stepped in front of her.

"You cannot put any weight on your foot, Miss Bennet. Please allow me to assist you."

"Very well," she answered. "What must I do?"

He knelt on one knee before her to remove the ice and folded the blanket over her lap, sliding one arm under her knees and the other behind her back.

"Hold on to me as you did outside."

Her heart seemed to lodge in her throat as she breathed his scent, but she did as he requested, and he soon had her in the Bath chair with her ice and cloths back in place on her foot and the blanket over her legs.

"Are you quite comfortable?" he asked, straightening up.

"Yes, thank you," she replied, fighting the flush creeping up her neck, trying to forget how safe and easy she felt in his arms, "though my foot is becoming quite cold."

"Perhaps if I put your sock back on for you, it would help to keep your foot warm. I would do my best not to hurt you."

"I trust you, Mr. Darcy. I know that you would not willingly cause me pain. Your idea is a sound one."

He retrieved her sock and once more took a knee in front of her, removing the ice again before gently taking her injured foot in his hands. He slowly worked the sock over her toes, pushing the blanket up a bit.

"You must tell me if you feel discomfort."

Elizabeth closed her eyes briefly as her breathing quickened.

I love him too much, and 'tis unlikely he will ever be mine. The ache in my heart is much greater than any pain he is causing me.

He paused, holding her foot in his warm hands with a look of consternation.

"Miss Bennet, are you well? Should I stop?"

She shook her head, struggling to slow her heartbeat and not think about how his brown curls caught the light.

As it is impossible to forget him, I shall hide these days in my heart; I will always remember him like this.

She took a deep breath. "I am fine. Please continue."

The gentleman carefully inched the garment over her foot, stopping when his hands reached the bottom of her trousers. He then replaced the ice pack, adjusted the blanket, and stood to his feet.

Darcy hesitated, a look of uncertainty on his handsome face. "May I ask you a question? I warn you that it might be construed as impertinent."

She turned her gaze up to his. "I cannot imagine your being so. What do you wish to know, sir?"

"Mr. Jones accused you of breaking a promise to him, and you said you had broken no promises. Would you mind telling me what you promised him?"

"Not at all. When Thomas left for the parsonage late yesterday, he asked me not to make any momentous decisions before he returned. I told him that I would remain as I was then until he came back to Rosings."

"And you did as you said you would do."

"I did."

Darcy was silent for a moment before he continued.

"Did I understand him to say he has offered for you?"

"Yes. Several months ago, he did."

He raised a brow. "And you did not accept?"

"I did not, and I will not. We are not suited."

"But you love him?"

Elizabeth nodded. "As a brother – a lifelong friend."

His eyes darkened.

"Just as I love Anne."

She felt as if her heart stopped altogether.

With an effort, she smiled, but she was unable to hide the quiver in her voice. "Probably so, though I think it may be easier to love Miss de Bourgh, as she does not try to compel you into matrimony."

Darcy chuckled. "Quite the opposite. Anne would not marry me if I asked her."

Is that what he wants? "Since we are being bold and open with one another, do you wish to marry Miss de Bourgh?"

He shook his head slightly, holding her eyes with his. "She and I are of like mind on the subject. Neither of us wishes to wed a person we view as a sibling. I will always care for her and protect her, but only as her brother."

Darcy was quiet. He cleared his throat and glanced away. "Are you still held to your promise with Mr. Jones?" he asked softly.

Elizabeth looked at her hands folded in her lap. "I do not consider myself to be so. After all, I did exactly as he asked."

Without another word, the gentleman bent and retrieved the handle of the chair, soon contriving to pull her from the room and into the hallway.

"I had the footmen bring in the greenery and leave it here, along with a ladder," he said. "Where shall we begin?"

She looked around the room and pointed to a spot.

"Let us begin with doorways. After we finish all of those, we shall move to the mantles. Fetch the ribbon and scissors for me, please, and I shall tie the bows while you hang the branches."

He nodded his agreement, handed her the ribbon, and moved the ladder into place.

"You, there," he said, gesturing to a footman. "Miss Bennet, if you will point out the boughs you wish me to place, Smythe's son will hand them to me."

She agreed, and the work began.

~~oo~~

After several hours, Darcy tied the final ribbon to the pine and cedar boughs over the doorway leading to the large dining room.

"What shall we do next?" Darcy looked to Elizabeth for his answer.

"Shall we have tea before we begin to decorate the tree?"

"A grand idea," he answered, smiling. "Do you agree that the ballroom would be the best place to host the Boxing Day celebration?"

"If you think your cousin would not mind. After all, there are very few furnishings in that room, so we have freedom to arrange everything to our satisfaction. There would be no danger of the children doing any damage to expensive furniture."

"Anne is quite practical," he answered, eyes merry, "and should my aunt be able to attend, she will have very little about which to complain. This evening, I plan to ask her to help us choose a room, guide her as to the feasibility of using the ballroom, and allow her to think it was her idea."

Elizabeth laughed aloud. "I had no notion you were such a schemer, Mr. Darcy! I see I shall have to be on my toes when dealing with you."

His expression grew serious. "You need have no fear, for I would never deceive you. I abhor disguise of any kind. I would not lie to my aunt, either. I merely let her appropriate my ideas as her own."

"I am not afraid of anything to do with you, sir. I may tease you, but I think I understand you better than I did when we first met. You are, without a doubt, the most honourable man of my acquaintance."

"I shall strive to deserve that compliment."

She smiled. "So, the ballroom it is?"

He inclined his head.

As they were agreed, Darcy spoke to the footmen. "Move all the greenery, fruit, and ribbon to the ballroom, as well as the tree. Then fetch a large bucket and fill it with rocks and water to serve as a tree stand. You must cut the small branches from the bottom of the trunk before you place it in the bucket."

After the matter was settled, he turned to Elizabeth. "My cousin and the ladies are likely still in the morning parlour. Do you wish to join them?"

At her nod, he picked up the handle to her Bath chair, easily pulling her chair towards the room.

~~oo~~

By the time they finished their tea, Darcy and Elizabeth were ready to return to the task at hand.

The ladies had already filled two large baskets with their handiwork, so the gentleman instructed the footmen to take the decorations to the ballroom.

"Do you wish to join us as we trim the tree?" asked Elizabeth, looking around the room.

Miss de Bourgh smiled complacently at her. "I fear we have not made nearly enough paper and silk flowers, and I just know the little girls will each want one. Do you not agree, Mrs. Collins?"

"Without a doubt, Miss de Bourgh. Maria has offered to take Mrs. Jenkinson's place with Lady Catherine and allow her the enjoyment of helping us. She has been up there all morning, and she must be tired of reading by now."

"How kind of you," replied Miss de Bourgh, nodding at Maria. "I shall order fresh tea for Mrs. Jenkinson."

"I am happy to be of assistance," answered Maria, curtseying before she left the room.

"It seems we must shoulder the burden alone, Miss Bennet," said Darcy, standing to walk to her side.

"'Tis no burden at all," she answered, looking up into his face. "Only think what joy we shall give to the children and their families."

"We are in one accord. 'Tis no burden at all," he replied, reaching down to retrieve the handle of her chair.

She watched him as he pulled her from the room.

He is everything I want in a husband — strong, agreeable, commanding, gentle, intelligent, kind, and warm. He is the handsomest man of my acquaintance, and I could have been married to him already. I would now be basking in the glow of being Mrs. Darcy.

She sighed. *How could I have misjudged him so completely? Will he ever forgive me?*

Chapter Eleven

The next morning at her usual time, Elizabeth carefully left her bed, mindful of her injury. She put her undamaged foot to the floor first, cautious as she attempted to stand on both feet. Frowning at the pain, she abandoned the idea and stood on one foot.

The housemaid entered quietly, carrying a basket of wood. She set it down on the hearth and curtseyed.

Elizabeth smiled at her. "Good morning, Meg."

"Good morning, miss. I see you must still jump about."

"Aye. 'Tis still too tender to put weight on it. I suppose I shall be in the Bath chair again today," she answered, sighing. "I do so miss my morning walk."

She remembered being carried by Mr. Darcy the day before, his strong arms around her. *Though being in the chair does have its benefits.*

Meg nodded, kneeling to see to the fire. She finished quickly and stood to face Elizabeth.

"I'll tell your maid to come straightaway and help you to dress."

Elizabeth hopped to a chair and sat down. "Thank you, Meg."

The girl hurried away.

Within a few minutes, the lady's maid entered. "Good morning, miss," she said as she curtseyed.

"Good morning, Michelle. You have such a lovely name. French, is it not?"

The maid nodded. "My mother was French. She married an English soldier and came with him to England. I was born not far from here," she replied as she set about readying Elizabeth for her day.

Before long, Elizabeth was dressed and seated in a comfortable chair.

Michelle smiled at her. "I told a footman to come after me to bring the chair and lift you into it, Miss Bennet."

Elizabeth thanked her, and shortly, someone knocked at the door.

Upon opening it, the maid stepped back and curtseyed. "Mr. Darcy!"

He walked into the room, nodding to Elizabeth. "Good morning. I was passing by and saw Henry at the door with the Bath chair, so I told him to wait. Shall we go, Miss Bennet?"

"Yes, thank you, Mr. Darcy," she replied, attempting to calm her racing heart.

He strode across the room and drew her into his arms, holding her firmly against his chest as he carried her into the hallway.

Elizabeth felt him inhale deeply and looked up at his face, surprised to see a tender expression there.

Without thinking, she began to raise her hand to touch his cheek, but the warmth in his gaze was gone so quickly, she thought she must have imagined it. She caught herself and tucked a curl behind her ear instead.

"Where is the chair?" asked Elizabeth, tilting her face to his.

"I had the footman take it to the bottom of the stairs. I'll settle you in it after I carry you down," he answered in a gruff voice.

Is he angry with me? Is he in pain? "Am I too heavy for you, sir? I can go slowly on one foot. I should not like for you to hurt your back."

He smiled down at her. "Elizabeth, do you think I would have you struggle when I am perfectly capable of carrying you? Is it so unpleasant to be held by me?"

The blush crept up her neck. "I should not like to be burdensome to you."

"Pray, do not fret. You could never be so."

When they reached the foot of the stairs, Henry was waiting beside the chair.

"You may return to your duties, Henry," said Darcy. "I can manage well enough."

The man nodded and walked away as Darcy lowered Elizabeth carefully, making certain she was comfortable before he pulled her to the small dining room.

He transferred her to a chair and walked to the sideboard, picking up a plate.

"May I get your food for you?"

She raised her brows. "That is very kind of you. Shall I tell you what I like?"

He shook his head, green eyes twinkling. "No need. I shall serve you, and you will see that I know very well what you like."

"You profess to know me well?" she asked, suppressing a smile.

He turned to the sideboard and busied himself. "Elizabeth, I have observed you closely under several different circumstances. I think I may safely say that I have become quite well acquainted with your likes as well as your dislikes."

After saying his piece, he placed a plate before her, filled with her favourites.

"How did I fare?" he asked.

"Very well indeed." She chuckled, looking at what he had chosen. "Shall I tell you what to put on your own plate?"

His lips twitched. "I suppose turn-about is fair play."

"Toasted bread with orange marmalade, eggs, ham, tea with sugar, and a small piece of Plum Cake."

Darcy quickly served himself the chosen foods and sat down beside her, taking a sip of his tea.

She pursed her lips. "Did I not select your preferences?"

"You did. I confess I am surprised." His voice was low.

"Why is that?"

"I had no idea that you observed me so intently."

"Mr. Darcy, I have allowed you to carry me about as no other man besides my father has ever done. Why would I have permitted that if I had not watched you enough to feel relaxed in such a position? And if I did indeed pay close attention to what your words and actions revealed about your character, would I not also see the details involved in those things which give you pleasure and what does not?"

"You must be very wily."

"Oh? How so?"

"I told you I have observed you closely for some time, yet I never noticed you studying me." He spread marmalade generously on his toast and took a bite.

She chuckled. "You forget that I did not see you watching me, either. Consequently, I must not be the only sneak in the house."

"It seems we have much in common." He smiled a little smugly as he took another bite.

"Apparently so."

They ate in companionable silence for a few minutes before he spoke again.

"As we finished making the tree ornaments last night, shall we hang them on the tree this morning? Or would you prefer a walk in the gardens?

She fairly beamed at him. "I should like to do both, if you agree."

"There is nothing I would like better."

"Should we finish the tree before we visit the glass buildings?"

He nodded. "The gardens will be warmer after a few hours of sunlight. You will be more comfortable then."

"And we could hang ornaments as we are. We shall need our coats to roam the orangeries."

"Then we are in harmony."

Before a half hour had passed, they were in the ballroom, laughing together as they finished trimming the tree.

~~oo~~

Darcy pulled Elizabeth down the hallway and stopped after entering the morning parlour where his cousin sat with Mrs. Collins, Miss Lucas, and Mrs. Jenkinson.

He placed the handle of Elizabeth's chair on the floor and bowed to the ladies.

"We have finished decorating the house, and Miss Bennet has expressed a wish to see the gardens again. Do you wish to come with us?"

Miss de Bourgh shook her head. "Thank you, my dear, but we shall decline. As you can see, we are all quite busy writing invitations for the Boxing Day celebration and wrapping presents."

Elizabeth smiled. "I should feel guilty enjoying the beauty of the flowers and foliage while you three labour. Maria, will you come?"

Maria glanced at her sister. "Thank you, but no."

Charlotte looked up. "If the invitations are to be delivered today, we must write them now."

"Then we shall help you," answered Elizabeth.

"But you are already in your coats and scarves," replied Miss de Bourgh smoothly. "The four of us are sufficient for the task, and you have worked so diligently at beautifying Rosings. Please enjoy yourselves for an hour or two. There will be plenty to do later this afternoon. I have sent to the village for scarves and gloves to give the children, and we shall wrap them. I do so want the party to be a grand success. I wish for them to have useful things as well as toys and treats."

Elizabeth's heart was touched. "You are very good. The children of Rosings Park and Hunsford are blessed to have you as a patroness."

The lady shooed them away with her hand. "Such nonsense! Go and have your walk."

Darcy bowed. "If you insist."

He picked up the chair's handle and pulled her through the halls to the back of the house.

Before long, they were in the glass buildings.

"It has finally stopped snowing!" exclaimed Elizabeth with joy.

Darcy smiled, pointing at the oaks in the park. "I believe the skies cleared yesterday evening. The ice is melting on the trees, and the roads are much clearer."

"'Tis so beautiful. The world is sparkling and quiet."

"Yes, and the families will have a much easier time coming to Rosings." He paused. "In a few weeks, you will leave for Longbourn."

She looked up at him and caught her breath, for his eyes were on her face, his gaze tender.

Darcy knelt in front of her.

"I dreamed of you again last night," he said so softly that she leaned forward to hear him.

"Again?" she whispered.

"Whenever I close my eyes, I see your beautiful face."

She held her breath.

"Elizabeth, I have been such an arrogant fool. Please believe me when I say I love you with all my heart and soul. I am completely under your spell; I am yours, and I know I always shall be so. You know I cannot make flowery speeches, but I hope you can forgive my inability to articulate what I feel for you."

She smiled through tears. "I believe you underestimate your abilities, for that was a lovely speech."

He took her hands in his, his expression earnest. "Do you think you could grow to love me in time? I am willing to wait for you."

"There is no need to wait, for I have long loved you, Mr. Darcy." She put a hand over his and softly stroked it.

He lifted her fingers to his lips, kissing them gently.

"I had lost all aspirations of ever having my feelings returned before I came to Rosings. I had given you up as lost."

"What happened here to change your mind?"

"My Aunt Catherine," he replied, laughing quietly.

She arched her brows in shock. "In truth? I expected her speech to turn you from me completely."

"'Tis what she assumed as well, though I must say, her words had the opposite effect. They taught me to hope as I never had since you refused me last April."

"How so?"

"You would not promise her that you would never accept me. I knew if you had decided against me irrevocably, you would have told her so." He caressed her hand with his thumb.

She laughed. "Aye. You have experienced enough of my frankness to believe that. After abusing you to your face, I would not have hesitated to repeat my words to all your relations."

"You spoke the truth to me as no one else would. I pray you shall do so for the rest of my life. And you have made my aunt very happy, for you know how she loves to be of use."

He leaned closer to her and cupped her face with his hands, touching his forehead to hers before feathering light kisses across her cheeks and lips.

"Scoundrel!"

Darcy rose immediately, dropping his fisted hands to his sides and turning to face an enraged Thomas.

"Sir! You have intruded upon a private moment. You are most unwelcome."

"I would wager I am, Mr. Darcy! You mean to take advantage of Elizabeth and ruin her for anyone else."

"Do you mean for you?" Darcy drew himself up to his full, intimidating height.

Thomas shook his head and glared at Elizabeth, his voice harsh. "No, not for me. I decided that Elizabeth will never love me, and this morning I visited Lady Metcalf to make an offer for her eldest daughter. Her dowry is quite substantial, unlike yours. Fortunately for me, she is not as pretty as her sisters, and she had no expectations of marriage due to her age. Therefore, she accepted me immediately. We are to be wed as soon as the banns are read."

"If you are betrothed," answered Mr. Darcy, "why are you protesting what happens between Elizabeth and me? How is it your concern?"

She stood to her feet, ignoring the pain, staring fiercely at Thomas. "Why, indeed! If I will not pledge myself to you, you wish me to reject everyone else. You care not at all for my happiness. You love no one but yourself."

He took a menacing step forward. "You have caused me nothing but trouble and pain. After you refused me the first time, I turned to drink and other pursuits unworthy of a gentleman. I nearly quit my profession, and it was all due to you! You nearly ruined my life, but my father took me in hand. He went to Mr. Hough and pleaded with him to give me a place in his practice, pledging himself to pay any expenses the gentleman would incur. That is love. You have no knowledge of what it is."

Darcy stiffened beside her, but she placed a calming hand on his arm.

"I have tried not to hurt you, Thomas, for you have been a brother to me for as long as I can remember. If you love Miss Metcalf, I wish both of you all happiness. I want only the best for you."

Thomas sneered at her. "Love! I am finished with sentimentality. Mr. Darcy may dally with you, but he will never marry you. I have told you that before, Elizabeth, because I was concerned for you. Now I think you deserve whatever you get from him. You have pursued him boldly, and I am ashamed of you. All friendship between us is over, for I would not expose my innocent wife to such a woman as you."

He turned to stalk away as Darcy stepped forward.

Elizabeth held his arm.

"Let him go," she pleaded.

"He insulted you in the vilest terms! It shall not stand. I will call him out."

"My foot hurts," she whimpered. "I need you to help me, for I can neither walk nor pull myself back to the house. Do not leave me here alone."

Darcy exhaled slowly. "You must sit."

He helped her into the chair and knelt before her again.

"I know what you just did, my dear."

She made her countenance as guileless as she could.

"Me? Pray, what did I do?"

He chuckled. "You stopped me from beating that insufferable ruffian to within an inch of his life. I hope you do not plan to manipulate me in such a way throughout our marriage. 'Tis a bit frightening to realize how easily you sway me."

Elizabeth managed to look shocked, though her eyes betrayed her mirth.

"Our marriage? I have no memory of a proposal. How did I miss such an auspicious moment?"

He bent to kiss her lips soundly.

"I fear I have compromised you thoroughly, and Mr. Jones was a witness to your shame and my villainy." He wiggled his eyebrows. "You must marry me as soon as ever may be, or he will spread the tale throughout Meryton as well as London. Would you ruin my reputation?"

She maintained a serious countenance.

"Well, I suppose I must agree since you put it that way. However, I did so want a romantic offer that could warm my heart when I am old."

He stood with his chin in his hand for a moment before he looked back down at her with eyes full of mischief.

"Flowers?"

"Oh, yes."

"Perhaps a piece of jewelry?"

Elizabeth clasped her hands together, smiled sweetly, and nodded with enthusiasm.

"Do I have your promise you will accept this time?"

She bit her lip and laughed softly.

"You know I am teasing you. I accept now, silly man. I do not need flowers or jewelry, for I would not go another minute without giving you my promise."

"Then you are mine now."

"As you are mine."

His countenance was triumphant as he leaned over and kissed her a third time.

Chapter Twelve

When Darcy and Elizabeth entered the parlour, Charlotte stood and crossed the room to greet them.

She bent to take Elizabeth's hands in hers. "Thomas has gone, saying he will not return. He told us that Lady Catherine has no further need of him and my husband is past the worst of his illness." She straightened up and looked from Darcy to Elizabeth. "Thomas apparently thinks his job is done, and Mr. Sims is now sufficient for both patients."

Charlotte sighed. "He appeared to be quite angry and announced he would return to London immediately."

Darcy placed a hand on Elizabeth's shoulder.

Elizabeth looked up at her friend. "I fear this is my fault, for Thomas is most put out with me. He broke off our friendship in a very unpleasant way."

Darcy made a small noise of disgust. "I wonder how he intends to travel back to Town, for he rode in my carriage with me, and the carriage will remain here until I choose to leave."

Charlotte glanced at his hand, still possessively placed on Elizabeth's shoulder, saying, "I see he has offended you, Mr. Darcy. Thomas's temper often gets the best of him. It has been so since he was a child. When he did not get his way, he could be most disagreeable."

"I think we may safely say that Thomas is no longer the Darcy family physician," said Elizabeth.

"Mr. Hough will fill that vacancy quite nicely," said Darcy decisively.

He leaned over to whisper to Elizabeth, then strode across the room to look out the window, arms crossed over his chest.

Miss de Bourgh looked from him to Elizabeth, arching an eyebrow. "Mr. Jones seemed to be in a great hurry to leave, so I sent for one of my carriages. I would not have him stay when he no longer wished to do so. His trunks were packed in all haste and brought down so as not to delay him. I daresay, Mr. Hough will come if we truly need him, and Mr. Sims is capable if we do not. Do you not agree, Cousin?"

He dropped his arms to his sides and turned to face her. "I do, and I thank you for your expeditious handling of the matter. I do not wish to have further contact with Mr. Jones."

Darcy cleared his throat, clasping his hands behind his back. "I shall talk no more of the physician, for I have much better news to reveal. I should like for you all to know that Miss Bennet has agreed be my wife. You shall decide when to tell your mother, Anne, as well as the best manner in which to present the happy news. I would go to Longbourn today to speak with Mr. Bennet were it not for the celebration day after tomorrow. As it is, I shall write a letter immediately and have it sent express. Please wait until I receive his reply before you inform my aunt."

Darcy returned to Elizabeth's side, leaning over to see her face. "Thomas must not be allowed to spread his lies before your father hears from me."

She smiled at him. "I shall write to him as well as my mother, and you may send both my letters together with yours. They can have no objection to our union."

He lifted her hand and pressed his lips to her knuckles before he straightened.

"May I be the first to wish you joy?" asked Miss de Bourgh, eyes shining with happiness.

"You may," answered Darcy, smiling broadly.

Charlotte, Maria, and Mrs. Jenkinson added their congratulations to Miss de Bourgh's, and the happy couple moved to a table where they could pen their letters together.

~~oo~~

Christmas day dawned, and Elizabeth was delighted to find that she no longer needed the Bath chair. Though her ankle was not so fit as to tempt her to run through the gardens, she was able to walk without too much discomfort.

The morning passed most pleasantly as everyone made final preparations for the Boxing Day celebration. There was an excitement at Rosings which had been extremely rare for the past twenty years at least.

The cook had outdone herself preparing Christmas dinner, and after enjoying it to their hearts' content, Charlotte, Miss de Bourgh, and Mrs. Jenkinson adjourned to the parlour.

In the ballroom, the Yule log burned brightly in the grand fireplace as Elizabeth, Darcy, and Maria gathered to enjoy the tree and place the last of the gifts on the branches.

When they had finished, Elizabeth announced her intention to stay in the ballroom, planning to practice her music for the celebration on the morrow.

Maria followed her to the pianoforte to turn her pages, but Darcy waved her off with a smile. She left the room, expressing her wish to go to the other ladies.

He pulled up a chair beside the bench.

"Merry Christmas, my love," he said. "Has it been a happy day for you?"

"You pretend you have not noticed my joy? I thought I surely must be glowing like the sun. My cheeks fairly ache from smiling"

His eyes were bright. "I have hardly looked away from you all day. I have a secret," he said, grinning with mischief.

She laughed. "You must not want to keep it, or you would not tease me so."

"I would have no secrets between us," he replied, attempting a serious expression without success.

"Then you must tell me immediately," she answered, chuckling. *He is like a small boy in his excitement.*

He took her hand in his. "This has been the best Christmas of my life."

"Truly? You have most likely been given everything you ever wanted. Ponies, toys, books, travel – what have you lacked?"

The corners of his lips quirked up. "Why, you, of course. No other gift could compare to you, Elizabeth. I have never loved anyone else as I do you, and for you to love me in return fulfills the fondest wishes of my heart."

His words took her breath away, and it took a moment for her to gather her thoughts.

"I have always been a disappointment to my mother. I was neither the prettiest nor the liveliest of her daughters. Jane and my father loved me as I was, and Charlotte has always been a faithful friend, but I fear the remainder of my family and acquaintances do not view me favourably."

He shook his head. "I must disagree as to your beauty and animation, for you are quite the loveliest woman of my acquaintance, and I know your sisters as well as your mother. For them not to adore you shows the defects in their own natures. Beyond that, I admire your mind and your character."

"I know you do, my dearest. Trust me when I tell you I cannot take that lightly. You are the perfect man for me."

"Yet you resisted me for nearly a year." His eyes dropped to their hands, dark lashes shading his cheeks.

"You must promise to forget that lack of judgment on my part," she whispered. "I misunderstood you. Once I knew you, I loved you with all my heart, and I was profoundly saddened to realize what manner of man I had rejected. I am sorry I hurt you."

He lifted his eyes, caressing her cheek with his fingertips. "Pray, do not be distressed. You were justified in your response to my proposal. My manner of offering proved that I did not deserve you. I am fortunate that you did not find a better man and marry him instead."

"As I could find no better man, I had determined I would never marry," she replied, turning her head to kiss his fingers.

"I should be unhappy to hear you say that, but I am a selfish man. May I ask why you had decided such a thing?"

She looked up at him with all the adoration she felt. "If I could not have you for my husband, I would have no other. The poor man would have forever lived in your shadow, as I could love no other as I love you. You are the best man of my acquaintance."

He took her face between his hands and lowered his lips to hers.

~~oo~~

Before a quarter of an hour had passed, the couple wisely decided it would be best to join the rest of the party in the parlour.

Elizabeth immediately saw that the Bath chair had been put to good use, for Lady Catherine de Bourgh was seated in it, attended by a footman.

Darcy bowed and Elizabeth curtseyed.

"It is good to see you, Aunt," he said calmly. "I hoped you would be able to come down for Christmas."

She frowned and narrowed her eyes. "I would rather doubt that, nephew, but we shall not quarrel again. Too much has happened while I have been indisposed. Anne has told me of your plans for tomorrow."

He escorted Elizabeth to a chair and stood beside her.

"Excellent. We all hope you will enjoy the decorations and the Boxing Day celebration. My cousin and the other ladies have all worked quite diligently to accomplish so much."

Her eyes locked with his. "I doubt I could bear the excitement of so many people in my condition, so I shall remain above stairs during the festivities."

"As you wish."

She shifted her attention to Elizabeth. "I have been told that Mr. Collins is doing quite well. You will be leaving Rosings soon to return to the parsonage with Mrs. Collins."

Elizabeth inclined her head. "I feel certain Mr. Sims will give us good news before long. Charlotte must be eager to settle herself in her home to await the birth of her child."

"We shall return to the parsonage the day after tomorrow, if Mr. Sims approves," answered Charlotte.

Lady Catherine looked from Darcy to Elizabeth. "Excellent. Mr. Collins surely must be in need of the company of his wife by now. He has had very little to occupy his time, I would imagine."

Charlotte smiled and nodded. "While I appreciate your generous hospitality, I confess I am eager to return to the parsonage. I have much to do."

"Do not walk home, Mrs. Collins," intoned Lady Catherine. "Though it is but a short distance, it is cold, and the ice is treacherous. You must take our carriage. I will brook no arguments."

"You are very kind," answered Charlotte.

"I am glad that you show proper appreciation," the lady replied. "So many people have no notion of gratitude." Frowning, she glanced at Elizabeth. "I suppose allowances must be made for a lack of proper decorum due to deficient training during the formative years."

Elizabeth lowered her eyes, knowing that her thoughts were betrayed too easily by their expression.

Darcy immediately offered her his arm. "We shall be quite occupied tomorrow, and as our guests will leave for the parsonage the day after, I should like to show Miss Bennet parts of the gardens which she has yet to see. Would any of you other ladies care to join us?"

"Please, come. I am certain you would enjoy it," said Elizabeth as she stood, placing her hand on Darcy's arm.

Maria crossed the room to join them, but the other ladies chose to remain with Lady Catherine, pleading fatigue.

As they walked down the hallway, Maria asked Darcy and Elizabeth to wait while she fetched her pelisse and bonnet, as well as Elizabeth's.

She hurried away, and Darcy turned to his betrothed.

"My aunt oversteps her boundaries. If she does not mend her ways regarding you, we shall not visit Rosings Park in the future. I will not have her treating you thus. Had I already received your father's permission, I would have told her so just now."

Elizabeth patted his arm. "We must think of Miss de Bourgh."

"She is well able to travel to London, and we shall meet her there. I will not come here without you, and I will never tolerate anyone's rudeness to my wife."

"I fear you may have to face many in the *ton* who share your aunt's opinion. Truly, it does not bother me, Mr. Darcy. I would not have you limit your circle because of me."

He bit the edge of his lower lip. "I will not allow you to be abused by anyone, Elizabeth. I have never cared for society or the *ton*, though I have endured it for Georgiana's sake. However, I will not stand by silently if any of our acquaintance chooses to be so foolish as to cut you. They are not necessary for my happiness. You are."

"What of Georgiana? I should not like to deprive her of her coming out."

"She shall have her Season. You forget that Lady Catherine is not my only relation. The Fitzwilliam family shall love you as I do, and they are quite powerful. Do not be distressed, my love. You shall adore Aunt Isabella, and she will take delight in you. She has never cared for Aunt Catherine, and it shall bother her not at all to thwart the lady."

"Do you speak of Colonel Fitzwilliam's mother?"

"I do. No one shall dare to be uncivil to you in her company. To displease her in such a way would be social suicide."

Elizabeth nodded, and, as Maria rejoined them, she began to speak of the celebration the following day in terms of great happiness and anticipation.

Soon they were smiling and laughing together, enjoying the beauty of the gardens.

Chapter Thirteen

Rosings Park bustled with activity well before dawn on Boxing Day. The servants were excited that there was to be a celebration, for many of them were family members of the tenants. Not only would they spend most of the day with their families, but also they would be a part of the festivities, enjoying the food, games, music, and dancing.

In an effort to make everything as easy as possible for the staff, Elizabeth had told her maid to come an hour before sunrise, so she was dressed and ready to break her fast well before her usual time. She opened the door from her room into the hallway and stopped in surprise.

Mr. Darcy awaited her there, holding several folded papers in his hand. He held them up and smiled with obvious delight.

"These letters were delivered by express quite early this morning. I thought we could read them together over our morning meal."

Her dark eyes sparkled. "You have not read them? I confess I am shocked by your lack of curiosity."

He shook his head. "I wished to share them with you."

"But what if my father refuses to give his blessing and my mother says terrible things about you?" she asked with exaggerated consternation.

Darcy cocked his head, apparently in deep thought.

"Then I suppose we shall elope. After all, we do not truly need their approval, though I should like to have it all the same."

She raised both eyebrows, genuinely surprised. "You would elope? You? The very proper Mr. Darcy? I confess I am astonished! What would people say?"

"Elizabeth, I nearly lost you by worrying about the approbation of other people. I now care more for your opinion than I do anyone else's." His gaze was earnest. "Would you elope with me if there were no other way?"

"Fitzwilliam, you surely know I was teasing. My parents will have no objections. My father will give his consent readily, and my mother shall likely be embarrassingly eager to have your family connected to ours. In fact, I am extremely relieved that you did not approach my father in person at Longbourn where you could have both seen and heard her jubilation."

"You have avoided answering my question. Would you elope with me?" He offered her his arm.

"Right now? We would miss the Boxing Day celebration, and we have worked so diligently." She chuckled as she tucked her hand into the crook of his elbow.

"I am perfectly serious."

Elizabeth looked up at him, curious. *Why is this so important to him?* "Of course, I would, my love, though the gossip would be unpleasant to endure. My reputation would be in shreds, but that would be a small price to pay. I would never risk losing you again."

His smile was wide, displaying his dimples. "'Twas all I wanted to know. Though I would happily marry you today in London with a special license, we can certainly wait for the banns to be read in Longbourn church. I want no hint of scandal to attach to you."

"Very wise on your part, for my father might call you out, and my mother would despair of her opportunity to play hostess on such an auspicious occasion."

"One month. I want to take you to Pemberley as my bride in a month. Do you agree?"

"If Charlotte's child cooperates."

"I shall order it, and the child shall obey." His face was solemn, voice deep.

"It appears to be a simple matter for the master of Pemberley."

"Who would dare to thwart such a noble personage, descended from the aristocracy of Ireland and England?" he thundered.

The jubilant couple continued on their way to the breakfast parlour, continuing to banter amiably.

~~oo~~

After they were seated at the table, Darcy opened his letter from Mr. Bennet while Elizabeth read hers from her mother. Finished, she turned her head to observe his expressions.

"What does my father say?"

"He gives his consent," replied Darcy, eyes twinkling. "It seems he is eager to add another man to the family, as he has been living with your mother and two sisters since you, Jane, and your youngest sister are gone, and he finds himself lacking any sensible conversation."

"I am surprised he misses Lydia and her husband. He was not overly fond of Mr. Wickham, even before he acted so dishonourably."

"Your father writes that she is no longer at home – not that he wishes she were back. However, it seems I have a standing invitation to Longbourn, so I should be happy to escort you and Miss Lucas there whenever you are ready. I put the idea to your father in my letter, and he approves, saying it will save him both the trouble and expense of arranging proper transportation for you. What says your mother?"

She folded the letter and laid it aside. "Suffice it to say that Mama is enraptured at the idea of our betrothal. Fortunately, you are not at Longbourn as a witness to her exultation. Finally, I have done something which pleases her, though she is quite anxious regarding the wedding clothes."

He chuckled softly. "Even though I am neither so handsome nor so pleasant as Bingley?"

Elizabeth looked heavenward. "My dear, you are now the handsomest man who ever was, and she admires your manners, courtesy, bearing, air – need I elaborate further? She absolutely adores you, though you probably should have married Kitty. She fears my independent, stubborn nature may cause you unhappiness."

"Did you just roll your eyes?" Darcy asked, laughing aloud.

She stared at him and bit her thumb very deliberately.

He laughed even more loudly. "Did you bite your thumb at me?"

"I do bite my thumb, sir."

"But did you bite you thumb at me?"

She grinned impishly. "No, sir. I do not bite my thumb at you, sir; but I bite my thumb, sir."

"I have heard you and your sisters revelled by acting out plays when you were younger. Exactly how many parts did you play in *The Most Excellent and Lamentable Tragedy of Romeo and Juliet*? Most importantly, did you take the part of Juliet, and, if you did, who was Romeo?"

"I think you know the answer to your questions, sir. I played many parts, and I was, indeed, Juliet to Thomas's Romeo. However, I refused to kiss him, so he kissed my cheek instead. I was but ten years old, and he was fourteen." She placed her hand on his arm. "I have always thought of him as a brother."

Darcy took a deep breath. "There is one small consolation. At least he died at the end. Quite painfully, I believe."

She giggled and put her hand over her mouth. "Wicked man!"

"We may have to read Shakespeare's plays together, and I will be Romeo, as well as any other character you romanced. I *will* kiss you, and not on the cheek."

"Oh, I hope so. I fervently hope so."

He looked behind himself, and seeing there was no one attending them, he quickly pulled a sprig of mistletoe from his pocket, held it above her head, and gave her what she hoped for.

~~oo~~

At Miss de Bourgh's request, the housekeeper and butler had arranged a schedule for the servants' work so that none of the Rosings staff would be excluded from the party. Furthermore, it was rumoured among them that there was a present for each of them on the tree, and they were amazed at the lady's generosity.

Miss de Bourgh had always been a favourite among the servants at Rosings, but their affection for her greatly increased at the proof of her thoughtfulness.

Darcy, Elizabeth, Miss de Bourgh, Miss Jenkinson, Charlotte, and Maria made their way to the ballroom just before noon, when the guests were to begin arriving. Rather than making a receiving line, they placed themselves in pairs throughout the room, ready to greet the families and direct them to the tables laden with seasonal fare.

As the room began to fill with people, Darcy leaned over to speak with Elizabeth.

"Perhaps 'tis a good time for some music while they eat." He offered her his arm. "I shall claim the honour of turning the pages for you."

She took his arm, and he escorted her through the crowd to the pianoforte.

Soon she was seated and playing "Silent Night," "The Holly and the Ivy," and other favourites while Maria engaged in games with the children.

A small girl came up to the piano and stayed, watching Elizabeth's hands.

Elizabeth stopped playing to look at the girl, smiling. "Do you have a request, my dear?"

The curly haired waif nodded, staring with large, blue eyes. "'I Saw Three Ships.' My brother and I sing it. 'Tis the one we like the most at home."

"Mr. Darcy, do we have the music?"

"Here 'tis," he replied after rifling through the stack on a table by the instrument.

"What is your name, sweetheart?" Elizabeth asked.

"Lucy Baker, ma'am."

"And your brother's name?"

"Luke."

"I shall play the song if you and Luke agree to sing it."

When Lucy nodded, Elizabeth sent her to fetch her brother. A few moments later, one of the stable boys stood beside the pianoforte, holding Lucy's hand.

Elizabeth began to play the tune, and soon the room quieted, listening to the siblings sing. Other children came forward to join them, and the lively tune inspired several couples to dance.

As soon as Elizabeth finished playing that song, she was besieged with requests, and she gladly granted every one.

An hour passed quickly before Miss de Bourgh stood in front of the tree. The room fell silent, and she asked Darcy and the three ladies to assist her in distributing the gifts.

Everyone, from the oldest to the youngest, received a gift, and as they left, they were given two pieces of fruit to take home. Darcy and Elizabeth made certain that those unable to attend due to age or infirmity were remembered with gifts and food, sent home with their family members.

Finally, the room emptied, and the tired host and hostesses retired to the parlour, all declaring that it was the best Christmas they could remember.

~~oo~~

Darcy accompanied Elizabeth, Charlotte, and Maria the next morning, expressing his wish to be certain that the carriage, as well as inhabitants, arrived at the parsonage safely.

At Charlotte's invitation, the gentleman followed them into the house, hoping that he might pay a short visit to Mr. Collins. The previous evening, Lady Catherine had expressed a wish to be apprised of her parson's condition, and Darcy wanted to set her mind at ease.

A half hour later, he was sanguine concerning the recovery of Mr. Collins, but not as confident in reference to the parson's wife.

Charlotte had gone immediately to her husband's side, but soon retreated to her own room, citing extreme fatigue and discomfort.

Seeing Elizabeth's worried face, Darcy sent for Mr. Sims.

The apothecary was soon in attendance and examining his patient. When he had finished, he approached Darcy, Elizabeth, and Maria, who waited in the hallway outside her room.

Mr. Sims rubbed his forehead. "It appears that the infant will make an earlier appearance than I originally thought. Since 'tis only two or three weeks before her full time, mother and babe should be fine."

Elizabeth's concern was evident in her tone. "I knew she had done too much in the past week. I tried to get her to rest, but she would not. How soon do you think it will be?"

"Tonight or tomorrow. Mrs. Smith had thought to go home today, but I shall tell her to stay. She will know when to call me."

The next morning, Charlotte gave birth to a small, noisy baby boy.

~~oo~~

Elizabeth and Maria stayed another week, and on their final day in Kent, Darcy came to the parsonage and invited Elizabeth to walk with him. She happily agreed.

Under the tree where he had given her his letter the previous April, he paused, pulling a box from his pocket.

"I stood under this oak tree during one of the lowest points in my life and handed you a letter filled with vitriol," he said quietly. "I should like to make a more pleasant memory here for the both of us."

He reached for her hand, and placed the box in her palm. "'Tis a late Christmas present."

"A late Christmas present?" she asked with a small frown. "But I have bought nothing for you."

"Please, open it, dearest. You will see that I spent no money."

She untied the string and tore away the paper. When she removed the lid, she found a lovely ring, set with emeralds and diamonds.

"It was my mother's," he said, his voice low. "I had it repaired and cleaned in London, and my man must have packed it in my trunk when I left to come here. Do you like it?"

He took it from the box and slipped it on her finger.

She held her hand out to admire it. "'Tis the most beautiful ring I have ever seen. I shall always think of your face when I look at it, for your eyes are just that colour. Emeralds are now my favourite stone."

Darcy grasped her hand and held it between his own. "My parents would have loved you, Elizabeth. They would be pleased I have found a woman who completes me so well. I cherish you with all my heart."

She withdrew her hand and placed it on his face, cupping his cheek. "The ring is exquisite, but you had already given me the best gift I shall ever receive."

He drew his brows together. "I have no memory of ever giving you anything, save for that bitter letter, though I have long wished to do so."

"My dear Mr. Darcy," she said softly, placing a finger on his lips. "You have given me yourself, and that is all I want. You are my forever Christmas gift."

She lifted her face to his, standing on her tiptoes, as he took her in his arms.

The world faded from around them, lost in their embrace as he kissed her.

He finally broke the kiss and whispered, "Forever. I like the sound of that."

She nodded. "Forever."

The End

If you enjoyed reading *Her Christmas Gift*, you may like these other books by Robin Helm, available at Amazon.com.

For news of her new releases, follow her on her Amazon author page.

Guardian, Soul Fire, Legacy (The Guardian Trilogy)
Yours by Design, Sincerely Yours, Forever Yours (Accidentally Yours Trilogy)
Understanding Elizabeth

THE MATCHMAKER'S CHRISTMAS

Laura Hile

THE MATCHMAKER'S CHRISTMAS

Copyright © 2017 Laura Hile

Chapter One

Charles Bingley looked as fatigued as Darcy felt, but there was no room for pity today. Bingley's sister was right. He must be packed off to London.

"Really, Darcy," protested Bingley, as he came down the steps to the drive, "a delay of only one day—"

"—would be most unwise," said Darcy. "One cannot escape business by hiding in the country, Charles. Trust me to know."

Bingley gave another yawn. "But I did not turn in until almost four. And my bed is calling—"

Darcy put a firm hand on his friend's shoulder. Bingley must not be allowed to talk his way out of this. There was too much at stake.

"I know, old man," said Darcy, more kindly. "It's cold and you're done in. But you've put this off long enough."

A footman held open the door, and Darcy guided Bingley to his traveling coach. "Once you are underway, stretch out on the seat. I've instructed Mrs. Nicholls—there, do you see? She has set you up nicely. Pillows and blankets and, unless I miss my guess, a warm brick for your feet and a flask for comfort."

Bingley looked unhappy. "I'm not an old woman."

"Think how much better you'll feel to have this behind you."

Bingley's red-rimmed eyes met Darcy's. "I intend to return tonight."

"Upon my word, man, why? Give yourself a few days."

"But there is so much to be done. Here at Netherfield, I mean."

"In late November? I think not."

"But you said— those improvements to the—"

"—can wait until spring. Besides, it's been raining all week. What exactly do you intend to accomplish?"

"But-but," Bingley babbled, "I must speak with Mr. Bennet as soon as may be. He's Jane's father, you know."

Darcy fought to keep from showing alarm. Things with Jane Bennet had become more serious than he realized. "All in good time," he soothed. "Bennet can wait." He closed the coach door behind Charles, and signed to the driver.

The coach rolled forward, with Bingley's dismayed face showing through the window glass. Darcy forced a smile and lifted a hand. There. The first step of his plan was underway.

Or was it Caroline Bingley's plan?

This thought brought a grimace. It was his plan, and yet—

Darcy dug his hands in his pockets. Only a madman would align himself with Caroline Bingley, but what else could he do? Charles had too soft a heart and was too easily influenced. Moreover, his fortune made him prey to the likes of Jane Bennet. Her mother's smug complacency last night was galling.

Another sigh escaped Darcy's lips. *Haven't I had enough of matchmaking women!*

No, his pact with Miss Bingley could not be helped, for who else had Charles's interests at heart? Oh, Caroline said sweet things about Jane—for indeed she was a gentle, kindly girl—but the idea of a marriage alliance with the Bennets was as repugnant to her as it was to Darcy.

At the door to the house Darcy hesitated; his gaze took in the expanse of park with its winding drive. After last night's ball, it had been lined with carriages. He had stood just here, in the flickering light of the torches, watching Miss Elizabeth Bennet descend to her family's carriage.

Elizabeth. Even now he could recall their dance together and each conversational exchange. Her eyes, sparkling with intelligence and wit; the enigmatic smile; the delicious trill of her laugh. Elizabeth Bennet did not simper or flirt. Indeed, she thoroughly disliked him.

And yet before entering the carriage, Elizabeth had looked back at the house—and at him. Their eyes met. Or had they? The distance was great. Perhaps he'd imagined that uncanny flash in her eyes.

Blast. He was as infatuated with Elizabeth as ever! Charles Bingley was not the only one who must leave the Bennet family behind.

Darcy went into the house, crossed the entrance hall, and mounted the stairs. This obsession with Elizabeth Bennet was nothing that a morning ride would not cure. He would change and send word to the stables.

Unfortunately, Darcy's trek took him past the open door to the dining room. Brittle laughter drifted out. Caroline Bingley. What the devil had she found to laugh about at this hour? He looked in. There she sat, close beside her sister, with a paper between them.

"Oh, Mr. Darcy," Miss Bingley sang out. He had been seen.

Politeness demanded a response. Concealing his irritation, Darcy entered the dining room. "You are up early," he remarked.

She rewarded him with a conspiratorial smile. How he wished she hadn't! Doubtless she would invite him to sit beside her. He'd see that! Darcy crossed to the buffet and took up a plate. Since he was here, he might as well eat.

"We are putting our plan into action, Louisa," she told her sister. "Charles is now on his way to London, is he not, Mr. Darcy?"

Darcy speared several strips of bacon. "He is."

Again he was rewarded with a smile. "It's a pity that Charles did not leave earlier. However, all is well that ends well, as the saying goes."

"That he managed to leave when he did is a wonder," said Darcy. "It was close on four when the last of the guests departed."

"Don't I know it?" Caroline Bingley gave a heavy sigh. "The Bennet clan. They simply *would not* go, Louisa. I was forced to make conversation with the mother. She is not one to take a hint."

"Dear Caroline," soothed Louisa Hurst. "How you have suffered."

"The things I do for Charles," Caroline went on. "A full month wasted in this dreary house—days and days! —just because he wished to shoot. And then, although I am feeling quite ghastly this morning, what must he do but leave me to entertain our countrified neighbours."

"Truly, you have been a saint," said her sister.

Darcy remained silent. *Saint* was not how he would describe Caroline Bingley. His morning ride was looking better and better, so long as the rain held off. A cup of coffee, a bite of breakfast, and then—

"I have written a little note to dear Miss Bennet." Caroline held out a sheet of paper to Darcy—the one they had been laughing over. "Do let us hear your opinion."

Must she relish the role of co-conspirator so openly? Those looks of hers made Darcy's flesh crawl. Had he cherished a *tendre* for Caroline Bingley— which he had not!—this shared *contretemps* would have cured him of it.

Nevertheless, Darcy knew his duty. He abandoned his plate and took the paper Caroline offered. He brought it to the windows to read.

Caroline continued to talk. "How I wish that we had left with Charles, and do you know why?"

"My dear, it was quite impossible," protested Louisa. "Mr. Hurst will sleep until noon, at the very least."

Apparently this was not the response Caroline was looking for. "Do you know why, Mr. Darcy?" she repeated.

Darcy lifted his gaze from the letter, but he did not look at her. "To escape the possibility of rain?"

She gave a sharp trill of laughter. "What care I for rain? It's the dreary round of morning calls I must endure. Our so-polite neighbours will come to express gratitude for the ball, and Charles has saddled me with the responsibility of receiving them."

Had she forgotten that Charles did not wish to leave? He would have enjoyed conversing with each person who came.

Darcy returned to Caroline's letter. It was laced with sweetly-worded snubs that even a gentle girl like Jane Bennet could not mistake. This was an ugly business. Darcy tossed the letter onto the dining table. "I take it that this note will be delivered after we are gone?"

"But of course. I trust I have made my point?"

"That it is doubtful whether Charles will ever return to Netherfield? Yes."

Much as Darcy deplored Caroline's crude tactics, Jane Bennet's matrimonial hopes—and those of her mother—must be quashed. He remained at the windows, gazing out the leaden November sky. Then a movement caught his eye: a coach pulled by four horses was coming up the drive.

He turned and glanced at Caroline, who was smiling over her letter. A three-cornered cat's smile it was, and wholly unattractive. "I believe," said Darcy, "that one of your callers has arrived."

"So early? They should not come until three, at the earliest." Caroline's tone became sharp. "It is Mrs. Bennet and her daughters, I just know it. Wretched woman! Come to steal a march on the others, and to plague me to death." She rose to her feet and reached for the bell pull. "I am not at home to callers. Indeed, were it not for the necessity of Charles' departure, I would still be in bed."

Louisa Hurst joined Darcy at the windows. "This is not the Bennet carriage, my dear. A traveling coach, nicely-appointed, and simply drenched with mud."

"Oh, heavens," said Caroline Bingley, and she turned away. Darcy hid a smile. He watched as the coach pulled up before the house. Two ladies—one young, one middle-aged—and a gentleman, descended.

Mrs. Hurst's tone became animated. "Caroline dear, I believe there is a crest painted on the door. Does Sir Lucas, or whatever his name is, have a crest? His title is so new."

From below came the sharp rap of the door knocker, then voices.

"Saints preserve us," said Caroline. "My poor head already throbs, and my throat is on fire. I do believe," she added, with a look to her audience, "that I am becoming ill."

The butler came in with cards: Miss Woodhouse, of Hartfield, and Miss Bates. And Mr. Thomas Bertram, of Mansfield Park.

Louisa Hurst looked to her sister. "My dear," she said softly.

Caroline responded with a toss of her head. "Of course we are not at home to them. The idea."

The butler went out, but returned almost at once. "The lady, Miss Woodhouse, refuses to go, Miss. She insists on seeing Mr. Bingley, and she wishes you to read this." He presented a folded paper.

Caroline opened it. Darcy itched to see what it said, for her dismayed expression as she read was comical.

"I know *nothing* of this invitation," she said at last. "Mr. Bingley is not here; he has gone to London. Tell these people to come back another day."

Meanwhile, Louisa Hurst had come to her sister's side. "Caroline, dear," she said fretfully, "we are acquainted with Sir Thomas Bertram; I believe this is the son. He is not to be, as Mr. Hurst so charmingly says, fobbed off. And Miss Woodhouse of Hartfield?" She murmured something in Caroline's ear.

"Oh, *very* well." Caroline paired this ungracious statement with a look at Darcy. "If I must see them, I must." She paused. "Show them into the front—"

But the butler had already gone out. Caroline spread her hands. "The staff in this house—hopeless, all of them! Receiving callers at the breakfast table?"

The door came open again. "Miss Woodhouse and Miss Bates," announced the butler. "Mr. Bertram will be joining you presently."

"Presently," said Caroline, aside. "How charming." Turning, she put on a polite smile. "So *unfortunate*, the timing of your visit. My brother is not at home. I," she added, "am Miss Bingley. This is my sister, Mrs. Hurst, and Mr. Darcy." She paused for emphasis. "Of Pemberley."

The younger woman appeared unimpressed. The older woman looked about the dining room in agitated dismay.

Darcy had the grace to feel ashamed for Caroline Bingley's intentional snub.

Miss Woodhouse, who was the younger of the two, came forward to take Caroline's hand. "How do you do?" She had a pleasant, musical voice. There was a pause. "Can it be that we are not expected, Miss Bingley?" To Darcy's surprise, Miss Woodhouse was smiling.

Such directness was disarmingly awkward, and Caroline began to stammer an answer. Although Miss Woodhouse shared the coloring of Jane

Bennet, she had none of Jane's gentle shyness. Here was no shabby country miss, but a well-heeled gentleman's daughter.

"Mr. Bingley's invitation," Miss Woodhouse went on, "was as much a surprise to me as it apparently is to you. I suspect its origin is found not in your brother, Miss Bingley, but in Aunt Jane."

"Who?" said Caroline faintly.

"Great Aunt Jane, our cousin on the Austen side? Surely you remember."

"We ... are related, you and I?"

Again Miss Woodhouse smiled. "Yes, very distantly," she said.

Caroline sought refuge from Miss Woodhouse's direct gaze by studying the invitation.

"It came about in this way," Miss Woodhouse continued. "I received a letter from Aunt Jane, describing a dilemma and requesting my help. I was obliged to refuse because of Father. He is an invalid, you see, and he quite depends upon me. Next, I received your brother's kind invitation. And then Mr. Bertram, whom you shall meet presently, arrived with his cousin, Miss Price."

"Such a helpful young woman, Miss Price," the other woman put in, with a nervous giggle. "She is to look in on my own dear mama from time to time."

There was nothing affluent or fashionable about Miss Bates. Caroline Bingley gazed at her as if she were vermin.

Miss Woodhouse went on with her story. "According to Mr. Bertram, our Aunt Jane commanded him—for there is no other word for it—to collect Miss Bates and me, and to bring us to you."

"So that you may solve Aunt Jane's dilemma?" said Darcy.

Miss Woodhouse gave him a bright smile. "Yes. Precisely."

"But you cannot stay with us," protested Caroline. "We are about to leave for London."

"Leave?" cried Miss Bates, flustered. "Oh dear me, no. You cannot wish to leave dear Netherfield. Not with three weeks left before Christmas."

"What has that to do with anything?"

Miss Woodhouse lowered her voice. "Why, no one spends Christmas in London if they can help it."

"Christmastide," said Miss Bates, warming to her subject, "is the glory of the country estate. How wondrous this old house was at Christmas, with so much gaiety and so many parties. Poor, dear Grandpapa," she added, "was very fond of parties. And gaming and horse racing, bless him."

She twisted her fingers together as she talked. "These led to his downfall—and to ours as well—and to that *most* unfortunate shooting accident. But we had, oh, so many happy times here. Bless me, that was close on forty years ago."

"*Here?*" cried Caroline. "Were you—in service—Miss, er, Bates?"

Frumpy, faded Miss Bates drew back her shoulders. "You would not know it to look at me now," she said, "but at one time I was Miss Henrietta Bates of Netherfield Park."

Silence filled the dining room. "There is a portrait of dear Mama on the wall just there," she went on, pointing. "How pretty she is! And goodness, there should be a portrait of me, as a mere slip of a girl, up in the gallery."

"With the frilled parasol?" said Darcy politely.

Miss Bates fairly beamed. "The very one! And now I have returned to Netherfield Park in time to keep Christmas."

"But you cannot stay," cried Caroline Bingley. "Indeed, you cannot."

Miss Woodhouse collected the invitation and folded it. "I do not think we have a choice in the matter, Miss Bingley," she said kindly. "Here we have come, and here we shall remain."

Chapter Two

Jane Bennet paced the length of the bedchamber she shared with her sister. "Lizzy," she said, "I am so very sorry. Truly."

"It's not worth fretting about," said Elizabeth. "Chances are it is here in the house; it will turn up."

"But it hasn't," said Jane mournfully, "and I have looked everywhere. It was lost at the ball last night; I just know it."

"That clasp has always given me trouble," Elizabeth pointed out. "I should not have loaned it."

"I should not have borrowed it."

"Nonsense. You did not ask; I offered. Amethysts are the perfect complement to your gown."

"They were," said Jane, with a sigh.

"Never mind. My bracelet will turn up somewhere."

"Somewhere at Netherfield," said Jane.

Netherfield. If Elizabeth did not see Netherfield ever again, it would be too soon! Last night's ball had been a disaster. In her mind's eye she could see the clumsy attempts at dancing made by her cousin, Mr. Collins. And she could hear his boastful speeches too—as well as her younger sisters' raucous laughter as they danced with the officers, and her mother's unwise (and rather loud) remarks made in the supper room. The unholy glee of Miss Bingley and Mrs. Hurst, as they observed all this, was palpable.

And then there was Mr. Darcy. True, she ought to have minded her tongue and left some things unsaid. But that expression of cold disdain, glittering in his dark eyes, she would not soon forget. It had been a horrid night. A wretchedly horrid night.

"I'll go down and write to Miss Bingley at once," said Jane, and she glanced at the window. "It is not raining. Ned can take it."

Elizabeth followed Jane out of the bedchamber and down the stairs. "Writing a note is not the way to find a thing," she said. "We must go to Netherfield ourselves."

Jane came to a halt. "Oh, Lizzy, I cannot," she said softly. "It would look as if I were grasping for a reason to—well, you know."

"—to see Mr. Bingley again?" Elizabeth could not keep back a smile. "Mama would approve."

Jane's eyes found the floor. "It-it is not like that. I am not chasing him, even though everyone says so. How mortifying to have Mama's ambitions displayed so publically."

"I fear Mama cannot help herself," Elizabeth said. "Your Mr. Bingley is quite the perfect match for you."

"If only he were not so wealthy! For people will say—"

"His wealth," interrupted Elizabeth, "is part of his perfection!"

"Lizzy!"

"I am only funning, dearest. I tell you what. I will go in your stead to Netherfield. No one can say that I am setting my cap at Charles Bingley."

"But Lizzy—"

"Believe me, I do not intend to force my presence on the Bingleys or the Hursts or Mr. Darcy. I had quite enough of their company when you were ill. I will ask at the service door for the housekeeper. And as I do not wish for Mama to know of my errand, I will walk to Netherfield."

"But the weather," protested Jane.

"You saw for yourself that it does not rain. Have no fear, everyone there will be asleep or at breakfast. The housekeeper will do all that is needed. I will be back before midday, you'll see."

But Netherfield's Mrs. Nicholls was not of a mind to search. "A little thing like that, Miss?" she said. "It could be anywhere. A very trying morning we've had." And then, because Elizabeth insisted, she brought her up to search the supper room and ballroom herself.

She passed to Elizabeth a dry mop and a lamp. "Mind, we've not cleaned, Miss, not properly, you understand. Not with two ladies and a gentleman arriving on our doorstep this morning, fine as you please, demanding to be housed and fed."

Mrs. Nicholls drew back one of the heavy draperies, sending a dust-filled shaft of light into the ballroom. "Moreover," she went on, "the mistress wishes to be packed up and gone as soon as may be. And the house closed for the season—all on the morning after the largest ball this neighborhood has seen in years. It's enough to drive a body to drink."

This from the dignified Mrs. Nicholls! What else could Elizabeth do but thank the woman and promise to stay out of her way?

How forlorn the ballroom was, with empty chairs grouped in corners and along the walls. Last night it had been alive with light and music and conversation. Now the glittering chandeliers were dark; the banks of flowers wilting. The air smelled of stale perfume.

Elizabeth removed her pelisse, set her gloves and bonnet on a chair, and took up the dry mop. She would begin with the area in front of the musicians' gallery and work through the room.

Straightway she saw the value of Mrs. Nicholls's lamp. By its light she found a button, several hair pins, and a spangled ribbon. The glitter of gold and amethysts was nowhere to be seen, but Elizabeth's memories shone bright. Here she had danced with Mr. Darcy—he had asked and she did not refuse him.

She ought to have done so! They had conversed together, and his answers were intelligent and even witty. Mr. Darcy was no fool, she gave him that. Even during Jane's illness, which kept her confined to this house, she had been impressed with his conversation. And he danced surprisingly well.

Here too she had danced with Mr. Collins—she had the bruised toes to prove it! The less she thought about him and his pompous conversation, the better.

And here Jane fell in love with Charles Bingley. Elizabeth paused in her search and leaned against the long handle of the dry mop. Beautiful, gentle, good-hearted Jane had found a kind man worthy of her love. In this Elizabeth rejoiced with all her heart.

Presently she heard a rattle of a latch, and the ballroom doors came open to admit someone. "Hello?" a man's voice called. "Mrs.—Hurst? Is that you?"

Elizabeth squinted at him through the dimness, but she did not answer. She did not dare, because she recognized his voice. It was Mr. Darcy.

"Who is there?" he enquired.

How like Mr. Darcy to be persistent! "It is I, Elizabeth Bennet," she said reluctantly. There. That would drive him away.

But he did not go. He simply said, "Miss Bennet."

And now an explanation was in order. "I—am searching for my sister's bracelet, or rather, my bracelet."

She was babbling. Heaven help her, she was babbling. "It was lost at the ball last night. Mrs. Hurst is not here."

"Have you searched the cloak room downstairs?"

This was an obvious location, but Elizabeth had not thought of it. "No. I—thank you for the suggestion."

Instead of leaving, Mr. Darcy came toward her through the dimness. "What sort of bracelet is it?"

"Amethysts set in gold. It—is not a great loss, Mr. Darcy. A mere trinket given me by my Aunt and Uncle Gardiner. Jane borrowed it, you see, and she is distressed because it went missing."

A gust of wind rattled the windows. The sky darkened noticeably.

The door came open again. "Mr. Darcy?" said a woman's pleasant voice. "Have you found Mrs. Hurst? Oh. Hello."

"Miss Woodhouse, this is Miss Elizabeth Bennet." Mr. Darcy paused. "Is she also related to Aunt Jane?"

Miss Woodhouse came forward in a decidedly friendly way and held out a hand to Elizabeth. "Of course she is related; we all are. How do you do, Miss Bennet? Forgive me; from what Miss Bingley was saying, I thought your name would be Jane."

"She is my sister," said Elizabeth. "And I shouldn't shake hands, as mine is rather dirty. I am searching for a bracelet Jane lost at the ball."

Emma grasped Elizabeth's hand anyway. "Then we must help you. Although," she added, "I should find Mrs. Hurst, for Miss Bingley must be stopped. She cannot be allowed to leave Netherfield, not when Aunt Jane so clearly wishes her to be here."

"Aunt Jane," said Darcy in a low voice, "is apparently some sort of guardian to us all."

"That is very nicely said," agreed Miss Woodhouse. "It is most unwise to trifle with Aunt Jane. No good will come of it."

A flash of lightning lit the room; in the near distance thunder rolled. Rain began to beat against the window glass. Elizabeth's heart sank. The minute she left Netherfield she would be drenched to the skin.

Apparently Mr. Darcy noticed her dismay, for he looked a question. "Yes, Mr. Darcy," said Elizabeth tartly. "As before, I scorned to use our carriage and walked." She gestured to the hem of her gown. "Behold, the mud. I had hoped to make my search privately, without attracting notice."

"You are stranded here?" said Miss Woodhouse. "Then we must persuade Miss Bingley to ask you to dinner, which would be a very good thing. Mr. Bertram is becoming rather tiresome."

"Oh, but Miss Woodhouse."

"Do call me Emma. Will you help me to find Mrs. Hurst and Miss Bingley?"

"Of course," said Elizabeth. "But I should tell you that Miss Bingley will not be pleased to see me."

"Nonsense," said Emma. "Now where could she and Mrs. Hurst be? The drawing room is already wrapped up in Holland cloth. Let us try the front parlour, a room Miss Bingley has set aside for receiving callers—most of whom she hopes will not come."

Darcy leaned in. "She means guests from last night's ball, who will come to express their thanks," he said to Elizabeth. "Caroline wishes them at Jericho."

"Caroline wishes to *be* at Jericho," said Emma pleasantly. "Which, I must say, is a very apt description for London." She waited at the door for Mr. Darcy to open it.

Elizabeth came into the front parlour in time to hear Mr. Hurst bellow, "Have I seen you somewhere? One of the clubs? The name is familiar."

A young man, dressed in what Elizabeth guessed to be very smart attire, was slouching against the mantelpiece. He straightened up and cleared his throat. "My father," he said, "is a member of White's, sir. But I prefer Boodle's."

"Fond of cards, are you? Whist, faro, quinze?"

The young man brightened. "I am a dab hand at hazard as well, sir, although the rules are devilish complex."

"Oho. Then we must have a game of whist, if we can find enough players. You there!" Mr. Hurst fixed a beady eye on Elizabeth. "You fond of cards?"

"I am afraid not, sir," she said. "No more than before."

"Ah, I remember you, the reader. Paugh." He swung round. "No use asking that gabble monger," he said of a middle-aged lady seated by the window. "No use asking Darcy either. Has to be Louisa and—say." He eyed Emma. "Do you play whist?"

"I play rather well, thank you," said Emma. "But at the moment I have no time for card games."

"Humph. Caroline will have to sit in. Now where did she put the cards? *Caroline?*"

"There is no need to *yell*," said a muffled voice. Apparently Caroline Bingley was lying on one of the sofas. She struggled to sit up. "I have no idea where your wretched cards are kept."

"You there, boy!" Hurst called to a footman. "Find us a deck of cards and bring in a glass and a new bottle for—what did you say your name was?"

"Bertram. Tom Bertram. My father is—"

There came a groan from Caroline. "For heaven's sake, speak more softly; my head aches dreadfully."

"And you would go to London today, would you, Missy?" said Mr. Hurst to her. He turned to Mr. Bertram. "Well, boy? You were saying something about your father?"

"His name is Sir Thomas. Sir Thomas Bertram."

"And you're Tom. Same as your father, eh? Eldest son?"

"That's right."

"Come take a seat, boy, and pit your skill against mine. And Caroline, if you know what's good for you, you'll play whist with young Tom, here. He's the eldest son." Mr. Hurst gave a braying laugh.

Emma leaned in. "Do you see why I am glad that you have come, Elizabeth? What sort of people have we fallen in with? I fear they are not gentlefolk."

Elizabeth bit her lip to keep from laughing. Had Mr. Darcy caught this remark? Yes, he certainly had. His expression was forbidding, but his eyes were alight with laughter. Somehow this gave her courage to approach the sofa.

"Good morning, Miss Bingley," she said. "I am come to search for a missing bracelet. It was never my intention to disturb you, but Miss Woodhouse and Mr. Darcy insisted that I pay my respects."

"How—lovely." Caroline's tone was arctic. Her gaze shifted to Elizabeth's hemline. "Dear me, Miss Elizabeth, is that mud *quite* dry?"

"It is," said Elizabeth. "Although this bit here"—she pointed to her smudged knee—"is from your ballroom floor."

"When in the country," said Emma, "one must expect a little mud now and again."

Caroline rolled her eyes heavenward, and this did not escape Emma Woodhouse. "Walking is a usual practice among resident landowners," she said. "I often walk about our park, or in the shrubbery, or to and from dear Highbury. Walking," she added, "seems rather odd to London people. I daresay that as you become accustomed to living on an estate, you will learn our ways."

Caroline's flushed face became even redder. "I'll have you know," she flashed, "that—"

The parlour door came open with a bang. "Hallo!" called a cheerful voice. "Here I am, home again. The bridge at Brunsley is washed out; can you believe it? So I had to turn back."

"Charles," cried Caroline hoarsely.

"Nonsense," said Mr. Hurst. "That bridge is made of stone; been there since Roman times."

"The bridge is as right as rain," said Charles, "it's the road on either side that's washed out. The river's overrun its banks."

"Could you not—what is the expression? *Ford* the river and press on? For you must go to London," wailed Caroline. "Our plan …"

"There's no crossing that river without a boat, dear girl," said Charles. "No harm done. The water should be down in a day or two."

"Unless it continues to rain," Emma pointed out. "I believe you are Mr. Bingley, the man who so kindly sent our invitation. How do you do? I am Emma Woodhouse of Hartfield."

Charles Bingley looked rather startled. He was kept from answering because of clucking noises made by the middle-aged woman, who had deserted her post by the window. She now hovered over Caroline Bingley.

"My dear," she said, "are you feeling *quite* well? I know it is not my place to say, but you look as if you are burning up with fever. My dear mother is prone to feverishness, so I know *all* about it. You ought to lie down again, with a damp cloth on your forehead. Is there someone here who can make a mustard plaster?"

"Caroline?" said Charles.

"I am fine," she insisted. But she lay back on the sofa cushions just the same.

"You do not look fine," her brother said. "As this lady said—I beg your pardon, ma'am, I did not catch the name?"

"This is Miss Bates, Charles," said Mr. Darcy. "Another of your invited guests. The gentleman is Mr. Tom Bertram."

"Of Mansfield Park," added Emma helpfully.

Miss Bates laid her hand on Caroline's forehead. "My dear child, you are burning up, positively burning up. And your cheeks …"

"Caro," said Charles, "your cheeks and your neck are swollen."

Caroline's hands flew to her neck. "They are not!"

"Indeed they are, and *very* much so," said Miss Bates. "And your head aches; you said so yourself. My dear, do you find it difficult to swallow?"

Caroline looked as if she were about to cry. "Of course not," she rasped.

"We'll see about that," said Charles, and he snatched Mr. Hurst's wine glass. "Drink this," he told his sister.

Elizabeth had to give Caroline Bingley credit. She did try to drink the wine.

"Of course I am not a physician—and you must have your own medical man in this area, although I daresay he cannot compare with our dear Mr. Perry," babbled Miss Bates. "It is a childhood illness, and you are not a child, but *all* the signs are present, indeed they are. I very much fear that you, Miss Bingley, have contracted the mumps."

"What?" shrieked Caroline. And then her eyes filled with tears, for her throat truly did pain her.

Mrs. Hurst shrieked too. "The mumps?"

"How—humiliating," wailed Caroline.

"But-but I have never *had* the mumps," cried Mrs. Hurst, "at least I do not think I have. And what if I am in the family way?"

Caroline wrinkled her nose. "Oh, surely not."

Mrs. Hurst gave her sister a look. "It *is* possible. And I'll not take the risk, thank you. Mr. Hurst," she called, "we must leave at once. Bridge or no bridge, we must get *away* from here."

"But Louisa—" rasped Caroline.

"I am very, *very* sorry, my dear, but it cannot be helped. We cannot host you for Christmas at Grosvenor Square this year. Come at Easter." She turned to her husband, who was deep in his card game with Tom Bertram. "Mr. Hurst!" she cried, and hurried from the room.

He rose to his feet and cast his cards on the table. "Just when I was winning," he complained. "First Charles steals my wine, and then I am cheated out of a game. And now," he added, "I must spend the night in some curst coaching inn." Mr. Hurst shambled off. The parlour door swung shut behind him.

Elizabeth went up to Charles. "If I might importune the Hursts, Mr. Bingley," she said, "the lane passes quite near to Longbourn. If your sister is ill, I should not trespass upon your hospitality by remaining. It would be so very helpful if I am not obliged to walk home."

"I'll see to it at once," said Charles.

"Have you had the mumps, Elizabeth?" said Emma anxiously.

"I believe so, yes. I do pity Caroline. I have heard that it is worse when one is older."

And so it was that Elizabeth found herself deposited in front of Longbourn House, as the wind howled and rain stung her skin. The bright fire in the drawing room soon set her to rights.

"Rain and more rain," lamented Lydia, gazing out of the windows at the downpour. "I do hope the officers will come this evening. Denney and Wickham promised so faithfully."

Elizabeth's lips compressed into a line. She had forgotten about Mr. Wickham—and the unjust treatment he had received at Mr. Darcy's hands. It was a very good thing to be gone from Netherfield.

"No bracelet, alas," Elizabeth whispered to Jane, "but my search was interrupted. The housekeeper knows of it, and when the rooms are more thoroughly cleaned, I daresay the bracelet will be found."

Jane's face crumpled. "Oh, Lizzy."

Elizabeth put her arms around her sister. "Do not cry, dearest. It was an accident. And just think, poor Caroline has contracted the mumps."

Mrs. Bennet came into the drawing room, with Mr. Collins hard on her heels. "Lizzy, where have you been? Whose coach was that?"

"I've been to Netherfield, Mama. The Hursts have kindly brought me home, because of the rain."

Mr. Collins cleared his throat. "But that coach was loaded for travel."

"It was, yes." Elizabeth paused. "It so happens, Mama, that Caroline Bingley has contracted the mumps. Mrs. Hurst has not had it, so she and her husband were off at once."

"A most sensible thing," announced Mr. Collins. "We do not want mumps here."

Mrs. Bennet kept silent, gazing at Elizabeth and Jane. "Mumps," she said at last, "spreads through a household like wildfire, the vilest thing."

"If that is so," said Elizabeth, "then it is likely that we have all had it."

Mr. Collins's eyes narrowed. "But are you certain? Because you, Miss Elizabeth, have brought disease into this house. And," he went on, "by embracing your sister, you have likely passed it to her."

"Mr. Collins—"

"Communicable disease is treacherous," he warned. "How it spreads from person to person is a mystery, but it is nothing to be trifled with."

"Why, that is very true," cried Mrs. Bennet. "Lizzy, what have you done?"

"Mama, we had the mumps as babies."

"Did you? We dare not take the risk. I agree with Mrs. Hurst, whom I have always thought to be a most prudent, sensible woman. You cannot stay here, either of you."

"What do you mean?"

"If there is mumps at Netherfield, then to Netherfield you must return."

"Mama! You cannot be serious!"

Mrs. Bennet gave the bell pull a series of tugs. "Hill will pack your things, girls, and Ned will drive you to Netherfield in the carriage."

"In the middle of a storm?"

"Indeed yes. What do the Bingleys mean by passing this highly contagious illness to you, and then sending you home like so much baggage? There you are, Hill. We need Jane's and Lizzy's best gowns and night things packed up right away—enough for three weeks."

"Mama, no!"

"For three weeks," repeated Mrs. Bennet. "Do you think a mother forgets how long her babies were ill? Mumps runs its course in three weeks. If we are lucky," she added with a smile, "perhaps you will be well again by the New Year."

Chapter Three

Not for the first time did Darcy wonder why he had become friends with the Bingleys. Charles was the best of fellows, but his sisters? What noise and nuisance! Neither of them possessed true elegance of mind, only pretension and posturing. Hurst was little better than a gamester—he would run through Louisa's fortune soon enough—while she clung to social ambition. As did her sister Caroline.

Darcy's lips twisted into a rueful smile. How right his grandmother had been! *An ape's an ape, a varlet's a varlet, though they be clad in silk or scarlet.*

Well, Caroline had taken to her bed, and the Hursts were gone away to their house in London. Darcy's plan to part Charles from Jane Bennet was thwarted, but at least there would be quiet in the house. As soon as the roads permitted, he would leave Netherfield. Charles and Caroline must remain until the New Year, for where would they go? There would be no celebrating Christmas with the Hursts.

But will she press me for an invitation to Pemberley?

"Ha," said Darcy aloud. He'd see that! Caroline Bingley had matrimonial ambitions, not only for herself but also for her brother. As if his fortune made Bingley an acceptable husband for Georgiana! That alliance would be as unequal as one between himself and, say, Elizabeth Bennet.

Which was plainly ridiculous. Elizabeth thoroughly disliked him, and no wonder. She'd believed whatever lies Wickham had told. Curse the fellow, he was never at a loss. The longer Wickham remained in Meryton, the more lies he would invent. Eventually the truth—and his debts—would cause him to flee, as a rat abandons a sinking ship.

Even so, Elizabeth Bennet would be difficult to forget. He'd seldom encountered so much intelligence and beauty and—to give it a name, sincerity—in a young woman. Moreover, she was refreshingly uninterested in pursuing him.

And then Darcy heard something—Miss Bates. Having seen Caroline put to bed upstairs—talking all the while—Miss Bates was now wandering the hallways of the first floor, singing. Her thin voice came warbling up the stairwell.

"Christmas is coming, the geese are getting fat,
Please put a penny in the old man's hat.
If you haven't got a penny, a ha'penny will do…"

There were a good three weeks until Christmas, and if she meant to keep singing that song …

Darcy made for the safety of the library and hastily closed the door behind him. Bingley was in a chair before the fire; he looked up with a smile.

"If you haven't got a ha'penny," said Darcy to Charles, "then God bless you."

"If I haven't got a what?"

"It's Miss Bates," said Darcy shortly. "She is not only anticipating Christmas, she is speeding the day by singing about it." He paused. "God only knows what she is doing here."

Bingley's smile disappeared; from a pocket he pulled a folded paper. "Here is Miss Woodhouse's invitation. I cannot understand it. This is my handwriting, but …" His eyes were pleading. "Darcy, I swear to you, I never wrote this letter."

Darcy pulled forward a chair. "Thus we are left with Miss Woodhouse's theory of Aunt Jane."

"Is there such a person?"

"Miss Woodhouse says so. According to Miss Bates, we are to celebrate Christmas together, observing all the old traditions."

"You are welcome in my house at any time, Darcy, but—"

"I am afraid not, old fellow. Georgiana waits for me to come to London, and we will travel north together. We will spend Christmas as we always have, at Pemberley."

Bingley passed a hand over his eyes. "Why have these people come? More to the point, how am I to be rid of them?"

"If the bridge at Brunsley is underwater, then—" Darcy was interrupted by a knock at the library door. He and Bingley exchanged a look.

"Come," called Bingley.

To Darcy's relief it was Emma Woodhouse who entered, not Miss Bates. She was followed closely by two others. Darcy rose to his feet, and then he heard Bingley's gasp of recognition. "Jane!" Charles cried. "Er—Miss Bennet!" There was no mistaking the joy in Bingley's voice.

And then Darcy saw Elizabeth. His heart begin to hammer. *Am I a schoolboy, that she should have this effect on me?* Yet he was powerless to do anything other than gaze at her.

"I am sorry to disturb," said Emma cheerfully, "but things have sorted out in a most interesting way."

Jane and Elizabeth were looking as flushed and uncomfortable as Darcy felt.

"It's—Mama," stammered Jane, close to tears. "Oh, Mr. Bingley, I was never so mortified. Indeed, I hardly know how to look you in the face."

Darcy glanced at Bingley. He looked as if he wished to take Jane into his arms! To prevent this, Darcy stepped forward. "Is Mrs. Bennet ill?" he said.

"Mama has—she has—"

Elizabeth spoke up. "It's this matter of the mumps. Because I was here this morning, Mama believes that I have contracted the disease. And because I embraced Jane, I have supposedly passed it to her." She hesitated.

"And therefore," Emma put in, "Mrs. Bennet does not wish to expose the family. She has sent Elizabeth and Jane to stay here while the sickness runs its course. Is this not delightful?"

"Oh yes," cried Bingley. "Indeed it is."

Elizabeth, living here? For several weeks? Darcy felt his mouth go dry. This was not good news. Why then was his heart rejoicing?

"But—the imposition," said Jane. "I would not put you out for the world."

Bingley spread his hands. "Darcy and I were just discussing Christmas. The bridge is out; we have nowhere to go."

"Actually—" Darcy began, and then stopped himself.

"We shall celebrate the season together!" cried Bingley.

Together for Christmas? That Charles would be in Jane's company was bad enough. But ... he and Elizabeth?

"Ring the bell, Darcy, will you?" said Bingley. "We must tell Mrs. Nicholls to set two more places at dinner—indeed, for every meal."

But before Darcy could obey, Bingley called him back. "We'll tell her ourselves; that would be simpler, eh?"

He offered his arm to Jane Bennet. "I am informed by Miss Bates," he said, "that we ought to observe Christmas with all the old traditions of Netherfield. The first Sunday of Advent is almost here. That is when we make the puddings, is it not?" The library door banged closed behind them.

Darcy found himself alone with Miss Woodhouse and Elizabeth. Miss Woodhouse was busy examining the bookshelves. "Mr. Darcy," she said, "do you know whether Mr. Bingley has a copy of Debrett's?"

She looked over her shoulder at Elizabeth "It is a guidebook for the peerage. Surely Miss Bingley has one," she said, before Darcy could answer. "Depend upon it, she means to marry well. Aha! Here we are."

Emma removed the book from its shelf and brought it to a table. "Something Mr. Hurst said interests me." She smiled at Elizabeth. "He is a funny one, is he not? The sort of person my brother-in-law would call a *rum'un.*"

"A what?" The words were out before Darcy could stop them. Hurst certainly *was,* but—

Elizabeth's eyes met his; she gave a gurgle of laughter.

Emma was untroubled. "He seems to be a *most* peculiar person. My brother-in-law *will* talk like that, because he is fond of jests and wordplay. I daresay it is also because he is a barrister. Mind, he is quite well-to-do, being a Knightley of Donwell Abbey. But such is the lot of a gentleman's younger son. He must have a profession."

"My Uncle Gardiner," said Elizabeth, "is in the same situation. He is in trade." She said this with a lift of her chin and a glance in Darcy's direction, as if it were a challenge. What did she mean by it?

Emma continued to turn pages. "But who is Sir Thomas Bertram? That is the question. Because young Tom is *not* a younger son. And so his presence becomes, shall we say, interesting?"

Darcy did not care for her implication. "In what way?" he said.

Emma gave him an ingenious smile. "I specialize in matchmaking."

She specialized in *what*? Somehow Darcy managed to keep his countenance.

"It is a most amusing occupation," continued Emma. "My first was ever so successful—my former governess and old Mr. Weston. They are happily settled at Randalls now."

"How nice for your governess," said Elizabeth.

"She is the dearest creature and quite the gentlewoman—as the best governesses always are. I have another match in progress, between my friend Harriet and our vicar. I do worry, however, because I am away. Matches, you see, need helping along."

"So I am given to understand," said Darcy dryly. A matchmaker in their midst. What next?

Then again, why should he object? Because dinner—without Caroline's repressive formality—was refreshingly agreeable. Charles sat in his place, and the others chose seats as they wished. Jane shyly slipped into the chair at Bingley's right, with Mr. Bertram beside her. Elizabeth sat at Bingley's left. Darcy could not help himself; he claimed the chair next to Elizabeth's. This meant that he had Miss Bates on his other side, but she was content to talk across the table to Mr. Bertram and Emma. Darcy hid a smile. Miss Bates could carry a conversation on her own, without stopping to draw breath.

And the wind and rain continued to beat against the house.

This meant that the bridge was still out. Darcy, imprisoned at Netherfield against his will, was forced to endure lovely, intelligent Elizabeth Bennet as his dinner partner. It was all he could do to keep a foolish smile from his lips.

This time—this time!—he would speak without stiffness or pretension. If Emma Woodhouse meant to match Elizabeth with Tom Bertram, she would have a fight on her hands!

After dinner Charles was intent on receiving the stream of callers his sister had predicted, and so he cheerfully led the entire party to the drawing room. But word must have had spread that there was sickness at Netherfield, or else the storm kept people at home. Only one person was waiting for them: Mr. Collins.

He rose to his feet. "My dear Mr. Bingley," he began, with impressive formality.

Still talking, Miss Bates came into the room, without noticing Mr. Collins. "Now then," she said, striking her hands together, "Christmas is a time for merrymaking. So we must play games in keeping with the holiday spirit."

"What sort of games?" Tom Bertram wanted to know. "Whist? Loo? Better yet, shall we set up a faro bank?"

"Goodness, no. Children's games, Mr. Bertram, the very best kind. Grandpapa and his friends were especially fond of Charades."

"My dear Mr. Bingley," began Mr. Collins again.

"Does anyone know how to play How, Why, When, or Where?" said Emma.

"A game of questions?" said Bingley. "Famous! Do teach us."

"Mr. Bingley," repeated Mr. Collins.

"My good fellow," said Bingley, "do sit down and enjoy yourself."

"Since there are so many of us, what about Reverend Crawley's Game?" said Miss Bates. "It is always most amusing, and not nearly as fatiguing as guessing. To play, we must stand in a circle."

"Oh, yes," cried Emma. "Let's do."

Immediately Darcy was on his guard. He had played this one before. Apparently Collins had too, for his expression was eager.

"We link hands," said Miss Bates, "but not with those on either side, or not both hands with the same person. And then we must untangle ourselves—but without letting go of the hands you are holding."

"Untangle ourselves?" said Elizabeth, laughing, "But how? We will be an enormous human knot!"

Vividly Darcy recalled the twisting and turning and stepping through, often at very close quarters. Collins—and Tom Bertram—must not be allowed to come smash up against Elizabeth Bennet like that.

He raised his voice about the babble. "What about dancing, instead?"

Had he truly suggested this? But the word *dancing* acted like magic. Darcy was voted a capital fellow; Bingley and Bertram began rolling back the carpet. "Will you play for us, Miss Bates?" Darcy enquired.

"Oh my, bless me," she fluttered and clucked. "I have not played in a good many years, not since I was a girl—a very long while ago——"

"I will play," said Emma, and she opened the pianoforte. "You must dance, Miss Bates. Country dances," she added, over Miss Bates's objections.

"I'm sure you remember how." She spread her fingers over the keys and played an opening chord.

Darcy took hold of Elizabeth's hand. "Do me the honour," he said in a low voice. "You suffered enough last night with Mr. Collins."

Elizabeth's startled eyes met his; he could see the refusal forming on her lips. "He is coming this way," Darcy murmured. Elizabeth looked round.

Sure enough, Collins was already making his bow. "My dear, *dear* Cousin Eliza," he said. "Will you do me the honour? As I have come all this way just to speak with you—"

Darcy saw Elizabeth stiffen. "I beg your pardon," she said. "I am, as you see, engaged to Mr. Darcy."

Darcy's brows went up. He grinned, and she broke out laughing. "Too late, Mr. Collins," he said smoothly. "Dance with Miss Bates instead."

Tom Bertram was left standing to the side, blinking. "What we *ought* to do," he said stubbornly, "is set up a faro bank."

Chapter Four

Usually Elizabeth enjoyed dancing—but at a private assembly or ball, where there were many partners from which to choose. Here, with four gentlemen and three ladies, it was more awkward. After dancing a set with Mr. Darcy, Elizabeth went directly to Mr. Bertram, knowing he would ask. After that, she planned to dance with Charles Bingley. Unfortunately, Mr. Collins edged in.

"I thank you for the honour," she told him, "but I ought to relieve Miss Woodhouse at the pianoforte." After that, Mrs. Nicholls brought in refreshments, and Elizabeth fled the drawing room.

Would Mr. Collins follow? Or would he be occupied with coffee and cake? Across from the drawing room were the double doors to the ballroom. Elizabeth pulled one open and slipped inside.

Inside it was dark and chilly; rain beat against the tall windows like fingers drumming on a table. Elizabeth pressed her back against the wall. Surely her busy cousin would not follow her here! Surely he would remember that she had been exposed to sickness.

Why, oh why, has he come to Netherfield?

Moments later the door opened to admit a gentleman carrying a candlestick. When she saw who it was, Elizabeth let out a sigh of relief. "Mr. Darcy," she whispered. "How you startled me!"

"Is something wrong?"

"It is so—close in the drawing room," she said. A weak excuse, but it was the best she could do. "Please, close the door before my cousin—"

Mr. Darcy did so at once, but he remained inside. Why did he not go out? Elizabeth turned her gaze away from him. And then, by the light of his candle, she noticed something. There, on the far side of the ball room—a glittering.

"What is that?" she whispered. "Just there, do you see the sparkle on the floor? Hold up the candle."

He did so.

"Could it be my bracelet? Under that collection of—what are they, chairs? Do you see?"

Together they crossed the ballroom, their footfalls echoing on the bare floor. Mr. Darcy gave Elizabeth the candle, pushed the chairs aside, and knelt to reach under a sofa.

Behind them, the drawing room door came creaking open. "Yoo-hoo," a voice called. "Miss Elizabeth?"

It was Mr. Collins.

"What luck, to find you here," he crowed. "Are you quite well, fair cousin?"

Elizabeth closed her eyes. "A trifle over-heated, that is all," she called back. "I am not ill, if that is what you are wondering."

"Your mama did mention that you have already had the mumps."

Her busy mother's tactics were thus exposed, and before Mr. Darcy of all people! Elizabeth felt a flush rise to her cheeks. "I wonder that you would dare to risk coming here," she said to Mr. Collins.

"I was a bit over-hasty in my advice," he admitted. "For most people have had the mumps, have they not?" He hesitated, and then gave an awkward laugh. Elizabeth suppressed a shudder; she could picture him moistening his lips. "It was in order to solicit a private interview with you that I have come," he said. "And providence has granted my wish."

Any honest answer Elizabeth could give would not be helpful, so she merely said, "So it would seem."

"It is very dark in here," Mr. Collins pointed out.

Elizabeth glanced at Mr. Darcy. From his kneeling position, he gazed up at her. She could see questions glittering in his eyes. "Don't you *dare* move," she whispered, and she held the candlestick higher.

"What is it you wish to say to me, cousin?" she called, more loudly. "Have you come to ask for a dance?"

Mr. Collins gave a little giggle. "Now that you mention it, yes! But come, you can hardly doubt the *true* purpose of my call. My attentions have been too marked to be mistaken."

Elizabeth held back a sigh and courageously crossed the room. She had been fearing a declaration for days. Behind her came a noise, rather like a cough—Mr. Darcy!

Of course, Mr. Collins would continue to talk. "Almost as soon as I entered Longbourn House," he said, "I singled you out as the companion of my future life."

So here it was: a proposal, made with that pulpit-trained voice. It penetrated to every corner of the room! And he was smiling; Elizabeth could see the glint of his teeth.

"Perhaps it would be advisable," he went on, "if I state my reasons for marrying. For you must know that I came into Hertfordshire with the design of selecting a wife."

"Mr. Collins …" said Elizabeth repressively.

But his enthusiasm would not be deterred. "First, I think marriage a right thing for every clergyman in easy circumstances. Second, it will add very greatly to my happiness; and thirdly—"

Was he preaching a sermon? Listing his reasons as one would draw up a list for the village shops?

"And thirdly," he repeated, smiling more widely, "it is the express wish of my noble patroness, Lady Catherine de Bourgh."

"In other words," said Elizabeth, "you have been commanded to marry."

He gave an awkward laugh. "You may have your little jest. But I am in earnest, dear cousin. Because I am to inherit the Longbourn estate after the death of your honoured father, I resolved to choose a wife from among his daughters, that the loss to them might be as little as possible, when the melancholy event takes place."

"You wish to marry me out of pity, sir?"

His smile disappeared. "Why, er, no. Certainly not."

By the light of the candle, Elizabeth could see the mulish set of his chin. "You," he said solemnly, "being the fairest and cleverest of your sisters (possessing both wit and vivacity), have caught my eye. My motive stems from chivalry, fair cousin—a fine and selfless purpose, which is to mitigate the evils of the entail. I flatter myself it will not sink me in your esteem."

In other words, Mr. Collins wished to assuage his guilt of casting his female cousins from their home!

"I am sensible of the honour of your proposals," she began, "however—"

Again he interrupted. "As to fortune I am perfectly indifferent. I shall make no demand of that nature on your father, since I am well aware that it could not possibly be complied with. One thousand pounds, yours after your mother's decease, is all that you may ever be entitled to."

Must he insult her by pointing out her deficiencies? A noise in the far corner reminded her that Mr. Darcy was listening.

Mr. Collins added, with an air of awkward gallantry, "Rest assured, no ungenerous reproach shall ever pass my lips once we are married."

This was a bald-faced lie! He was reproaching her even as he proposed!

"I am sorry to give you pain," said Elizabeth carefully, "and I thank you for the compliment you are paying me, but I am convinced that we shall not suit. Moreover, at the present time I have no intention of marrying."

"None at all? Nonsense. Will you become like that haggish spinster in the drawing room? The laughingstock of Meryton, supported by the charity of friends? Come now." Mr. Collins rubbed his hands together. "I am well aware that it is usual with young ladies to reject the addresses of a man whom they secretly mean to accept—"

From the corner of the room came was a loud clattering, as if items of furniture—the chairs? —were being tossed aside. Mr. Darcy came striding through the darkness, smash up to Mr. Collins.

Elizabeth's candle threw Mr. Darcy's features into sharp relief. "The lady," he said sternly, "has told you no."

Mr. Collins gave a scream. "What are you doing here?"

"That," said Mr. Darcy, "is beside the point. As a clergyman and a gentleman, it is now your part to thank her for her time."

"But—"

"And then take yourself off. At once."

Mr. Collins looked from Elizabeth to Mr. Darcy and back again. His face was twitching like a rabbit's.

Mr. Darcy turned to Elizabeth. "If this person continues to trouble you, say the word and I will gladly throw him from the house."

Elizabeth's eyes widened in surprise. "Could you?"

"Now or at any time," he said promptly. "And with the greatest pleasure."

This remark was answered by hurried footfalls and the slam of the drawing room door. So much for Mr. Collins's courage!

Elizabeth nearly collapsed with relief. "Thank God!" she cried. "And if you *dare* to breathe a word of this to anyone …"

"Your secret is safe with me. And most especially from Miss Woodhouse, our resident matchmaker."

"Good gracious," said Elizabeth, "she cannot mean to match me with Mr. Collins—"

"I think not. Besides, you have cut the ground from beneath her feet rather neatly. Your cousin will not be renewing his addresses."

"I devoutly hope that you are right. I—am ashamed that you had to listen to all that."

Mr. Darcy's grim expression dissolved into a grin. "I have never yet had the occasion to propose to a lady," he told her. "But now, thanks to Mr. Collins, I know precisely what *not* to do."

"Oh dear, he was rather insulting, was he not?"

"As to Miss Woodhouse, you are not the only sufferer. No doubt she has a match in mind for me as well."

"Not Miss Bingley," said Elizabeth, before she could stop herself.

His eyes met hers, but they were smiling. "Definitely not Miss Bingley." There was a pause. "Shall we sit for a moment? There is something I would like to talk over with you."

He stepped away, and Elizabeth heard the scrape of chairs being brought forward. She sat in the one he placed for her, and he set the candlestick on the floor between them. His handsome face was now lit from beneath, rather like a ghoul's, while fantastic shapes danced on the ceiling. And yet somehow it was easier to face Mr. Darcy like this, half-hidden by shadows.

He sat silent with his hands on his lap; Elizabeth noticed that the tips of his fingers touched one another.

"Miss Elizabeth," he said suddenly. "Who or what is 'Aunt Jane'?"

Chapter Five

Darcy saw Elizabeth's expression change, and instantly he regretted his words. Here he was, in a darkened room with her—a most excellent state of affairs, his cousin Fitz would say. And what must he do but spout the first foolish thought that came into his head? Why couldn't he converse about the weather? It was raining hard enough to wake the dead!

He felt his lips twist into a rueful smile. "You must think me quite mad, Miss Elizabeth. Indeed, I hardly know how to explain what I mean."

She returned his smile—a singularly beautiful smile, he thought. It was sincere and engaging, with none of Caroline Bingley's tight politeness. "You are not *yet* a candidate for Bedlam," she pointed out. "Although I dare say, if it continues to storm for the next fortnight, we shall each be joining you there."

"We'll fill a van," he agreed. "What I said about Aunt Jane is unimportant. I was thinking aloud."

"A profitable way to occupy your time."

The lifted brow, the twinkle in her eyes—under the spell of her charm, Darcy could feel his reserve evaporating. "Oh, certainly," he quipped. "I babble nonsense, thereby causing my friends to look askance or leave the room. *Most* productive."

"I promise to do no such thing, Mr. Darcy. Pray continue. I would like to hear what you have to say about Aunt Jane."

Her tone was decidedly friendly; perhaps he should risk it. Moreover, this was a prime setting for speaking freely. And yet—

"After all," she went on, "you can scarcely embarrass yourself more than I have embarrassed myself tonight."

"Upon my word," Darcy burst out. "Do you consider your cousin's actions to be *your* fault?"

"N-o," she said slowly. "But as he *is* my relation—"

"You are responsible for *nothing* that he does. As for relations, I dare say every family has a Collins or two—we certainly have. I have promised to forget what happened earlier, so I suggest that you do the same. Now then, let us discuss Aunt Jane."

The candlelight enhanced the anticipation in her gaze. Darcy drew a long breath and began. "Have you had someone in your life who was—how shall I say it? A deuced managing busybody?"

"Indeed, yes," she said promptly. "Mr. Collins fills the role admirably."

Darcy gave her a look. "I had in mind someone like a governess," he said lightly. "Or a steward or a groom. A masterful sort of person whom it is impossible to get round."

"It wouldn't be a groom. I never have learned to ride."

I'll teach you.

Darcy blinked. Where had this thought come from?

"But I do know what you mean," she went on.

He worked to regain composure. No more stray thoughts! Moreover, he must take special care not to embarrass her. "What I mean to say is, have you ever had the suspicion that you are being managed by a force outside yourself?"

"Do you mean being compelled to take a certain course of action? Such as," she added, twinkling, "how we must all remain here until Christmas? By order of this Aunt Jane?"

"Exactly. The rainfall and the bridge—and the mumps—have conspired together."

She tilted her head. "Coincidence?"

"I would be inclined to agree, if it were not for the letter. Charles Bingley claims that he never wrote the invitation that brought Miss Woodhouse and her friends here."

"How very odd."

"Isn't it. I've seen the letter. The writing is his."

Elizabeth's brow furrowed. "Perhaps he did write, and then forgot?"

"I devoutly hope so, Miss Elizabeth." Darcy leaned forward. "And yet, my own experiences cause me to wonder." He paused. She would certainly think him mad if he continued. And yet, the temptation to confide in her was almost overmastering.

"Yes?" she said. "Do go on."

Darcy cast caution to the winds and plunged ahead. "Have you ever taken matters into your own hands? Run with an impulse? And then, quite suddenly, it is as if the situation is *erased*, and you discover that you are back where you were originally? That what you did has simply disappeared?"

She did not answer right away, and he liked her for it. At length she said, "Perhaps you dreamed it."

If only he had! But Elizabeth was intent; she wished to understand him. There was nothing scornful in her tone. He could not resist—he must continue.

"I have wondered that, yes," said Darcy. "But I recall the erased events vividly." He hesitated. "This is a faulty metaphor, but it is as if pages were removed from a storybook."

"Are you one of the characters in the story?" she said, smiling. "Perhaps what you are referring to is an act of God."

Darcy returned her smile. "Ah, but He has a very different feel. We worship and pray; we confess and are forgiven. But this other—this manager—merely alters things. Rather ineptly, sometimes. Not at all like the Almighty would."

"Then it must be coincidence."

"Like coincidence in a storybook?" he countered. "There are rather too many of those to be believable. Cinderella loses a slipper, and it fits no one else in the kingdom. Sleeping Beauty is kissed by a prince, not licked by a hedgepig. Beauty returns just as the Beast is dying."

"Or a letter is delivered at a critical moment," suggested Elizabeth.

"Precisely. A letter did come, just before Wickham ran off with my—" Darcy stopped, aghast at what he had been about to say.

"Dear me, is even Mr. Wickham under your manager's command?" Elizabeth sounded amused.

Darcy felt his jaw tense. "Apparently so," he said stiffly.

He saw her eyes widen in surprise. "I—do not follow you," she said slowly.

Of course she did not. She would never understand unless he was specific—and that meant being forthright. There were risks with complete frankness. On the other hand, perhaps it was well that Elizabeth learn the truth about Wickham.

"Look here," he said, showing her the knuckles of his right hand. "A year ago April I had an, er, altercation with George Wickham, wherein his nose and jaw were broken."

He heard her intake of breath. "Broken by you?"

He shrugged—what else could he do? "Behold the scar."

Her eyes blazed into his. "Of all the unjust, hateful, barbaric—"

Darcy cut her short. "I had my reasons, Miss Elizabeth. Wickham attempted an elopement with my—" Again he stopped. Georgiana must be kept out of this. "I arrived in time to confront him face-to-face. The elopement was halted—by me."

Elizabeth pressed her hands to her cheeks. "An elopement," she repeated. "Oh, this does not sound like him at all."

"He stood to gain a substantial fortune," said Darcy. "But I digress. The point is not that I hit him, but that after I did so, I found myself back at Pemberley. It was as if I'd never gone to Ramsgate at all."

"But you did hit him."

"In truth," he said ruefully, "it was rather worse than that. He struck his head sharply as he fell; the amount of blood was ghastly."

"So you killed him."

"To be honest, I do not know. As I told you, almost at once I was back at Pemberley. When I did journey to Ramsgate—for the second time, which had somehow become the first—I arrived two days earlier than before. There was no confrontation then, for Wickham had not yet come."

"A happy circumstance," cried Elizabeth.

"For the state of his face, yes. I must confess," Darcy admitted, "I brought a pistol that second time, for I had every intention of shooting him. Instead, I—merely wrote a letter. I negotiated a settlement, for I had my sist—"

Blast his unruly tongue!

"I had the reputation of another to consider," he amended. "I did not wish to broadcast his infamy to the world, on account of her. But here is the curious thing: the scar made when I struck Wickham remains, do you see?"

To Elizabeth's credit, she leaned in to study the back of his hand.

"When next you see Wickham," Darcy added, "you might notice the slight notch to his left ear, made by my ring."

"You say you hit him," said Elizabeth, "but it turns out that you did not."

"The managing force—Miss Woodhouse's Aunt Jane, if you will—stepped in and changed things. But she forgot a few details. Such as the cut to my fist and to Wickham's ear."

He saw her doubt, and yet she was not dismissive. "And this same force is at work here?"

"I believe so, yes."

"Stopping something from happening? Or else rearranging something that has already happened?"

Darcy felt his cheeks grow warm. How fortunate for the concealing shadows! "I believe it is the former. To be frank, yesterday afternoon I was to travel to London," he said, "and my intent was to keep Charles Bingley there for as long as possible."

He saw Elizabeth consider his words. He also saw irritation flash in her eyes. "To keep him there," she repeated. "In spite of his growing affection for my Jane? You wished to keep them apart?"

"To be fair, I saw little evidence of her regard for him."

"You saw little—Oh! How *blind* you are!"

"If I am blind," he countered, "then you are *naive*. You have no idea the number of women who have pursued Charles Bingley simply for his fortune. He has an affectionate heart; I have often seen him in love. Can you blame me for assuming that your sister had mercenary designs?"

"I can and I do!" she cried. "Jane sincerely loves him. He is not a prize to be won!"

"Now that I have seen them together," Darcy said more mildly, "I am inclined to believe you."

"Who made you an authority on—" She stopped. "Oh. You—approve of the match?"

Darcy had to smile. "Let us say that I have revised my opinion somewhat. They seem to be well-suited," he said. "And she does sincerely care for him. But I believe Miss Woodhouse is to be the final authority. Give me your left hand."

He saw her quick intake of breath, and the surprise in her eyes as her gaze flew to his. Slowly she put out her hand. Darcy realized his gaffe and hid a smile. The poor girl! Did she think he was offering her a ring?

And yet she held out her hand to him.

Darcy felt the blood rush to his face. He lightly clasped Elizabeth's wrist, and from a pocket brought out the missing bracelet. "I believe it is the left you favor for bracelets, is it not? You wore this at Sir William Lucas's party, as I recall."

"I—yes," she said, a little breathlessly. "But how did you—"

Darcy ignored the question as he enjoyed the warmth of her. "This is rather pretty," he said, and he opened the clasp. "It is fortunate that you noticed it there in the corner."

"I—thank you."

He frowned over the clasp. "The latch appears to be broken. Shall I ride into Meryton and have it looked at? Is there someone with the skill to mend this?"

"I do not know. Perhaps Mr. Wade, who looks after clocks and timepieces. But there is no need, Mr. Darcy, truly. It is not altogether broken.

I know to be careful when wearing it." She leaned in, and he inhaled her scent. "Do you see, just here," she said, "how the catch—"

The drawing room door came roughly open. Bingley came in, with Jane close behind. "There you are!" he crowed. "We've been looking everywhere."

Darcy kept a light hold on Elizabeth Bennet's wrist. He felt her pulse quicken. "Do not move," he murmured. "Brazen it out."

"What's all this? Alone together—and holding hands, are you?"

"You have been reading too many novels, Charles," said Darcy lightly. He released Elizabeth's wrist.

Behind them edged Miss Bates, Emma Woodhouse, and Tom Bertram. "This is very nice, I must say," quipped Bingley. "My sister is not here to act as duenna, and what must the pair of you do but slip away together!"

"I was helping to locate Miss Elizabeth's lost bracelet," said Darcy evenly. "And here it is."

"Mr. Collins was with us," Elizabeth hastened to say. "Until very recently."

Bingley was smiling widely. "Alone," said he, "with a single candle between you. Indicative! Highly indicative!"

Darcy refused to rise to the bait, staring down even Miss Woodhouse's interested gaze. He rose to his feet and assisted Elizabeth to do the same. She hesitated, and then placed her hand lightly on his proffered arm.

"We shall never hear the end of this," he confided in a low voice, as they left the drawing room together. "But it could be worse, you know."

She looked an enquiry.

"I could be Collins."

"Oh—you!" she whispered.

Was a playful blow to the arm a good thing? Darcy rather hoped it was.

Chapter Six

Into the drawing room they trooped together, with Mr. Bingley teasing his friend all the while. Elizabeth concealed a sigh. She and Mr. Darcy would never live this down.

And what must Mr. Darcy do but take the chair beside hers? "It is the only way to silence him," he murmured.

"By confirming his suspicions?" she whispered back.

"No, we spike his guns by playing along. Would you care for coffee?"

Miss Bates's clucking voice rose above the conversation of the others, like a hen marshalling her chicks. "What say you to a round of Spillikins?"

Another noisy game. It would be a welcome diversion, but—

She dared not glance at Mr. Darcy to see what he thought. From the corner of her eye, Elizabeth saw him rise to his feet. He placed a small table before her and then came back with the backgammon board. "Shall we play a game?" he said pleasantly, moving his chair to face hers.

"No!" she whispered urgently. "We shall never hear the end of it."

His response was to open the board and begin placing the checkers. "When everyone sees how thoroughly you are trounced, Miss Elizabeth, speculation of a romance between us shall cease."

Trounced? Elizabeth lifted her chin. "If I do agree to play, I have no intention of losing, sir."

Mr. Darcy's eyes glittered. "We'll see about that."

Elizabeth discovered that she was smiling. "I'll have you know that I am rather good at backgammon."

"Ah, but are you good enough?"

Was he taunting her? Silent, taciturn Mr. Darcy? And there was more. When he smiled, his cheeks dimpled attractively. Why had she never noticed this?

"I am not afraid of you, sir," she countered.

"You should be," he said, and he held out her dice. What could she do but take them?

Her bare fingers brushed against his palm. "*En garde*, Miss Elizabeth," he said.

Did he think to confound her with fencing cant? He would soon discover that she was no green girl. "*Allez*, Mr. Darcy," she smilingly retorted, and boldly tossed the dice onto the board.

It was very late when the party broke up. What an evening! Mr. Darcy was a formidable opponent, but Elizabeth held her own. Best two out of three became best three out of four—and they ended in a tie. Backgammon might not serve to quell gossip, but it had been most entertaining.

And the storm continued to batter the house. Elizabeth was never more grateful for warmed sheets—and for the cheerful fire in her bedchamber, by Longbourn standards a luxury. Lulled by the pattering of raindrops against the window glass, she settled into sleep.

Some hours later a clock chimed—not there in the room; it was the longcase clock in the passageway. Elizabeth shifted in bed, pulling the blankets higher. It was still raining out, but—there was light in the bedchamber. Elizabeth opened an eye. Sure enough, her candlestick was lit.

She knew she had blown it out earlier, and yet there it was. Moreover, Elizabeth discovered that she was propped up in bed; in her hands she held a book. Had she been reading?

She turned the spine to see the title, but the lettering was indistinct. It occurred to her that she was waiting—but for what?

Or for whom?

Footfalls sounded in the passageway, and then the door slowly came open. Whoever it was carried a candle; she could see its light advancing into the room. Elizabeth felt herself close the book, a smile hovering on her lips.

It was a man who entered—and she felt no apprehension! He kept his back toward the bed, as if using his body to shield the candlelight.

"You are in rather late," she heard herself say. "Did you enjoy your evening?"

"Elizabeth! Have you been waiting up all this time? I did not wish to—"

He put down the candlestick and laid his greatcoat on the chair. "It must be almost three." He turned, smiling an apology. It was then that Elizabeth saw his face. It was Mr. Darcy.

Mr. Darcy! In her bedchamber? Elizabeth heard her voice calmly say, "I do not mind. I could not sleep."

He pulled his timepiece from his waistcoat pocket and studied it with a groan. "It's terribly late. In the first place, dinner was delayed—not that it mattered to us—and after that, well."

He shrugged off the frock coat and unknotted his cravat. "You know how these navy fellows are. Each had to tell his favorite story," he said, "embellished with new and barely-factual details." She watched him unbutton his waistcoat. It joined the pile on the chair.

"There were tales of India and Portugal. And several prosed on about"—he deepened his voice—"The French Menace. At last we fell to discussing what Bonaparte might be up to, which is what I wished to hear in the first place."

He moved to her side of the bed and paused at the bedside table. She heard him place his sleeve buttons in the porcelain bowl. He began unbuttoning his shirt.

He was undressing right in front of her!

But Mr. Darcy was treating this as commonplace—and so was she! Indeed, her only response was to place her book on the table.

"You might like to know," he went on, "that Captain Simmons is now engaged to Miss Rutherford. I believe we can expect to hear wedding bells this Christmastide." He twinkled at her. "As you know, I'm rather partial to Christmas weddings."

Elizabeth averted her eyes, shy under the intensity of his gaze. Reserved Mr. Darcy, smiling at her like that! She adjusted her position, and a flash of gold caught her eye; something twinkled on her hand—her left hand. Elizabeth stared at her fingers, and her heart began to hammer. It couldn't be, but it was!

A gold wedding band.

"I'm glad you've been enjoying your book," Mr. Darcy continued. "When I left tonight you seemed rather low."

She heard herself say, "Not low, exactly."

He paused, with his brows raised. A questioning look, but without scorn. Now it was her turn to smile an apology. "It's this dreary, endless rain…"

Elizabeth felt herself shrug—and suffered another shock. Her hair! It was loose, tumbling over her shoulders. Where was her cap? For that matter, where was her thick flannel nightdress? She was wearing, no, she couldn't be wearing—a silk chemise! Thin and clinging, it was positively indecent! Why did she not seem to notice? Didn't she care?

Mr. Darcy sat on the bed, smiling down at her in a most unsettling manner. Elizabeth found herself gazing at his adorable dimples and at the cleft in his shapely chin. Why had she never noticed how handsome he was?

His fingers gently brushed a stray lock of hair from her eyes. "Shall we escape?"

"To a land bathed in sunshine?" she said. "Your Mr. Bonaparte has made travel difficult…"

Now Mr. Darcy was leaning over her, tenderly kissing her neck, then her chin and the lobe of her ear. "Ah," he murmured. "But there is nothing like staying at home for real comfort."

At home. With him.

"Fitzwilliam," she heard her voice whisper. This was his Christian name; why had she never before used it?

Eagerly her arms reached to return his embrace, pulling him closer. She felt herself surrender to the pleasure of his lips upon hers.

Kissing Mr. Darcy. She was kissing Mr. Darcy.

Elizabeth no longer cared that she wore a thin chemise, or that her hair was tumbling down—only that the door was securely locked.

A gust of wind hurled rain against the window panes. Elizabeth, overcome with desire, did not care. There was a blinding flash of light. An explosion of thunder followed.

And then, screaming.

Elizabeth gave a start—and Fitzwilliam Darcy disappeared.

The screams continued.

Elizabeth lay still for a moment, stunned by aching loss. He had been here, in this bed, kissing her. And she had welcomed him, desired him…

A dream. Only a dream.

Elizabeth pressed her palms to her cheeks. A dream. Not real. *This* was real: this room, this storm—and the screams. Whose screams? Jane's?

At once Elizabeth scrambled out of bed—thank heaven, she now wore her flannel nightdress—shrugged into her woolen dressing gown, and tied the sash securely. Out the door she stumbled, heedless of her bare feet.

The passageway was not deserted. There were Jane and Miss Bates. And Caroline Bingley, with her neck wrapped in cloths. At the far end stood Mr. Bingley and Mr. Darcy, with his candle.

The passageway was cold and draughty, hardly a surprise since the wind was howling against the house. There, another flash of lightning! Thunder rattled the window panes. The storm was right overhead.

A door opened, and Emma emerged with a candle.

"Did it strike the house, do you think?" Mr. Bingley was saying to Mr. Darcy. "Should we check for fire?"

"Fire?" said Caroline hoarsely. "In this deluge? Impossible!"

"The roof tiles are of slate," Elizabeth heard Mr. Darcy say, "but one cannot be too careful. Perhaps it would be wise."

Mr. Bingley took the candle and made for the staircase, but Mr. Darcy remained where he was. Elizabeth felt the back of her neck—but her hair was in its usual braid, not tumbling over her shoulders. Shyly she checked her hand, but the gold wedding band was gone. Even so, it was difficult to meet Mr. Darcy's solemn gaze.

It was a dream, only a dream!

What it was not—what it could not possibly be! —was Aunt Jane at work. And yet the thought persisted: What if? What if it had been real?

What if Mr. Darcy had experienced the dream along with her?

Chapter Seven

The following day dawned clear and bright—a rainless day—and today would be much the same. Bit by bit, their isolation at Netherfield began to lessen. Yesterday morning Bingley went off on horseback, presumably to speak with Jane's father. And Tom Bertram disappeared as well—and did not reappear for dinner that night. Darcy suspected that he was looking for more robust gaming than Netherfield provided. He would find this with the militia. As birds of a feather...

Like a lapdog, Darcy loitered about the house. He knew this was unnecessary. The flooded bridge at Brunsley would soon be repaired, enabling him to travel to London and then on to Pemberley. And yet how could he leave Netherfield? How could he leave Elizabeth?

For he had kissed her—he had. It could not have been only a dream. Truth to tell, he longed to kiss her again.

So here he was, hovering about, hoping for another kiss. And wasn't this a noble enterprise? Like those curst fellows at the London assemblies— Almack's even—ogling the heiresses. Waiting for the chance to drop a charming line or a romantic compliment...

Like Wickham.

Or worse, like Collins.

With a sigh, Darcy retreated behind his newspaper. People could say what they wished about a reserved temperament. There were some things one was protected from doing!

Therefore he and Elizabeth spent the rainless days as people at a house party do: leisurely breakfasts; mornings spent in the company of books and newspapers; strolls through those parts of the garden that were not underwater—usually in the company of Miss Woodhouse and Miss Bates. But Darcy did try to be more sociable. Wickham—blast him—was known for having happy manners. It was galling to learn anything from the man, but Darcy knew he ought to try.

And Elizabeth's beautiful, intelligent gaze followed Darcy—provoking him, enchanting him, holding him prisoner. Across the room, or across the table at meals, their eyes would meet and she would smile. Or perhaps it was he who would be smiling. Yes, it was certainly him. Sometimes he could not help himself.

Miss Bates would set them to playing childish games or they would read aloud from books. Sometimes there was dancing, and always there was music.

Elizabeth or Jane would play the pianoforte and sing simple ballads. Darcy enjoyed these most of all.

It no longer mattered that Elizabeth's mother was noisy and ambitious—and her younger sisters too. Or that her portion was considered contemptable. He admired her. No, he loved her.

Love. There, he had said it. Or rather he had thought it—which was almost the same thing.

The only question left was what to do. How to tell her what was in his heart? Would she respond in kind? Or did she dislike him as much as ever?

But she had kissed him in that dream. Surely this counted for something!

His thoughts were interrupted by Lydia Bennet's voice. She, along with her sister Kitty, had come to call.

"We are supposed to be shopping in Meryton," Lydia was saying. "And so we shall be—later." Apparently the driver of the family carriage had been bribed to silence, a source of much hilarity.

"We've already had the mumps," Kitty pointed out, "so it makes no difference. We simply had to come, Lizzy, for we've such *news!*"

Lydia took up the tale. "Mr. Collins leaves for Hunsford tomorrow, but oh, Lizzy, you will never believe it. He is engaged—actually engaged—*to Charlotte Lucas.*"

Elizabeth appeared stunned. "You—cannot mean it," she said.

Apparently her sisters did. "Lady Lucas held the engagement dinner yesterday night," Kitty assured her. "The wedding is set for early January."

And then Darcy noticed Miss Woodhouse. She was looking hard at each of the sisters. "How very odd," she said. "I could have sworn that Mr. Collins's interests lay elsewhere. Not that I wish ill on Miss—Lucas did you say?"

Lydia kept talking. "And dear Wickham sends his love. He says it is not the same without you, Lizzy, although I cannot see why. We have the merriest evenings together."

"It's all tipsy dance and jollity," gushed Kitty.

"I *beg* your pardon?" said Elizabeth.

"It's—the name of a song, Lizzy," Kitty protested. "You needn't look so cross."

Actually, it was a line from Milton's *Comus,* but this fact would be lost on Kitty Bennet.

Elizabeth's sisters soon took their leave. Darcy watched Elizabeth cross to the far side of the room and stand before the windows.

Emma Woodhouse, meanwhile, was frowning at the carpet. "I do not understand it," Darcy heard her tell Miss Bates. "Mr. Collins's interests were so clearly in another direction. Ah well, I have someone else in mind for *her*, at any rate."

"You are always so clever, Miss Woodhouse," said Miss Bates. "Christmastide, as we well know, is *such* a time for weddings and engagements. It is a *wonderful* time of year."

Would his own engagement be included with the rest? Darcy turned a page of his newspaper.

"I take no credit for dear Jane and Mr. Bingley—that match was already well underway. But his sister?" Although Emma lowered her voice, Darcy could still hear. "An alliance with Mr. Darcy would be very nice; it would bring both families together. As you know, when our Isabella married John Knightley, it answered in every way."

Darcy knew that he should excuse himself and go out, but Emma was bent on talking. He kept still behind his newspaper.

"My dear, dear Miss Woodhouse," began Miss Bates, "far be it from me to raise an objection—of any kind. But Miss Bingley is not a soft-spoken sort of person, is she? And dear Mr. Darcy—"

"And Mr. Darcy *is*," said Emma, interrupting. "Opposites attract! Now then," she went on, "if we could only manage to keep Mr. Bertram at home of an evening, he and Elizabeth could get on. He is much too fond of card-playing."

"As was dear Grandpapa," lamented Miss Bates. "Although horse racing was his downfall—as it is with so many gentlemen."

Darcy turned another page. Tom Bertram could go to the devil, for all he cared. He'd had enough of the man's simpering ways and fashionable manners. But as the husband of Elizabeth? Preposterous!

"I dare say he will learn to outgrow it, although Mr. Knightley would probably disagree. He has the most old-fashioned notions as to character." Emma hesitated for a moment. "But no, Elizabeth is too lovely and too charming to marry just anyone. She deserves to be the next Lady Bertram, and if I have my way, so shall she be."

Young Tom did appear for dinner that night, probably for reasons of economy. Meals at whatever tavern he'd found in Meryton cost money, and money seemed to be in short supply. And what was this? The man's gold timepiece, with its collection of dangling fobs, was missing from his waistcoat tonight. Card games could be costly, particularly if one was as stupid as Tom Bertram looked to be.

Caroline Bingley was carried down to dinner, much to everyone's surprise. "Her fever has been gone since morning," explained Jane, as she helped the footmen guide Miss Bingley to her usual seat at the table. "Mr. Jones says cheerful conversation will help restore her spirits. It is disheartening to be shut away."

But did Miss Bingley wish to be cheered up? Darcy had his doubts. She appeared pale and cross, and her throat was well wrapped up—although not enough to conceal a necklace of glittering emeralds and a rope of pearls. Darcy gave a sidelong glance at Tom Bertram. Yes, he was staring at her. How could the man not notice such an opulent display?

Caroline looked on, open-mouthed, as the company trooped in. *Trooped* was the only way to describe their noisy entrance. Under her brother's management, the Netherfield guests sat where they wished, talked across the table, and generally ignored Miss Bingley's ceremonious niceties.

Darcy had his usual seat beside Elizabeth. "Tell me again," he heard Caroline say to Elizabeth, "why you and Jane are staying here?"

Elizabeth attempted to explain, but Miss Bingley was not having any. She rounded on her brother. "My dear Charles," she called down the table, above the hum of conversation. "You ought to be in London."

For someone who was supposed to be sick, there was certainly nothing wrong with her voice! Darcy leaned toward Elizabeth. "Now we're in for it," he murmured.

"You must leave at once, do you hear? Now that the rain has stopped, that rubbishy bridge is passable."

The others fell silent. Charles spoke up. "I've decided to pay that mantua maker's bill, Caro," he said. "A few pounds is not worth squabbling over."

"But I say that it is. The gown was made in the wrong fabric, Charles. I cannot possibly wear it. Moreover, the mistake was not mine, but hers. I refuse to pay."

The silence became awkward, and Miss Bates stepped in to fill it. "When I was a girl," she began, "we learned to make our own dresses. It was difficult at first, for we made the *most* amusing mistakes. Later, when we were older, my sister and I *turned* dear Mama's gowns and made new ones for ourselves."

Caroline's thundering glare showed what she thought of shabby-genteel economies. Darcy exchanged a laughing look with Elizabeth.

Tom Bertram spoke up. "Hear, hear," he cried. "You should not have to pay, Miss Bingley. At least, not right away. Make her wait." He broke into a wide grin. "What's she going to do, dun you?"

Caroline Bingley looked down the table at him with wide eyes.

"Better and better," Darcy murmured to Elizabeth.

"In six months' time she'll sing a different tune," Bertram went on. "Ten to one she'll buy the thing back. What's to keep her from selling that curst dress to someone else?"

Caroline brightened. "You see, Charles? What is a mantua maker after all?"

"Debts of honour," said Tom Bertram, "now those are a different matter. But tradesmen's bills?" He shrugged.

"Never mind having a good name," Darcy pointed out.

Caroline rounded on him. "A good name has nothing to do with it," she said. "The fault was hers, not mine. And this is not the *only* way in which I have been wronged." She turned a wrathful eye on Elizabeth.

At that unfortunate moment, Elizabeth's fork dropped onto the floor.

Darcy saw her glance down at it and wince. Immediately he gave her his unused dessert fork.

This did not escape Caroline Bingley's notice. "Really, Mr. Darcy. The footman ought to be the one to replace that. You, of all people, should allow him to do his job."

"Lucky him," said Darcy. But instead of smiling at her, he allowed his eyes to narrow. "Let us hope this oversight does not cause him to be—what is the expression? Sacked?" Caroline's chin came up.

"Miss Bingley," called Emma Woodhouse, "it is such a pleasure to have you here at dinner with us. I trust you are feeling better?"

Caroline Bingley passed a hand over her eyes. "Why," she said crossly, "are these people in my house?"

"Indeed," said Darcy pleasantly, "that is something I ask myself. Why am I here?"

"Not *you*, Mr. Darcy. I did not mean—"

"I trust that in future you will say what you *do* mean," said Darcy mildly, "and leave unsaid those things that you do *not*."

She gasped, she actually gasped. Darcy did not care. Caroline Bingley could look as angry as she liked. Illness did not give anyone the right to be rude to guests.

Darcy now became aware of Emma Woodhouse's dismayed expression. This was not the most promising exchange for a budding matchmaker to observe! The sooner she abandoned her scheme to pair him with Caroline, the better.

At the conclusion of their meal, Bingley rose to his feet. "A-hem," he announced. "As we have callers waiting in the drawing room, perhaps we should go in together and have our port and coffee brought there. What say you, Caroline?"

Miss Bingley did not bother to disguise her irritation. "Which callers would these be, Charles?"

Bingley lifted a calling card from the salver. "For one," he said, "the Reverend Philip Elton, Vicar of Highbury."

"What?" cried Emma Woodhouse. "Mr. Elton, here?"

"And then we have Ned Parks, of Longbourn Estate." He smiled at Elizabeth.

"That cannot be right," Elizabeth whispered to Darcy. "Ned Parks oversees our stables."

"And Mr. McGready, whoever he is," Bingley went on, moving through the cards, "and our good neighbour Sir Hugh, and Mr. George Wickham."

Wickham!

"I know it's late, Caro," added Bingley, "but Mr. Elton has come some distance. And Sir Hugh is the magistrate. We can't very well turn him away."

The magistrate—and Wickham. What luck! Darcy directed an enquiring look at Elizabeth. "Who is McGready?" he said in a low voice.

"He is—that is to say, I believe he is a businessman," she whispered back. "Who happens to lend money to people."

Oho! Darcy directed a quick look at Tom Bertram. The man was definitely looking white about the gills.

Wickham and a moneylender and the magistrate! Darcy rose to his feet and offered an arm to Elizabeth. "Sounds like a most interesting evening," he remarked.

"Mr. Darcy," said Caroline, in a die-away voice. "Have you failed to notice, sir, that I require assistance?" She wound her pearls around her fingers and made a play with her eyelashes.

Darcy gazed at her for a long moment. "Your footmen look to be strong enough and quite capable of carrying you in," he replied. Politeness caused him to leave the remainder unsaid: *You, of all people, ought to allow them to do their jobs.*

Caroline Bingley's eyes flashed. "I, being quite exhausted," she said coldly, "find that I am not up to receiving guests. Do ring the bell."

And then Darcy heard a slight sound. Tom Bertram stood alongside Caroline's chair. "My dear Miss Bingley," he said, making a bow, "I beg you will allow me."

Keeping a straight face at that precise moment was one of the most difficult things Darcy had ever done.

Chapter Eight

Into the drawing room they went. Elizabeth kept her gaze averted. If Mr. Wickham were present, she had no desire to converse with him. Emma Woodhouse followed so closely behind that she nearly tread on Elizabeth's heels.

"Are you acquainted with our vicar, Mr. Elton?" whispered Emma into Elizabeth's ear. "Is that why he is smiling so?"

Mr. Elton had to be the dark-haired man in clerical attire. When he caught sight of Emma, he fairly leapt from his chair. "Miss Woodhouse! How wonderful to see you, and in such good health." He impulsively put out a hand, but Emma did not take it.

"How do you do, Mr. Elton?" she said solemnly. "May I present Miss Bennet and"—Emma glanced behind her—"and Mr. Darcy?"

Mr. Elton's smile dimmed to politeness.

No wonder Emma was flustered! For wedged into Mr. Elton's buttonhole was not a silk flower but a sprig of Christmas mistletoe! Elizabeth's gaze shifted to Emma. Had she noticed this?

Mr. Elton turned a glowing face to Emma and dug in a pocket of his frock coat. "I have a letter from your father—er, somewhere." He gave an awkward laugh.

"And one from dear Harriet as well?" said Emma. "How is she faring?"

"Who?" said Mr. Elton blankly. "Oh, Miss Smith? Well enough, I suppose. To be honest, I have no idea. Here is your letter."

"But—" said Emma, taking it, "you have seen nothing of Miss Smith?"

"Perhaps at one of the services," he said, shrugging. "It must be at least a fortnight since—"

"Mr. Elton," said Emma, interrupting, "why are you wearing mistletoe?"

Mr. Elton's cheeks grew pink. He removed the sprig, twirling the stems between his fingers. "'Tis the season, don't you know."

"The season for what?" said Emma.

"Why, for kisses. And—you know—for love."

Elizabeth heard Mr. Darcy disguise laughter in a fit of coughing. Wretched man! And yet, how could she blame him? What a dreadful situation! For Mr. Elton's mannerisms were very similar to what Mr. Collins's had been—the nervous twisting of his fingers, the flushed cheeks and too-bright smile.

"Mr. Elton," demanded Emma. "Was it Father who sent you here? Or did you receive a letter from—from someone else?"

Someone else? Elizabeth caught her breath. Did Emma mean Aunt Jane?

Mr. Elton just stood there, blinking. "Why, er, I ..."

Emma's face paled. "Pray excuse me while I read this," she said—and fled from the drawing room.

Elizabeth did not mean to catch Mr. Darcy's eye. She did not mean to laugh, either. He promptly offered his arm and led her toward one of the sofas—and away from Mr. Elton. "Poor Miss Woodhouse," Elizabeth whispered.

"She has attracted quite a suitor," he remarked. "He'd best mind his teacup, as those mistletoe berries are poisonous. Not the most effective courtship technique, dying."

Again Elizabeth had to swallow laughter. Who knew Mr. Darcy could be so witty? "He reminds me of—of Mr. Collins, don't you think?" she confided. "Not in appearance, but in manner."

Almost Mr. Darcy's lips twisted into a grin. "I wonder," Elizabeth continued. "Among clerics, is Christmas the season for courtship?"

He laughed outright at that, and she gracefully took a seat on the sofa. "Would you care for coffee or tea, Miss Elizabeth?"

"Tea, I think," she said unsteadily. "Thank you."

As Mr. Darcy moved away, Elizabeth gave a quick glance around the drawing room. There was Mr. Wickham in his red coat, smiling as he rotated the stem of his wine glass. Ned Parks, Longbourn's stable-man, sat beside Sir Hugh. He looked very out of place.

At a low table, apart from the men, Jane was pouring out. Of Caroline Bingley there was no sign, which was just as well. She would not like seeing Jane as acting hostess.

Mr. Darcy returned with Elizabeth's tea. As she lifted the cup, George Wickham's familiar laugh drifted across the drawing room. Elizabeth hesitated, caught by a memory. If what Mr. Darcy said about him was true, then—

Again Elizabeth's gaze wandered, this time moved by curiosity. *Was* there a scar on Mr. Wickham's ear? If he would just turn his head, she might be able to see. Unfortunately, the man caught her gaze, and he boldly lifted his wineglass in salute.

Elizabeth felt the blood rush to her cheeks. And then Mr. Wickham winked at her.

What brazen insolence! How could she have thought him charming?

And how dreadful that Mr. Darcy had noticed the exchange! "I can see no scar on his ear," she said to him, "and yet I cannot disbelieve that you struck Mr. Wickham. Indeed," she added, "it would be a wonder if you did so only once."

"The temptation," Mr. Darcy replied gravely, "presents itself often."

Just then Sir Hugh, the magistrate, rose to his feet. "No doubt you are wondering why I have come," he announced. "As you may have guessed, this is not precisely a social visit."

At once conversation stilled. Sir Hugh placed a chair facing the group and settled into it, with his hands resting on his knees. "Nor does it involve a serious criminal matter," he went on. "Still, I would like to solve the mystery here, as civilized people, without having to involve the courts of assize."

The stopper rattled in the decanter; Tom Bertram was helping himself to another glass of port.

"We had an incident in Meryton this afternoon," Sir Hugh continued, "involving Mr. McGready here, and this officer of the militia." He indicated Mr. Wickham.

Mr. Wickham was smiling; of course he was. How could have Elizabeth thought the man attractive—or sincere? Emma Woodhouse returned to the drawing room just then; at once Mr. Darcy surrendered his seat on the sofa.

Mr. Wickham rose to his feet and made a bow. "George Wickham," he said pleasantly, "of the ___shire Militia, at your service."

After he was seated, Mr. Wickham's gaze wandered to Elizabeth, and Emma came under his notice. Elizabeth saw his eyes widen and then narrow, as he took in every detail of Emma's appearance. The string of pearls, clasped carelessly about her neck, held particular interest.

Why, the man was a rogue! Sizing up Emma's worth in that odious way! Poor Emma must have noticed, for she did not remain long in the drawing room.

"The conundrum involves *this*," said Sir Hugh. From a pocket he drew a sparkling bracelet—Elizabeth's very own amethyst bracelet.

Elizabeth gasped aloud; she could not help it.

"Mr. Ned Parks," prompted Sir Hugh. "Are you able to identify this item?"

Ned cleared his throat. "That there bangle is Miss Elizabeth's, sure as I'm alive. And what it was doing in the hands of that maggoty person, as he was a-selling it to the likes of McGready, is what I'd like to know."

A rush of whispering swept the room. "Not you, your honour," amended Ned. "That there officer is the maggoty person I mean."

Elizabeth could only stare. There must be some mistake. Her bracelet was in the drawer of the dressing table upstairs! And then she remembered. The day the rain stopped she had worn it—

"Continue, Mr. Parks," said Sir Hugh.

"That fellow"—Ned indicated Wickham—"was in Mr. McGready's office for to pawn it. I happened on them by chance. It's thievery, that's what it is."

All eyes shifted to George Wickham. He was continuing to smile, without a trace of shame. Elizabeth wished that she could say the same for herself. And yet she knew she must speak. She had no other alternative.

"May I see the bracelet, please?" she said. Everyone remained silent while Sir Hugh brought it to her. "This is mine," she admitted. "How it came to be in Mr. Wickham's possession I do not know. Jane wore this the night of Mr. Bingley's ball."

Mr. Wickham said not a word. Did he care nothing for her reputation? A man whom she had counted as a friend would leave her with no defense?

Ned spoke up. "Did you give this officer your bangle, Miss? Or did he steal it?"

Wickham made an impatient gesture. "As I told the magistrate," he said, "and you, if you care to recall it, this bauble was staked as a wager by a gentleman. It became my property in the course of the game."

Elizabeth saw Mr. Darcy turn to Tom Bertram. Mr. Bertram's face and cheeks were pink; he took a large swallow of wine.

Sir Hugh held out the bracelet. "You admit that this your property, Miss Elizabeth?"

"I do."

"And how did it leave your possession?"

"I—must have lost it while I was walking outside the other day. I—was not paying attention. The clasp is faulty."

"I will attest to the broken clasp," said Mr. Darcy.

His support gave her courage to continue. "To be honest," said Elizabeth, "I did not realize that it was missing until now."

The magistrate did not look impressed. "You were walking outside in the garden? In the rain, Miss Elizabeth?" He lowered his voice. "It will do no good to shield this officer. If he stole it, he must be made to admit it."

"I did go out, Sir Hugh. Yesterday morning, after the rain stopped."

"Rather mucky for a walk, wouldn't you say?"

"We had been shut up in the house for so long. It was a relief to go out."

"So you did not give your bracelet to Mr. Wickham?"

"I did not, sir."

Sir Hugh turned to Mr. Wickham. "And you say that it came into your hands in the course of a game?"

"Very pretty, that," remarked Ned.

Mr. Wickham rounded on Ned Parks. "Gaming debts between gentlemen are something *you* would know nothing about."

Ned gave a snort. "You, a gentleman? That's rich."

Sir Hugh interrupted this exchange. "But who staked the bracelet? That is what I want to know."

"My lips," said Mr. Wickham primly, "are sealed."

"You will keep silent and call into question a lady's reputation?"

"So it would seem." Mr. Wickham's smile reappeared. "Mine honour as a gentleman must take precedence."

"Oh, come now." It was Mr. Darcy who rose to his feet; clearly he was annoyed. "Since when have you cared for honour, Wickham? You've fleeced some poor fellow, that is all. And you hope to do so again. So you keep your mouth shut about his identity."

Wickham spread his hands. "A faithful friend, who can find?" he recited.

"You've already won the money in his pocket—and his timepiece too, am I right?" Mr. Darcy went on. "In flat despair, he returns to Netherfield and finds in the shrubbery a honeyfall—an amethyst bracelet. So he lets that stand against his debt." He turned. "Isn't that so, Bertram?"

Tom Bertram's pink face was now scarlet. "It—it was in the mud," he stammered. "Buried-like. How was I to know it belonged to Miss Elizabeth?"

Mr. Wickham was now scowling. "I am no thief. I stole nothing."

Darcy stepped forward and laid a hand on Tom Bertram's shoulder. "A simple mistake," he said. "The sort of misunderstanding that can happen when one is desperate. Miss Elizabeth now has her bracelet. All that remains is for Mr. Wickham to return the money to Mr. McGready."

"But—" said Wickham.

"That's it, Mr. Darcy," said Sir Hugh. "What of it, Mr. Wickham?"

"That bracelet was rightfully mine! The money is mine as well."

"But you pawned Miss Elizabeth's bracelet without her permission."

"I—I," stammered Mr. Wickham. For the first time he looked uncomfortable. Elizabeth saw him give a tug to his collar.

"Return Mr. McGready's money," said Mr. Darcy mildly, "and then settle up with Bertram some other way. What's the figure, Mr. McGready?"

"Five pounds."

"There you are, Wickham, five pounds. A small price to redeem a lady's reputation—and your own." Mr. Darcy rocked back on his heels, studying Mr. Wickham.

There was a short silence, during which Mr. Wickham went very red in the face. "Really, Darcy," he protested. "I don't carry money—"

Mr. Darcy smiled; it was a cold smile, Elizabeth thought, but not unattractive. "Is that so?" he said. "You have been in Meryton for a month? Tradesmen become impatient for payment. I do hope that some of them have been paid with that five pounds ..."

Wickham opened and closed his mouth like a fish. He wheeled on Tom Bertram. "You!" he cried out. "You'll pay for this."

Sir Hugh lifted his voice. "Now that Mr. Darcy brings it to mind, I have heard a thing or two about outstanding debts, Mr. Wickham. Your outstanding debts."

Elizabeth had heard enough. Amid the raised voices of the men, she slipped out of the drawing room and into the cool of the upper hall. She pressed her fingers to her cheeks and willed herself to think. Where to find refuge quickly? Her bedchamber? No, it was too far. Better yet, the ballroom? The doors were ajar ...

Behind her, the drawing room door came open and closed. Elizabeth stood like a statue. She did not dare look to see who came out.

"Here is your bracelet, Miss Elizabeth," said Mr. Darcy's quiet voice.

Elizabeth turned to him with a sigh of relief. He was holding it out to her, so she opened her hands to receive it. "I—oh, Mr. Darcy," she confessed. "I was never so embarrassed."

"I thought you handled the situation very well," he said mildly. "To my mind, Wickham takes the prize for humiliation. He does not have the money to pay McGready."

She lifted her eyes to his. "What of Mr. Bertram?"

"That young fool? A salutary lesson. If he'd been content to play for Miss Bates's penny points, this would never have happened. I will give Bertram the five pounds, if it comes to that."

Elizabeth could not return his smile. "It is I who have been the fool, Mr. Darcy."

He looked at her rather searchingly. "You don't mind about Wickham too much, do you?"

"Meaning, is my heart broken? Surprisingly, no. I was charmed by him, that is all. I should have known better than to believe everything he said."

"He excels at being plausible. Even my own father was taken in."

Elizabeth discovered that Mr. Darcy had taken her hands into his own. His were warm and surprisingly gentle. She would have returned their clasp if not for the bracelet she held.

"Elizabeth," he said softly. She lifted her eyes to his.

And then Emma Woodhouse's voice carried sharply into the upper hall. "Mr. Elton!"

Elizabeth and Mr. Darcy shared a startled look. Was Emma in the empty ball room?

There was more. "You forget yourself, sir!" Emma cried out.

Then came the sound of a stinging slap.

Mr. Darcy lifted an eyebrow. "So much for the power of mistletoe," he remarked.

Chapter Nine

And so much, Darcy thought wryly, *for my feeble attempt at romance.* For Elizabeth had at once stepped away, pulling her hands from his. He felt the loss keenly.

Out from the ballroom came Emma Woodhouse, with flaming cheeks and blazing eyes. Had Elton thrown caution to the winds and forced a passionate kiss? Darcy knew he ought to feel pity for the man, but alas. It was all he could do not to laugh.

"Oh!" cried Miss Woodhouse. "Insufferable man!"

Darcy leaned in and caught Elizabeth's eye. "Romance novels," he told her, "are most unhelpful. Once a fellow takes to reading those, he's doomed."

"I *beg* your pardon?" cried Miss Woodhouse.

"I merely mean," explained Darcy, "that novels are not a reliable guide to courtship. If a man's suit is unwelcome, a display of passion only makes matters worse."

As if on cue, Elton appeared at the open doorway, looking remarkably angry, with a scarlet patch on his left cheek. Without meeting Darcy's eye, Elton put up his chin and stalked down the stairs to the entrance hall. He could then be heard demanding his hat and coat.

Darcy glanced down at Elizabeth's hands. Surely there was no chance of holding them while Emma Woodhouse was here. Then too, she was still holding her bracelet.

"Shall I keep your bracelet in my pocket?" said Darcy softly. She passed it to him at once.

He murmured something about having the clasp mended, but was interrupted by shouting in the drawing room. "Dear me," he remarked. "Apparently Wickham's charm is unequal to the occasion."

Miss Woodhouse drew near to Elizabeth. "If you saw how Mr. Elton looked at me, heard how he spoke to me!" Darcy heard her say.

"I quite understand," said Elizabeth. "You have no idea how well."

"Why is it that men are so—so stupid?"

"It is because we cannot help ourselves, Miss Woodhouse," Darcy said. He looked to Elizabeth. "We men are hopelessly inept when it comes to matters of the heart."

"Matters of the heart?" cried Miss Woodhouse. "Mr. Elton loves Harriet, not me! He gave every sign, every indication, of sincere and heartfelt attachment. Well," she amended, after a pause, "if not precisely *every* sign, near enough. I was thoroughly taken in. What I shall say to poor Harriet I do not know."

"It is awkward, yes," agreed Elizabeth.

"Mr. Knightley did say that this might happen with Mr. Elton—that he preferred me. But I would not believe him."

The drawing room door jerked open. "I'll not stay and be insulted," shouted George Wickham.

Darcy kept his face expressionless as Wickham came striding out. "Then again," he added, over his shoulder, "what can be expected from ignorant, prejudicial rustics?" Wickham had the audacity to look at Elizabeth then— was he seeking her support? Darcy put a possessive hand to the small of her back.

Wickham's lips twisted into a sneer. Like Elton before him, he strode to the stairs and descended. Ned Parks and Mr. McGready followed with a purposeful gait. Darcy hid another smile. It would be best for Wickham to travel the road back to Meryton at a run!

Sir Hugh appeared next. "I'm sorry for the fracas, Bingley," he said, taking his leave. "Better to have the rumpus now than to wait for the assizes. The sooner that fellow is gone from the district, the better. Good evening."

Darcy nodded to Sir Hugh and, in answer to Charles' mute inquiry, slightly shook his head. Bingley returned to the drawing room; Sir Hugh made his way down the stairs.

"All my fine plans," said Miss Woodhouse to Elizabeth, "are quite ruined. I had so wished you to be a titled lady, but now I see that it would never do. Nor will the match I had in mind for Miss Bingley." She sighed heavily. "I wonder why Aunt Jane sent me here at all."

Darcy lifted an eyebrow. "A match could be coming Miss Bingley's way. She rather fancies being a titled lady."

"Do you mean with Mr. Bertram? I was much deceived in him. Why, he is little better than a gamester. Why did I not see this?"

"We all have our areas of blindness," said Elizabeth. "For my part, I was taken in by George Wickham's glib charm."

"Him, charming?" Miss Woodhouse wrinkled her nose. "He is quite commonplace, is he not?"

Darcy gave a crack of laughter. To a man of Wickham's stamp, there was no worse insult.

Below in the entrance hall, there were voices—Sir Hugh departing, Darcy assumed. The main door closed and was bolted. Then came the butler, ascending the stairs with a small silver tray.

A caller? Darcy peered over the bannister rail. Sure enough, a man in a greatcoat stood below, hat in hand.

"Ah well," said Miss Woodhouse, "he is gone now, and so is Mr. Elton. I suppose the last laugh belongs to Mr. Knightley."

"Miss—Woodhouse?" The man below gazed up at them and then began to mount the stairs.

When he reached the landing, Emma Woodhouse gave a gasp of recognition. "Mr. Knightley," she cried and ran down to meet him. He stepped back a pace, gripping the banister rail with a firm hand. His hat fell behind onto the stairs.

"Oh!" she cried. "How I *wanted* you!"

"You—did?" said the man, who was obviously Knightley.

"Yes, for it was just as you said. Mr. Elton—oh. I am not supposed to say what happened, am I? But I daresay you can guess what he said to me."

"I daresay I can," said Mr. Knightley pleasantly. His arm slipped round her shoulders. "Poor Emma."

"And that is not the worst of it," she confessed, as they ascended together. "All my schemes, every one of my matchmaking endeavours, have ended in disaster."

"That is only to be expected, you know."

"But—Mr. Knightley, you are wet." Miss Woodhouse brushed droplets from the lapels of his coat.

"It is raining again, I'm afraid," he said.

"A wet trot to Meryton for Wickham," said Darcy to Elizabeth.

Miss Woodhouse then became aware of her surroundings. "Do come and meet my delightful new friends, Miss Elizabeth Bennet and Mr. Darcy."

Mr. Knightley's head came up. "Darcy? You don't say." He shook Darcy's hand warmly.

"Do you know one another?"

"I—have heard of him," said Mr. Knightley, smiling.

Darcy was not sure what to make of this. The drawing room door opened and Miss Bates came rustling out. "Mr. Knightley," she called. "How delightful to hear your name announced. Do come in and warm yourself. Everyone else has gone away. Save for Mr. Bertram, but he is in the sulks."

Darcy saw Knightley hesitate, but he answered with perfect cordiality, "A cheerful fireside will be very welcome, thank you." He looked down at Emma, who nestled against his shoulder. "I am come to take you home, you know," he said. "You and Miss Bates."

Miss Woodhouse looked at him shyly. "Did Father send you?"

"Yes, my dear, he did. Along with, ah, someone else." The drawing room door closed behind them.

"In the sulks, is he? Poor Bertram," said Mr. Darcy.

"And poor Emma. It is hard to have schemes go awry. As well as being sized-up by suitors. He certainly did so."

Darcy smiled fondly down at her. "He?"

"Mr. Wickham. I caught him looking at Emma—as if he were judging the merits of a horse!"

The drawing room door opened, and the butler came out. So did Mr. Knightley.

"Darcy," he said, "I have something for you. Being situated so near to London, I am often called upon to perform errands for our aunt."

Darcy's eyes narrowed. "Aunt," he repeated softly. "Aunt Jane?"

"Aunt Jane Austen, yes." From a pocket Knightley removed a folded paper—a letter? "She was most insistent that I give this to you as soon as I arrived. To save time, she said. I surmise that she is rather in a hurry."

"For what?" said Darcy, all at sea.

"For the happy ending. You know, a merry Yuletide for one and all. Apparently there was too much angst building up. Too many complications."

"Complications," said Darcy.

There was something in Knightley's smile that made Darcy uneasy. He unfolded the paper he'd been given. The letterhead was unmistakable: *Vicar-General, The Faculty Office of the Archbishop of Canterbury*—

Darcy's cheeks began to burn. "Doctor's Commons?" he whispered. "You went to Doctor's Commons?"

"If I were you," said Knightley pleasantly, "I'd not delay beyond tomorrow. There's snow in the air."

"Impossible. It's not nearly cold enough—"

"I daresay it will be," said Knightley, smiling again. "Your sister and Miss Annesley will be ready to depart for Pemberley as soon as you arrive in London. As for what should happen before that time, you know best." With a nod, Mr. Knightley returned to the drawing room.

"What is it?" said Elizabeth, drawing nearer. "Is something wrong?"

At once Darcy refolded the license. "Nothing is wrong," he managed to say. "To the contrary, everything has suddenly come right."

Chapter Ten

That license fairly burned a hole in Darcy's pocket. He must speak! After all, where was the risk? He had Aunt Jane's blessing.

Or—perhaps not? For a questioning expression now lurked in Elizabeth's beautiful eyes. Darcy drew a long breath. He dare not assume a victory; Collins and Elton had made that mistake. Was it now his turn to be roundly refused? Would Fitzwilliam Darcy, the prize of the matrimonial market, face the cruel irony of a rebuff?

And yet he dare not delay, for this private moment would not last. Even now he could hear someone playing the pianoforte in the drawing room. With a hammering heart, Darcy reached for Elizabeth's hand. Her fingers were cold; he covered them with his own to warm them. "Elizabeth," he began.

And then he stopped, for there was a clattering in the hall below. "What now?" he muttered.

Elizabeth's eyes twinkled. "A footmen has dropped the teapot?" she suggested. "Or perhaps it is Mr. Wickham, returning to challenge someone to a duel?"

Darcy felt his lips curve into a smile. "Never that. Wickham is not a crack shot—and he knows that I am."

"*Are* you?"

His smile turned into a grin. "Near enough." He took another long breath and said, "Elizabeth." Again he stopped. Was he mad, to be proposing in a public passageway?

Darcy released Elizabeth's hand. "I won't be a moment," he told her. "Wait right here." Into the drawing room he went. On a table beside a sofa was what he needed: a branched candlestick.

Jane was at the pianoforte, with Miss Bates standing behind. "Christmas is coming," sang Miss Bates in a warbling soprano, "the goose is getting fat…"

That song again! Darcy's fingers closed around the candlestick's column, and Miss Bates paused. "Mr. Knightley," he heard her call, "do come and sing with me. You too, Miss Woodhouse."

Heaven help them! And him too, if he was noticed! But he had no such luck, for Darcy heard her say his name. "You're *just* the man we need," gushed Miss Bates. "I would so love to form a choir for wassailing, but Mr. Bertram refuses to join us. Do say that you will."

"Ah, presently, perhaps." Darcy snatched up the candlestick, sending a shower of wax onto his sleeve, and fled. Elizabeth met him on the other side of the drawing room door. Thank goodness she was smiling!

"Miss Bates is singing?"

"I fear so." Darcy turned to secure the door. "I pity that Christmas goose. And us, if Miss Bates comes out and finds us. She is laying plans for wassailing."

"Oh, surely not until Christmas …"

He answered with a speaking look. "She thinks," he said, "that we ought to practice."

Elizabeth gave a gurgle of laughter. "Oh dear."

"Come," said Darcy. "Quickly." He caught Elizabeth's hand and drew her across the passageway and into the ballroom. He set the candlestick on the floor and turned to close the doors. As before, rain tapped steadily at the windows.

Darcy kept still, listening for sounds of pursuit.

"Are we safe?" Elizabeth whispered.

"I—believe so."

But what this? Something was wrong with his voice! He could not propose sounding like a goose! In other words, like Collins …

Darcy drew forward a chair for her. "So we return to the scene of the crime," she said laughingly. "Poor Emma. Look, here is Mr. Elton's mistletoe." She bent to pick the fallen sprig.

"And poor you, as well," said Darcy.

He saw her eyes find the floor, and he heard her sigh. "I was hoping that you would forget about Mr. Collins and what he said to me. His list of my deficiencies was painfully accurate."

Darcy felt himself wince. He'd embarrassed her, the last thing he intended. Gently he removed Elton's mistletoe from her grasp and let it fall to the floor. "I realize," he said, "that this is neither the time nor the place …"

And it wasn't. Everything about this proposal was wrong. He had not spoken to her father, he had no ring, and—heaven help him!—he ought to be kneeling.

The rain continued to strike the windows, but it now occurred to Darcy that it was a gentle sound. *Right as rain.* Yes, everything about this proposal might be wrong—but at the same time, everything was right. Even though he did not know what her answer would be.

He gazed at Elizabeth's face, made more beautiful by the rosy candlelight. "Hear my soul speak," said Darcy softly. The words were Shakespeare's—not, perhaps, the most eloquent beginning, but heartfelt. His gaze never left her eyes as he lowered himself to one knee, his heart thundering in his chest.

Elizabeth became very still. He reached for her soft hand, cradling it in his own, pleased to find it was cold no longer. He felt her fingers tremble. Darcy trembled too!

"I love you dearly, Elizabeth," he said simply. "With all my heart."

And then he found that he could speak—for she was smiling. "I am as great a fool as Collins," he confessed in a rush, "and I have been in mortal fear of sounding as ridiculous as he, in desiring such a prize. But I do love you, Elizabeth, truly."

Did she give his fingers a gentle, reassuring squeeze?

"You may dislike me as heartily as you do Collins, and I would not blame you," he went on. "But I wonder if ..."

Here Darcy paused, for upon this question hung all his future happiness. "I wonder if you love me enough to consider becoming my wife."

"If I love you enough?" cried Elizabeth. "Of *course* I love you enough!"

Darcy could not help himself; he stood to his feet and caught Elizabeth in a crushing embrace, pressing his lips to hers.

He was overwhelmed as she cupped his face with her hands. Only the threat of imminent discovery made him break the kiss.

After that, there were glorious wedding details to work out. Darcy did not intend to wait if he could help it. "Since you are unable to return home—" he began.

"Because of the mumps," Elizabeth put in, smiling. "And Mama's interference."

"I rise up and call her blessed," said Darcy. "Now then, what I am wondering is this: would you enjoy spending Christmas with me at Pemberley?"

"With you," she repeated.

"And with my sister."

"As your—or rather, her—guest? With Jane?"

"Not with Jane," Darcy said gently. "And not as my guest. As my wife, dear heart."

"But—but that is impossible, Fitzwilliam. How can we be married so soon? Moreover, what will people think?"

Darcy could not help grinning, for she used his name, his Christian name. "I care nothing for what people will think. But there is something I need to show you." He brought out the folded license and gave it to her.

Elizabeth opened it and read it through without saying a word. "A special license," she said at last. She raised her astonished eyes to his. "How long have you had this?"

"Not long," he said truthfully.

"Of course not," she said, as if to herself. "It takes time; you had to send for it. But—Fitzwilliam, why did you not tell me sooner? Was it—oh, I disliked you for the longest time!"

"And with good reason." He put an arm around her; she leaned her head against his shoulder.

"And all the while you loved me," she marveled. "But when you heard Mr. Collins propose—? What must you have thought? No wonder you threatened him with violence."

"Did I?" said Darcy, bemused, watching the expressions flit across her lovely face.

"You did. And Mr. Wickham, too."

"I seem to have been quite busy." Darcy allowed himself to caress a lock of her silky hair, breathing in her scent. "Do you know," he said, "uppermost in my mind—once we settle the details of our wedding day—is discovering where my silver sleeve buttons are."

She pulled away, knitting her brows. "Your what?"

Darcy studied her expression. Perhaps it would be better if he did not bring up the dream? "It makes no difference; they will turn up somewhere."

"Sleeve buttons," she repeated. "For—your shirt?"

She remembered!

"Actually," he said, "they could well be in my bedchamber at Pemberley. That is where I saw them last."

He heard her gasp. "In your—?"

"But I digress," Darcy continued smoothly. "I will call on your father in the morning and, if possible, start for London in the afternoon. Along with your family—those who are free to make the journey."

"That would be every one of us. And Jane. I won't have Jane left behind."

"Nor I, Bingley. If all goes well, on the third day from this we shall be married." He could barely contain his elation.

"Married," she breathed. "Will wonders never cease?"

"After a sumptuous wedding breakfast at a hotel of your choosing," Darcy went on, "we'll be off for Pemberley." He paused. "What say you to this plan?"

Elizabeth pressed a hand to her cheek. "It is all so sudden …"

"Is it too sudden, my dear? Would you prefer to wait?" This was the right thing to ask, but deuced painful just the same.

"People will say—you know what they will say."

"I do indeed," he agreed gravely. "No doubt it is the same for every couple. But we know the truth, you and I. Dearest Elizabeth, would you rather remain here with Jane?"

Elizabeth was now frowning at the floor. "I cannot return home because of the mumps," she said. "Moreover, Miss Woodhouse and Miss Bates will be leaving, whereas Mr. Bertram—" She looked up. "Fitzwilliam, what of him?"

"I fear Bertram is out of funds, stranded here until Quarter Day. And while I am willing to redeem his sorry watch from Mr. McGready—and reimburse the man for the money paid to Wickham for your bracelet—I draw the line at transporting Bertram to wherever he lives."

Elizabeth smiled impishly. "So he must stay at Netherfield. With Caroline."

It was all Darcy could do not to laugh. "It could do Bertram good. Bingley is not a gamester and, as you know, he likes everyone. As for Miss Bingley, she might welcome the diversion. For once Charles tells her of his engagement to your sister—"

"A not-so-happy Christmas for her."

"Must it be so for you?" Darcy said gently. "Would you prefer to spend Christmas at Netherfield? Or with me at Pemberley?"

She was silent for a time, and Darcy held his breath. Aunt Jane or no, the choice was Elizabeth's.

"To say truth, Fitzwilliam," she said at last, "I would much rather spend Christmas with you." Blushing, she fingered the license. "Even if it means marrying you in two days' time." A coy smile reappeared. "I'll have you know, sir, that I am not usually so brazen," she added, with a twinkle. "Or so impulsive. But in this case—"

The only thing to do was to kiss her. More than once and rather more passionately than before.

Impulsiveness, Darcy decided, became his Elizabeth very well. Theirs would be a very happy Christmas indeed.

The End

More books by Laura Hile are available at Amazon.com

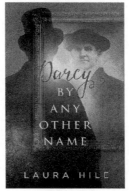

NO BETTER GIFT

Wendi Sotis

NO BETTER GIFT

Editing suggestions by Gayle Mills and Robin Helm.

Chapter One

Monday, December 16, 1811

"This was a mistake." Fitzwilliam Darcy's strained baritone echoed off the brown leather-upholstered walls of his coach, empty except for him. The sound was hollow — very much the way he foresaw his future.

He snapped the book on his lap closed and pulled the rug up around his neck to ward off the wintry nip in the air. The past few weeks had been colder than ever, or was it the prospect of a life void of the challenge, passion, and comfort *she* could provide that chilled him to the bone?

Darcy raked a hand through his hair. When had his thoughts become so fanciful?

He shook his head, already knowing the answer. It began soon after Michaelmas, that fateful evening at the assembly ball, the moment he took a second look at *her* and recognized his first impression was completely wrong.

"Ridiculous," he huffed with a cloud of breath. Again with the whimsy! He barely knew himself lately.

The impression that *she* was special or that she alone could soothe the ache within his soul was irrational. And yet, with each hoof step his team took towards the village of Meryton, his awareness increased, as if his mind had been in a fog since his hasty retreat from Hertfordshire several weeks ago. The further away he had been from *her*, the stronger the strain on their connection had grown, decreasing the likeliness of his concentrating on anything else. Now, as he travelled closer, the tension in his chest eased. Relief swelled through him.

No! He must stop thinking along these lines. The idea they were linked somehow was ludicrous. There had to be a perfectly good explanation for his response.

But if it were some sort of trick of his mind, why did not the illusion originate from where he would expect her to be? From the direction of Longbourn, which would be ahead and to the right, instead of to the left?

Perhaps in his mind's eye, he presumed she would be on a stroll with her sisters, heading for Meryton, or even on one of her solitary rambles?

His heart thrashed against his ribs as he pulled the window curtain aside. Gaze combing the woods, he searched for a hint of unnatural colour — her gown or mayhap her bonnet.

His well-sprung coach's wheels hit a rut so deep, the movement threw him against the seatback. The cloth dropped back into place.

This woman — this nobody — how had she cast a spell on him, so strong he was losing his mind?

It was a question he had asked himself many times since leaving Hertfordshire in late November. These three weeks in London, he had yielded to an all-encompassing, irrational dread that if he so much as *thought* the name of the lady who had captured his heart — let alone spoke her name aloud — his soul would be so completely weighed down with regret that he would never know a moment's peace for the rest of his life.

He would prove the fear wrong. He must. Now.

Darcy steeled himself. "Miss Elizabeth Bennet."

He held his breath for several moments and released it.

There! Nothing had changed. The lady held only as much power over him as he allowed. He would tolerate it no more.

However, the voicing of her name *did* conjure up a torrent of recollections he had struggled to suppress when awake, but which tortured him nightly in his dreams. Elizabeth's light and pleasing form skipping through a jig at the Assembly ball. Her porcelain skin, glowing with health and vigor whenever she came in from her beloved outdoors. Her delicate hand resting in his during the one and only dance they had shared. Her graceful movements, leaving a swirl of lavender in the air. Her voice, rising in song, filling his spirit with joy. Her eyes, alit with a flash of challenge or sparkle of lively wit, causing his heart to throb. The cleverness behind each of her words as she debated an opinion, forcing his own intellect to sharpen.

Darcy closed his eyes and fingered his signet ring — a symbol of all he had been taught to protect. Duty to his family name reigned above all else. He must select the proper mate, and Elizabeth was irrevocably unfit to be a Darcy.

Although his soul might be altered forever by meeting her, with time, he would have to forget her.

With that seemingly impossible goal in mind and hoping for an effective distraction, he headed for Matlock. He mentally corrected himself. No, he went primarily to spend Christmas with his relations. Three days hence, after months away from his sister, Georgiana, the siblings would reunite. Georgiana had indicated in her letters that spending time with their aunt and uncle had helped to heal the wounds left behind after learning the man she had loved had been interested only in her dowry. Perchance his spending time with family would cure *his* broken heart, as well?

Darcy's eyes snapped open. Broken heart? He was becoming nonsensical.

He shook his head. His aunt's naggings were correct. It was high time he settled down. Then all these absurd longings for Elizabeth would disappear.

When he returned to London in March for the Season, he *would*, at last, find someone worthy to become his wife.

There was one hitch to his plan. During his hurried flight from Netherfield, he had forgotten a gift he had purchased for his sister. Since he would be passing near the turnoff to his friend's estate whilst travelling north today, he chose to stop to retrieve it. To prevent temptation ruling over logic, for Longbourn — Elizabeth's home — was only three miles away, he would not even leave the confines of his coach. His driver would apply to Netherfield's housekeeper, and they would be on their way in less than five minutes.

The coach banked to the right, the signal that they would soon enter Meryton.

Darcy pulled the window curtain aside once more and tied it back.

One of the reasons he had approved Bingley's choice of leasing Netherfield was that Meryton reminded him of Lambton, the thriving community near his own estate. Last autumn, the sight of this village — always bustling with members of the four-and-twenty genteel households Mrs. Bennet boasted of entertaining, along with their servants and tenant farmers — often quelled the homesickness he faced whenever he was away from Pemberley.

However, as they pulled into town this time, his heart sank.

Something was wrong. Very wrong.

The village was deserted — peculiar for this time of the morning. No cheery boughs of greenery hung over the shop doors, as would be expected so close to Christmas. Window panes lacked the holly leaves and berries usual for this time of year. Absent were the pedestrians and carriages which had always been present before, save one lone cart sitting before the inn, but even that was abandoned with no horse attached. Shutters or drapes were tightly shut in every upper window facing the street, and "CLOSED" signs hung on many of the shop doors. The bookshop with which he had become so familiar during the time he stayed with Bingley, now had two boards nailed in an X across the doorway.

Darcy struck his cane against the roof. As the coach rolled to a halt, he opened the door and stepped down.

An icy breeze kicked up a whirlwind of dust near the butcher's shop. It rose, picking up stray leaves as it made its way down the empty road toward where it forked, one lane leading to Netherfield, the other to Lucas Lodge and Longbourn. At the end of the row of buildings, the eddy collapsed, scattering its contents near the sign he knew proclaimed "Welcome to Meryton."

He shuddered.

A door slammed, and Darcy spun. A man with a kerchief tied around his face exited a door near the milliner's shop and hurried along the boarded walkway.

"You there!" Darcy called out, but the man ducked into the next door without looking in Darcy's direction. A bolt clicked into place.

"What in blazes is going on here?" He glanced up at the coachman.

Roberts shook his head and pulled a rifle out from under his seat while the footman slid down from his bench and took a tentative step towards Darcy.

"Don't know, Mr. Darcy," Baxter said, "but it don't seem right."

Darcy nodded as he scrutinized the upper floors of the buildings across from him. Had the village been taken over by highwaymen? Had the French invaded England and now occupied Meryton?

A curtain moved in a window above the bookshop.

Darcy took a step closer. "Hello, Smithers? Is that you?"

The window opened a hands-width.

"Mr. Darcy?" The bookshop owner's voice bounced off all structures in the vacant street. "You best leave now, sir. Before it's too late!"

"Too late for what, Smithers?" He paused. "What is going on?"

The window closed with a bang.

Darcy caught Baxter's eye.

The coachman called down, "Want me and Baxter to knock on some doors, sir?"

Darcy shook his head. "Let us proceed to Netherfield as planned. Perhaps we can find out what is happening from the housekeeper."

As the horses followed the fork to the left, Darcy's gaze strayed down the lane leading to Longbourn. Was Elizabeth at home? Was she safe?

Why was there no tug at his heart coming from that direction?

An unpleasant weight settled in his stomach.

Whether this stop at Netherfield held any answers, and no matter how he longed to erase her from his mind, he could not leave the area until he was certain she was well.

The mile to Netherfield seemed interminable. When the coach jerked to a halt, Darcy bolted from it and up the staircase leading to the front door.

Since Bingley was not in residence, the knocker had been removed, so Darcy thumped the thick wooden door with the head of his cane.

Bingley had told him several servants were retained to keep the house in order until his lease ran out. So why, then, did the place seem deserted? Had the same fate come upon Netherfield as Meryton?

He paced the landing… it seemed forever. The tug on his heart began anew, from his right. Longbourn was in that direction.

He knocked again, to no avail. Not a trace of acknowledgment came from indoors, but the scraping of a rake sounded somewhere off to the right of the building.

Descending the stairs, he called out to the driver, "Remain here in case someone comes to the door."

Darcy motioned to Baxter to follow him, and they headed towards the stables.

He increased his pace to a jog. To a run. He *must* find answers.

Rounding the barn door, Darcy stopped short.

A lady stood still, rubbing her back, arched in a way that displayed her figure to its best advantage. One long chestnut curl escaped a simple bun. Her gown was of decent material and cut; the dirty hem was pulled up and tucked into the tie of a full-length apron, revealing both ankles and a hint of her right calf. After a few moments, she moved, and pulled a rake towards her again and again.

Darcy blinked several times, but the apparition did not disappear. His heart stuttered.

It was the most beautiful sight he had ever beheld.

Miss Elizabeth Bennet, safe and well… and vigorously mucking out a horse's stall.

Chapter Two

Would Mr. Bingley send assistance?

Elizabeth Bennet pulled the rake upright and leaned onto it. Just one moment of rest, that was all she needed. In truth, it was all she could afford.

A breeze swept through the barn, washing away the stench, if only for a moment. A few stray pieces of straw cartwheeled down the main corridor between the horses' stalls. When she first came out here, she was shivering, but after raking the soiled bedding from several compartments and all the way out the door, the cold air felt delightful against her overheated skin.

She had seen her father's stable boys do this work a hundred times. It had always seemed like such an easy job. But now she eyed the pitchfork, certain that the next step, laying out a thick layer of fresh hay, would be more difficult than it seemed, as everything she had done over the past few days had proven to be.

Her mother — so proud to be a gentleman's wife — had always laughed when she mentioned that the Lucas daughters helped their cook in the kitchen. What would her mother say if she knew her own daughter had spent the last few days dusting, changing linens, washing clothes, emptying basins, and sweeping floors?

And now she was cleaning stables.

Elizabeth would have to keep the details of her current situation a secret, or her mother's nerves would fray completely.

Meanwhile, privately, Elizabeth would take pride in doing her best at whatever she did, whether it was socially acceptable for a gentleman's daughter to do or not. Her compensation would be returning the sick to health. Hopefully with no lives lost.

A whinny floated through the window. The three horses Mr. Bingley left behind stretched their legs, galloping in circles around the pasture.

Her chest tightened. Those poor horses. How pleased they must be to finally be out of the barn, even for a short while.

Elizabeth shook her head. She must forgive herself. There was a good reason estates had a large staff — two people could not do it all alone. Not for long, anyway.

She rubbed at the small of her back. Every part of her ached from trying, even muscles she never knew she had before this week.

When all was restored to normal, she would personally thank every member of her father's staff at least once a week for the rest of her life.

That was enough of a rest.

Elizabeth extended the rake to pull filthy hay toward her. She must continue, must finish and return to the house.

A noise sounded behind her. She spun around and gasped.

"Mr. Darcy!"

Of all people, why was *he* here?

Without thinking, her hand fluttered to her hair and tucked the loose lock she had ignored as she laboured into the chignon at the nape of her neck.

She closed her eyes. Nothing short of a miracle would remove the grime her gown, face, and hair must have accumulated while cleaning out the barn. Besides, even if her appearance was perfect, Mr. Darcy would always find fault in her. She might as well give him an excellent reason this time.

Hearing footsteps, Elizabeth expected to see Mr. Bingley, but a man dressed in Darcy livery came into view instead.

Darcy bowed. His gaze darted to her ankles and stayed there, as if glued, reminding her she had gathered up the length of her gown to keep it out of the manure.

Lowering her head, in part to hide her burning cheeks, she curtsied in response. As discreetly as she could, she pulled her skirts loose from the tie of her apron.

"Miss Elizabeth." Darcy cleared his throat. "May I ask why you are mucking out Bingley's stables?"

Was his haughty attitude the only thanks she could expect for all she had done?

To tame her tongue before speaking, she took a deep breath and counted to five before releasing it. "Since everyone at Netherfield is ill, sir, and I am practically the only one who dares to venture near the estate, anything the maids who are helping me cannot do, I must do myself." She straightened her spine. "*Including* mucking out the stalls."

He stepped forward.

Elizabeth held out her hand, palm outward. "That is close enough, sir, unless you wish to contract the pox. I have been surrounded by the illness for six days."

Darcy's entire body stiffened. His face drained of emotion, an expression she had become quite familiar with a few weeks ago. "Not smallpox," he breathed.

She shook her head. "Chickenpox, sir."

His shoulders relaxed markedly. "I am immune. I assume you are, as well, Miss Elizabeth?"

"I had it as a child during a visit with my aunt and uncle in London."

Darcy turned to face the footman. "Baxter?"

Baxter answered, "Yes, sir. It made the rounds at Pemberley years ago when I was a stable boy." He startled, blanched, and cut a wide-eyed gaze towards Darcy.

Why had the footman reacted so strongly?

Darcy approached, took hold of the rake, and held it out to the footman. "Since you have experience, take over where Miss Elizabeth left off."

As Baxter went to work — almost too eagerly — Darcy motioned for Elizabeth to precede him out the door. She welcomed the opportunity for fresh air and began to move in that direction.

Elizabeth said, "I thank you for the assistance, sir."

Darcy bowed slightly. "It is you who should be thanked, not I."

Elizabeth examined his face. Surprisingly, he meant it.

Once outside, Darcy offered his arm.

Elizabeth swallowed hard. As tired as she was, she could have used his support, but the gloves were filthy. If she took them off, her mother would never forgive her for allowing Mr. Darcy to see the blisters she was sure had formed there, and judging by the pain, she was sure they had broken and were bleeding by now. "I do not wish to soil your suit, sir."

He stared at her hands. "Those gloves…"

Her stomach jumped. "Oh! Yes; I forgot." Her face heated again. Goodness, all this blushing must be from being so tired. Sleeping more than a half-hour here and there had been impossible since Mr. Jones had become ill. "I hope you do not mind that when I told Sarah, Netherfield's upstairs maid, that I was going to clean the barn, she explained where to find these gloves in your former rooms, sir. You must have left them behind. They have been a great help."

Darcy's nostrils flared.

What had he expected her to do, rake bare-handed? "I apologize for taking the liberty, Mr. Darcy. I had no other choice but to make do with what was at hand. My father will replace them, I am sure."

He stared straight ahead. "That will not be necessary."

They walked on in strained silence. Elizabeth stumbled and flailed. Darcy moved quickly, pivoting in front of her and placing one hand on each of her upper arms. He was so close, her hands ended on his chest. A sudden urge came over her to lay her cheek there and lean against him. She looked up into his eyes — perfect, dark brown pools that always made her insides melt.

She stiffened. *Control yourself, Lizzy. He has no interest in you.*

Darcy cleared his throat and stepped away from her. "You are obviously exhausted. I insist you take my arm, Miss Elizabeth."

"But..." she held up her hands, then gestured to the front of his coat. Oh, dear. At least she had soiled only his topcoat.

He followed the line of her gaze. "It matters not. Please, allow me to assist you."

Since he did not seem upset, she did as he asked. It occurred to her that a man as wealthy as Mr. Darcy probably had more than one topcoat.

When she took hold of his outstretched arm, his muscles flexed, sending a tremor through her to her core. They proceeded towards the house, his every movement reminding her of his physical presence.

It was so much easier to hate him when he was not here in front of her, so handsome he set her heart to race and her breath to catch in her chest every time their eyes met — so long as he kept his mouth shut. Since he had left Hertfordshire, any time her attraction to him haunted her thoughts or when her dreams betrayed her, she reminded herself of everything he had done to prove his character was wholly disagreeable. But it was too difficult to do when he was right in front of her, particularly as he was being pleasant at the moment.

Not that it mattered. He could never have any designs on her, made entirely clear by all the little things about him that practically screamed that she was far beneath him in every way possible. Every time she detected it, she could not help but become defensive and say something she would later regret.

Darcy barked, "How many are ill?"

His tone almost demanded that she salute him. Good! She could more easily dislike him when he behaved in such a way. Sometimes she feared she had made up his haughty attitude to protect her heart, but the proof that she had not imagined it was evident in his manner now.

"Sixteen," she answered.

"Sixteen children?"

"Ten children and six adults."

Darcy paled. "It is much worse in adults."

"Which has been well proven these past few days." She sighed. "The adults have suffered complications that I do not remember experiencing myself and, so far, have not affected the children. Their fevers are higher, and all have coughs. One woman has developed pneumonia."

She could feel the muscles of his arm tense. His voice was a bit husky when he asked, "Has Bingley been contacted?"

"It is my understanding that since most people affected were servants and tenants of this estate, Mr. Jones wrote to Mr. Bingley to inform him it was necessary to use the manor house to quarantine the patients."

Darcy shook his head.

With what could he possibly disagree?

"You must understand that since this neighborhood has had little experience with this illness, many are wary. *Someone* had to help these poor people, Mr. Darcy. They are too ill to take care of themselves. Though it is difficult for them to be away from their families just before Christmas, it was easier for Mr. Jones if the sick were all in one place."

She glanced at him and then away. "May I ask, if you are not here on Mr. Bingley's behalf, then why ..."

He fidgeted with a ring on his finger. Had the question made him uncomfortable? "I was travelling to Derbyshire for Christmas and realized I had forgotten something here. I stopped to retrieve it, but nobody answered the door — "

Elizabeth gasped. "Oh! The gloves? Were they meant to be a gift, sir?"

"Please do not let that trouble you, Miss Elizabeth. I have another gift for my sister."

The sound of birds in the distant trees seemed quite loud until he spoke again. "Has Mr. Jones received a reply from Bingley?"

"A letter from *Miss* Bingley was included in the basket of food left at the door this morning. They enclosed a five-pound note as payment for the apothecary."

Darcy stopped walking. "Do you mean to tell me that Bingley's staff and tenants are ailing and all he sent was a five-pound note?"

"Yes, sir." Elizabeth nodded. "Miss Bingley made it clear there would be no other aid offered."

His face reddened, and his eyes looked as though they might pop out of his head. He inhaled deeply. "What of your family?"

Elizabeth raised her chin. Was he saying her family should be responsible for the welfare of Netherfield's tenants and staff? "My sisters and Charlotte Lucas wished to provide assistance, but none of them have immunity."

Jane's, Mary's, and Charlotte's offers were expected, but it struck her as very odd when Lydia volunteered to come with her, too.

She continued, "As soon as my mother heard Mr. Jones's diagnosis, she took my sisters to London. Other than a few notes exchanged without any physical contact, I have not spoken with my father since coming to Netherfield six days ago, for Mr. Jones has forbidden him to come near."

"So you are saying that you alone are charged with caring for sixteen patients, Miss Elizabeth?"

"Longbourn's scullery maid was able, so she is assisting me." *Thank God for Emily.* If it were not for her, Elizabeth would have to deal with chamber pots, as well. Elizabeth had an oddly crushing need to justify her actions. "At first, I came simply to assist Mr. Jones, but it seems he did not have a resistance to the illness as he had thought. Since Mr. Jones took to bed, he directs me from there as to what to do for each patient.

"Our food and supplies are from Longbourn and the Lucas household. Some of the children's parents or older siblings, who can spare a few minutes and are immune, come when they can, which allow one of us to manage some chores. My aunt and uncle's maid is now here to offer further assistance. She arrived this morning, and as soon as one of the parents came to visit, I immediately came out to the barn. I have been feeding and watering the horses and other animals every day, but the needs of the sick had to come before the more time-consuming tasks involved in caring for the animals."

He began walking again. She had to hurry her steps to remain even with him.

"We need some supplies, sir. After I clean up, can I trouble you for the use of your coach to take me into Meryton? Generally, I would enjoy a walk into the village, but now … I do not wish to leave Hannah and Emily alone for long with so many under their care."

Darcy furrowed his brow. "I am sorry, Miss Elizabeth, but we just came through Meryton. All the shops are closed."

Elizabeth's stomach tightened. "What do you mean, Meryton is closed?"

Darcy shrugged. "I imagine it has something to do with the illness here at Netherfield."

She gasped. "Are they all unwell?"

"I saw one man, who would not speak to us, and the bookshop owner only yelled out his window saying we should go away. Both seemed healthy. They do know to come to Netherfield if they are ill, do they not?"

"Yes, Mr. Jones had a boy go to every household in the area, directing them to bring their sick here, but only two from outside the estate have come." Elizabeth sighed. "When the illness first began, everyone thought it was smallpox and hid in their homes. I assumed that when they heard it was chickenpox, they would have felt more at ease. But now, after seeing how ill some of the adults are, I do not blame them."

"I am surprised the regiment of militia has not offered support."

"I have to assume the colonel does not want his men exposed further than they already have been. The ailing man from outside the estate is a lieutenant." She looked away, not wishing to betray the identity of the man.

"Draw up a list of needed supplies. My coachman will fetch a doctor and a nursemaid or two from London. I will authorize the purchase of anything else you require, as well."

Elizabeth's step faltered, and Darcy pulled his arm closer to his side to steady her.

A pleasant warmth filled her chest. Netherfield was not his responsibility — nor was it hers, but this was her community, not his. He should not feel obligated. It said something for the man if he would do so anyway. "Thank you, sir."

His gaze was directed forward, but she could see a twitch at his jawline as he nodded.

Until this moment, if someone had told her she could ever be *this* grateful for the arrival of Mr. Fitzwilliam Darcy, she would not have believed them.

Chapter Three

The moment Elizabeth had looked in his eyes, he realized all previous efforts to cast her from his soul were defeated, utterly and completely. Never would he forget her. It had been foolish even to try.

Something as simple as seeing her wear a pair of gloves he had chosen, though for his sister, had caused such a sense of satisfaction to take root within him, that he found it exhilarating. He barely managed to hide his reaction. Her determination to do all she could to help those who depended upon her—the people, and even the animals—fixed her deeper in his heart than ever before.

His father had always prided himself on overseeing the lands and buildings of Pemberley, but caring for those who relied on the estate was his mother's passion.

Darcy had always striven to emulate both these qualities with his own behaviour. In his opinion, his mother's enthusiasm for ensuring the well-being of the community was one of the most important traits his future wife could possess, but it was a characteristic rarely found among the ladies who moved within the *ton*.

Yet, it was a quality Elizabeth possessed and did not hesitate to act upon, even though this was not her estate.

He glanced over at her. Even in her disheveled state, she was more attractive to him than ever. He was concerned that she seemed exhausted, and it was taking a great deal of willpower not to sweep her off her feet, carry her into the house, and put her to bed.

Unwittingly, his imagination ran wild, visualizing that scenario.

Darcy ground his teeth, reminding himself that the dark circles around her lovely emerald eyes confirmed she needed sleep desperately. She would be safer if he concentrated on something else, instead.

He refused to think of the ailment that was currently at Netherfield, which so many adults had contracted. He could not allow such raw, bitter memories to surface in company.

How could Bingley leave it up to his neighbors to care for his tenants and servants? Had Bingley ignored everything he was taught while they were here together a few weeks ago? One rule that Darcy had repeated over and over was that, whether it be convenient or not, the people who worked the estate were under their master's protection, even when the property was leased.

Darcy had never thought of Bingley as unfeeling before now. Immature? Yes, in some ways. Too easily led? Without a doubt. So eager to fall in love that he could be taken in by just about any pretty face? Absolutely.

Nevertheless, leaving his charges to fend for themselves during an epidemic was more than unsympathetic, it was hard-hearted. It did not sound at all like his friend. But why else would Bingley not even have taken the trouble to write to Mr. Jones himself?

The answer struck like a lightning bolt. It was more likely, and much less shocking, to believe Miss Caroline Bingley noticed the return address on Mr. Jones's letter and intercepted it before her brother even knew of the letter's existence. To prevent Bingley's being reminded of Miss Jane Bennet when he saw from whom the letter came — the very apothecary Bingley had called when Miss Bennet had been overcome with a cold whilst visiting at Netherfield — Caroline must have answered the letter herself, not realizing how far the ramifications her act of deceit would reach. Darcy doubted she would wish her brother to be labelled as a negligent clod, which is exactly what he would be called. Indeed, Darcy himself had just been thinking the worst, even though he knew Bingley better than most. Badly done, Caroline.

The shifting of Elizabeth's weight off his arm brought him to the present. With each step she had taken, she had leaned on him a little more, but now, as they approached the doors leading to the servants' entrance, she straightened. Perhaps his arm had helped her to regain a portion of strength?

The idea that Elizabeth had needed him for something so personal, even for such a short period, played havoc with the rhythm of his heart. It was a remarkable sensation, one he wished he could experience every day of his life. He could not, but at least for now...

His decision was made. While he would not lead her on in any way, for he could not marry her, since Bingley was absent, he could lighten her burden during this crisis.

When all was under control on the estate, he would leave — get on with his life — after collecting a few more memories of Elizabeth, which he would secretly cherish forever.

~%~

Revitalized by her wash water and a change of clothing, Elizabeth hurried from the rooms she had appropriated for her use. When she reached the stairwell, Mr. Darcy exited the same rooms he had occupied this past autumn. She was relieved they had not borrowed the mattress from that bed. He was wearing the same clothing in which he had travelled, but he must have taken a brush to it, for the dust from the road on his trousers was now gone. Of course, he would not have been able to change for there was nobody to bring his trunk upstairs. It was of no matter — he would not be here for long.

She waited for him, hands clasped behind her. It would do no good for him to see them.

"Excuse my appearance, Miss Elizabeth." He touched his simply-tied cravat. "I am unused to tying these myself."

"I am sorry we have no servants to assist you, Mr. Darcy. Did your valet not travel with you?"

He shook his head. "No, he was to visit his sister and meet me at Matlock after Christmas."

"Matlock?"

"Yes, my uncle's estate, where my sister has been staying these past months."

She paused. "Your uncle is the Earl of Matlock?"

He nodded.

She had heard Caroline Bingley boast that her guest was the grandson of a late earl, but her mind had not concluded that Mr. Darcy's uncle must be an earl now. No wonder his sense of self-worth was so pumped up; his relatives were peers of the realm.

Mr. Darcy interrupted her thoughts. "I expected you would rest for a while, Miss Elizabeth."

"There is no time for that, now, sir, for who would see to what needs to be done?" Why was she so angry? He was only trying to make conversation. She purposely softened her tone. "I only meant that any of my own needs which *can* be delayed, *must* be, for now."

Without taking the banister, she descended. He kept up with her pace.

"You need sleep, Miss Elizabeth. If you wish to continue helping these people, it would not do for you to become ill yourself."

She stopped on the landing between staircases and turned to face him. Her tone was tightly controlled. "Thank you for your concern, sir, but I am well."

"You are exhausted. Perhaps there is something I can do, such as assist in making up the supply list?" Mr. Darcy suggested.

Elizabeth hesitated. After freshening up, she expected he would head straight for the library until it was time for his coach to depart for London. However, she needed some sort of relief, and if he wanted to assist, she should accept, though doing so would mean exposing her hands to the man.

Her mother would never forgive her, but the needs of the many outweighed those of the few.

He gestured for them to continue down the remainder of the staircase. She complied.

Making up the list would go quicker if he wrote while she went through the pantry to see what was needed, and then she could return to caring for the sick. And perhaps the shop owner would take the requests more seriously if the list was in his handwriting instead of hers. She was unsure she could write just now, anyway.

"I thank you, sir. Why do you not gather the writing supplies from Mr. Bingley's study whilst I check with Hannah, Emily, and Mr. Jones to see if they need anything?"

Mr. Darcy stepped down from the staircase and turned to face her. "Certainly."

His smile was genuine and reflected in his eyes. Elizabeth's world brightened as if the sun had come out from behind the clouds after a month of rainy days. A shiver passed through her.

His eyebrows knit together. "Are you sure you are well, Miss Elizabeth?" Mr. Darcy touched her elbow.

Elizabeth blinked several times and looked around her. She had frozen on the last stair. She peeled her gaze from his face and stepped down and away from him. "I will meet you outside the kitchen. There is a table in the corridor."

"Am I not allowed in the kitchens?"

"I am afraid there will be no one there to chaperone, Mr. Darcy."

"These are trying times, Miss Elizabeth. I doubt anyone would even notice."

The idea of being alone with Mr. Darcy so far away from everyone else in the house made her nervous. She trusted he would not try to take advantage of her, but if someone were to accuse them of behaving improperly, her reputation would be in tatters, not his. Her cheeks heated — again. "I – I would not wish to take that chance, sir."

She hurried away towards the door of the sitting room, where the females were being housed.

As she entered, she glanced around to see how her patients were doing. In both sickrooms, the smaller children lay on the sofas, while the older children and adults reclined on several mattresses, brought down earlier in the week. A fire blazed, and the patients were laid out in a semi-circle, like arms stretching out from the hearth so all could benefit from its heat. The few dressing screens that were light enough to bring down were set up between some of the beds, providing as much privacy as was possible, especially for the adults.

She coughed at the sour scent of illness that nearly overwhelmed her. Elizabeth strode to the window furthest away from the patients and slid it open just a little. In her opinion, foul air never helped anyone, ailing or not.

Emily stood from a six-year-old girl's makeshift bed and waved her over. "Miss Elizabeth. Rose has a crop of fresh marks."

Elizabeth stooped to check under the cloths they had wrapped around little Rose's arms to hold in place the salve of oatmeal, vinegar, and honey that Longbourn's housekeeper had sent, as well as to keep Rose from scratching. "Is Mrs. Hill's remedy working?"

"Yes'm, Miss Lisbeth. It's not nearly so scratchy." The girl's brows pinched together as she stared at Elizabeth's hands, wrapped similarly to Rose's arms. "Do you have the pox, too?"

Elizabeth smiled. "They are just sore, dear, and so I put some of Mrs. Hill's salve on them." She hoped it would heal the blisters as it did the rash. "Nothing to worry about."

She straightened to speak to Emily. "How is Rose's fever?"

"Hers and Lucy's fevers are gone. As for the rest, 'tis always better during the day."

It seemed Rose and Lucy's older brother had brought the chickenpox into the area when he came to visit his family for the holidays. He was in the other room. Elizabeth nodded, then said to Rose, "Well, then, this should be the last round of new marks. Mr. Jones says they come in threes. You will feel better soon."

"Does that mean we can go home?" Rose stared up at Elizabeth with round, tear-filled eyes. All the children missed their families horribly, but their parents had work to do and other offspring at home who needed them. It broke her heart that they might be away from their families for Christmas.

"We have to be home in time for Christmas Eve." Lucy, older than her sister Rose by a year or two, puffed out her chest. "Our Papa said I can help light the yule log this year. And we don't want to miss Christmas service."

Emily and Elizabeth exchanged looks. Today was the sixteenth of December. Usually, the illness lasted one or two weeks, and they had been first to show signs of the rash six days ago. With a new round of pox breaking out on them now, it would be a few days before they could go home.

Particularly important since yesterday, the midwife had left a note for Mr. Jones on the steps outside. Two nights ago, the girls' mother had a baby — delivered too early. The newborn's health was quite poor, so Mr. Jones and the midwife agreed Lucy, Rose, and their brother should not return home until all their pox had scabbed and no new marks had appeared for at least two days. It was a hardship for the whole family to have them away from home when their parents could use their assistance, but to keep the infant safe, it had to be.

"I am not sure…" Elizabeth's heart squeezed as both children sank back against their pillows. "But I promise I will get a yule log, and you may light it early, Lucy, as practice." She had no idea how she would manage to bring a large log from the woods into the manor house. Of course, she could not ignore the boys and men, so that meant two logs.

Rose's eyes lit up. "And a kissing bough? Mama always makes a kissing bough."

Elizabeth smiled. "Yes, and I will give you both lots of kisses so you can pluck a berry every time and toss them onto the fire."

Rose's and Lucy's smiles were worth any trouble it would take to procure the evergreens and logs.

"I know you are not very hungry, but do not forget that Mrs. Hill made you some special soup with lots of carrots that Mr. Jones promises will benefit your healing."

Both girls, and a few of the others who had been listening, took a little soup right away. Elizabeth grinned. Everyone wished to be home in time for Christmas.

After checking with Emily about what she needed, Elizabeth crossed the corridor to the parlour where the males were staying to check with Mr. Jones and Hannah. When she came again into the hallway, Mr. Darcy lingered there, his writing supplies gathered on a side-table.

Elizabeth stifled a giggle. "This is not the kitchen, Mr. Darcy."

He raised his brows. "I have been waiting for you." His colour rose. "If you asked me to meet you at the entrance to the kitchens at Pemberley, I would have known where to go, but at Netherfield …" He shook his head.

"Oh, of course. Why would you?" She left the door to both rooms open so that the maids could come out into the hallway. It was the best she could do to avoid being alone with Mr. Darcy. She crossed to the table, picked up some of the supplies, and gestured for him to follow her. "It is just down the hall, sir."

His gaze caught on her bandaged hands, and he took in a sharp breath. "The rake?"

She turned away. "Yes." Goodness. Would donning a blush become her normal appearance?

Without looking at him, she indicated the table he should use then disappeared into the kitchens.

A few minutes later, their list began to take shape. Elizabeth asked, "Do you know which of Mr. Bingley's horses is the gentlest, sir?"

"Will you be going riding, Miss Elizabeth?" The twinkle in his eye told her he was teasing, which shocked her momentarily.

"I have promised the children I would collect greenery for trimmings and a yule log for each of the rooms where the patients are staying. I will need a horse to pull the logs to the house, but I am not quite *comfortable* with horses."

"They were in the pasture when I arrived ..."

Did he not believe her? Why on earth would she try to deceive him?

"The stables have a door that opens into the pasture, opposite to the one you used to enter. I simply opened it and then unfastened the stall doors. The horses were more than willing to comply with my wishes."

Mr. Darcy raised his eyebrows. "And just how were you going to get them back in?"

She bit the corner of her bottom lip. "I admit the timing of your arrival was perfect, sir. I was just beginning to worry about how I would manage it."

His eyes crinkled at the outer corners, displaying amusement, but she did not detect any mockery, which delighted her right down to her toes.

Elizabeth ducked through the kitchen door before revealing the emotion.

She must be completely exhausted if she was not taking offense at his every word, as she usually would. In fact, she was enjoying his company. It was strange ... and dangerous.

The next time she re-entered the hallway, he said, "If you can point me in the right direction, I would be happy to gather the plants for you, as well as the yule logs."

She shook her head. "I know exactly where to get what we need, but it would be difficult to explain. Besides, though I appreciate the offer, sir, I would rather have the doctor and supplies here sooner than that you should delay your departure until we return from the woods."

"My departure?" He paused. "Miss Elizabeth, I thought you understood ... I am staying."

She opened her eyes wider. "Staying, sir?"

"Yes. I am sending my coachman to London, but I will remain at Netherfield. Roberts and Baxter are bringing up my trunk as we speak."

"But sir, we have no servants to — "

Mr. Darcy waved off her concern. "I understand. With my valet absent, I had every intention of doing without his assistance while we travelled for the next three days. This will be no different. I can take care of my own needs, as long as you will forgive me for not being perfectly dressed every moment of the day. And unless I am mistaken, with no time for formal dining, it will not be necessary to change, which is perfectly fine with me. I have always considered changing for dinner a bother."

"But, sir, it is more than just being without a valet. For instance, I barely have had the time it takes to pump water for my own use, but have not had the energy to heat it. Please, do not expect —"

"Miss Elizabeth, I do know how to use a kitchen pump, a skill which is especially useful now that I know where the kitchens are." Darcy stifled a grin. "And incredible as it may seem, I even have experience with drawing water from a well, if it comes down to that." He hesitated, his eyes bright, the corners of his mouth twitching.

Elizabeth's heart fluttered at his teasing, but then it jumped. Goodness! When they came in from the stables, she had gone to the kitchens and brought up water for herself, but she had not gotten *him* any water to wash with. She examined his appearance. He seemed freshly groomed.

"Speaking of which, Mr. Darcy, if you did not know where the kitchens were …" She blinked. How did she ask this question politely?

"I did not wish to take anyone away from their duties. When I was here last month, I noticed there is a pump at the stables used to water the horses."

He brought his washbasin and pitcher all the way out there?

She snapped her mouth closed. "Quite resourceful."

"Thank you." He bowed his head slightly.

Mr. Darcy was certainly full of surprises today. At least he was honest about being able to get his own water.

"Truly, Miss Elizabeth, I do not intend to create more work for you, and I expect no special treatment. I wish to help, not hinder your efforts. Baxter will assist with bringing in the yule and greenery, and then you may give him whatever task you wish. Perhaps I can entertain the sick men with conversation and play some games with the boys to keep their minds off their troubles."

She believed his intentions were sincere, but even in her case, the situation had taken some getting used to, and she could not wait for this trying time to end. If *she* was having trouble, how would fastidious Mr. Darcy survive even one day without any servants at his beck and call? Besides, there were quite a few tasks that, once this was all over, she had no intention of admitting she mastered. If Mr. Darcy remained, he might witness her performing these chores. That would be humiliating.

Then again, she could use any help she could get.

If he did not cooperate, she would remind him of this discussion and offer him one of the horses so that he could continue his journey to Derbyshire on horseback.

"All right, then. I welcome your assistance, Mr. Darcy."

A niggling feeling in the back of her mind warned her this was probably a mistake.

Chapter Four

As Darcy wrote down the last of what Elizabeth — not Elizabeth, *Netherfield* — needed, an urgent thumping sounded from the front door. As he rose from his chair, he watched Elizabeth. She took a step in that direction.

"Let me." He moved down the corridor.

Elizabeth followed.

Darcy opened the front door just as a man with a cloth tied over his mouth like a highwayman raised a fist to pound again.

Darcy stepped forward, blocking the opening to protect Elizabeth.

The man took a step back. "'Scuse me, sir."

Confused by this behaviour, Darcy looked more closely at the man's clothing. He wore the Bennets' livery.

Elizabeth called out from behind him, "Wilson! You should not be here — you have never had the chickenpox."

Darcy relaxed a little and slid to the side, allowing Elizabeth to step forward.

"Miss Elizabeth." Wilson swiped the hat off his head and bowed. "I brought Mr. Bennet, miss. 'e's come down with the pox. Mrs. Hill said ta bring 'im here."

The colour that had just begun to return to Elizabeth's lovely face during their task now drained from her complexion. One bandaged hand fluttered up to her open mouth while the other took hold of the doorjamb.

Thinking she might swoon, Darcy reached out to steady her, but the lady was made of sturdier stuff. Before he touched her, her spine straightened. Darcy was two paces behind as she rushed down the steps to the carriage. The servant hung back.

"Papa!" she called out as she opened the carriage door. Elizabeth, along with a portly woman inside the carriage, assisted Mr. Bennet, covered in fresh marks, to slide towards the door.

As Elizabeth's father disembarked, Darcy took over. Reaching for Darcy's shoulder, Mr. Bennet said, "Mr. Darcy? What are you doing here?"

"It is a long story, Mr. Bennet. I will come to pay my respects later and explain. For now, please allow me to help you into the house."

Mr. Bennet raised both eyebrows and observed his daughter.

Elizabeth nodded.

Stooping to allow Mr. Bennet's arm over his shoulder, Darcy slid an arm around the older gentleman's back. Even through many layers of clothing, he could feel the fever burning through the man. Mr. Bennet covered his mouth with a handkerchief and coughed violently.

Darcy switched his gaze to Elizabeth, who was staring at her father with fear clouding her eyes.

When Mr. Bennet stopped coughing, she put her father's other arm over her own shoulders and an arm around his waist.

Earlier, Darcy had warned Elizabeth it was worse for adults to contract chickenpox. That unfortunate knowledge had come firsthand.

The sound of Mr. Bennet's wheeze near Darcy's ear had him fighting off a shudder. Memories of his own mother's battle with the same illness, which quickly led to pneumonia, flooded his mind, as did the sorrow of losing her.

Mr. Bennet's situation did not look good.

Elizabeth spoke to the woman, "Mrs. Hill, you are immune to chickenpox, are you not?"

"Yes, Miss Elizabeth. Mrs. Bennet ordered me to stay with Mr. Bennet, and stay with him I will. It'll be easier to cook from here and not send food in baskets every day. Now I can do it the other way 'round — less people, so less of a need for food at Longbourn, anyway. But Wilson's gotta leave right away after unloading some things I'll need, miss."

"Of course." She called out to the man in Bennet livery, who was backing away to the furthest corner of the landing as they climbed. "Wilson, as soon as we are in the house, do what you must and then return to Longbourn. There is no sense in your catching this. Mrs. Hill will leave a basket for you with food every day, in the same place as before. Take care of Longbourn while my father is here."

Wilson bowed. "Yes, miss. I will."

Mr. Bennet could barely stand. The activity was causing the gentleman's breathing to become even more laboured. Darcy almost suggested that he be carried, but he suspected Mr. Bennet would rather endure this discomfort than suffer indignity before his servants and daughter.

Finally indoors, Elizabeth motioned to a bench in the entry hall. All the noise must have attracted the maids' attention because they both came out of the sickrooms.

Elizabeth said, "Stay here for a few minutes, Papa. Emily must help me bring down a mattress."

Her father slumped into the chair, and another coughing fit began. Mrs. Hill busied herself tucking a blanket around him.

Darcy spoke up. "I will go with Emily, Miss Elizabeth."

Elizabeth blinked rapidly.

He could only imagine she was surprised he would lower himself in such a way. Every time he indicated he could do anything without a servant, or teased her in some way, she was shocked.

He brought this on himself. When she stayed with Bingley whilst her sister recovered here last October, though he was drawn to her so completely he could not avoid her, he fought his attraction to her by remaining aloof and at the same time, tried to communicate the differences in their social status. Between the way Caroline Bingley treated her and the way he had behaved, he obviously had done too thorough a job of it. Yes, he was above her socially, but he was not pampered, and he was not a dandy. Nevertheless, it was the way she thought of him. It would not do.

"Stay with your father."

The soft light in her eyes conveyed her thanks. He gestured to Emily and headed up the stairs.

Apparently, Emily had been here the entire week and knew exactly which rooms still had mattresses. He had to steer her away from his own, but they found another in good time.

When they made their way downstairs again, Elizabeth was sitting with Mr. Bennet in a chair in the men's quarters, and Mrs. Hill was nowhere in sight. Judging by the heavenly scent already floating down the corridor, Darcy guessed she was in the kitchens.

Resting seemed to have given Mr. Bennet a little more strength. Elizabeth and Hannah were in the process of shifting one of the beds over to make room for the new arrival.

Darcy was near Mr. Bennet when the older gentleman waved Elizabeth over. He rasped out, "Not there, Lizzy!"

Darcy tried not to listen, but he was too close to avoid it.

Confused, Elizabeth examined the room. "But there is more space on this side — "

"Absolutely not, Elizabeth. I would rather be placed in the entry hall than next to that rascal."

Elizabeth's eyes widened. Darcy could feel his own expression mirror hers.

Darcy's gaze darted to where Hannah still moved things about. When he saw who was in the bed nearest that area, he almost dropped the mattress. His gut clenched. Good Lord, it was Wickham.

When Darcy was here last, he had understood Wickham was welcomed by everyone in the Bennet household, including Mr. Bennet. What had happened to turn him against Wickham?

He listened on purpose now.

Elizabeth lowered her voice, but Darcy could still make out what she said. "Papa? I do not understand. You have always enjoyed Mr. Wickham's company."

"You have not received a letter from any of your sisters lately, have you?"

"Hannah brought letters, but I have not yet read them." Elizabeth shook her head. "Why, what is wrong?"

"Lydia brought the chickenpox with her to London, and now all your sisters and youngest cousins have caught it."

"Oh, no!" She shook her head and looked at Emily, who held the other side of the mattress angled away from the pair and did not seem to be able to hear what they said. Elizabeth glanced at Wickham again, then returned her gaze to her father. She appeared to be avoiding directly meeting Darcy's eyes. "But what does that have to do with Mr. Wickham?"

"He is the one who gave the illness to Lydia." Mr. Bennet's nostrils flared. "You know how Kitty lets loose all her secrets whenever she has a fever? Let us just say that as a result of her babbling, Jane informed me that Lydia has been meeting with the man secretly."

Darcy almost let go of the mattress.

Wickham could not have been hunting a fortune this time, for the Bennets had none. Perhaps he should have run Wickham through when he had tried to elope with his sister, Georgiana, so the rat could not have become a threat to any other young ladies.

Sick or not, Wickham deserved a thrashing.

~%~

Elizabeth's knees gave out, and she sank into a chair next to her father.

"Kitty has been chaperoning their encounters, but it seems he has been trying to convince Lydia to meet him alone."

"So Lydia is not…"

"Ruined? No. They have never been alone," Mr. Bennet said.

"Thank God." Elizabeth placed a hand on her forehead and closed her eyes. If Lydia had been ruined, it would have tainted all of her sisters' reputations, as well. No respectable gentleman would have wanted anything to do with any of them.

A moment later, Elizabeth raised her head. "But knowing Lydia and her obsession with red coats, if left unchecked ..."

"Yes, exactly." Another coughing fit necessitated a pause. "A week ago, the day before so many became ill, I overheard three shopkeepers in discussion with the tavern owner, all speaking about Wickham."

Elizabeth's chest tightened, both in response to her father's discomfort and the subject of conversation. How could she have been so wrong about Mr. Wickham's character? Her heart did not want to hear any more details of this rogue's misdeeds, but Papa wished to tell her, and her mind knew she had to listen.

"It seems he has used his charm to run up credit all over the village. One of the shopkeepers had been in the militia a few years ago and said that unless Wickham was independently wealthy — and by his own admission, he is not — he could never earn the amount of money needed to repay what he owes already, even just to those four, before the regiment leaves the area."

She helped her father take a drink.

Good heavens! This — all of it — must have been what Mr. Darcy alluded to when he had tried to warn her against Mr. Wickham. *Mr. Wickham is blessed with such happy manners as may ensure his making friends – whether he may be equally capable of retaining them, is less certain.*

Her father continued, "I joined their conversation, asking them to speak to the other shop owners and bring me a list of what he owes to them all.

"Then so many became ill, and I have not seen anyone since. When I am feeling better, I will go to speak to the colonel about this. Do not worry, Lizzy — of course, for the sake of all my daughters' reputations, I will leave out his *other* offence.

"It is a good thing there is no rush and Wickham is laid up, for I began feeling ill two days ago. My marks broke out yesterday. This morning, I had trouble breathing, and Mrs. Hill practically man-handled me into the carriage to come here."

"She was right to do so." Elizabeth touched her father's sleeve. "I will place your bed between Mr. Jones and the wall on the opposite side of the room."

"That will be safer for everyone, my dear Lizzy. I do not have the energy to cross such a large room on my own right now in order to beat the man senseless." Mr. Bennet drooped against the chair back. "I believe I am in need of a nap."

Elizabeth scurried away from her father. She had to get his bed set up as soon as possible.

~%~

Darcy told Emily he would call her if he needed her assistance again, but for now, she should see to the patients in the other room.

He crossed to where Elizabeth was busying herself. Taking a water pitcher from a table along the wall, she turned and almost ran into him.

He stooped and put a hand on each side of the small table. "Where do you want this?"

She hesitated a moment, then pointed. He moved it there.

She approached. "You heard all that?"

He shifted from one foot to the other. "I was in a position where I could not help but hear it."

Her countenance was tense as she placed the pitcher on the table.

He said, "I apologize, Miss Elizabeth."

"For listening to a private dialogue?"

"For allowing that scoundrel to live long enough to ... to *bother* anyone else."

She examined his face for several moments and then looked away, blushed, and again met his gaze. "You did try to warn me about him at Mr. Bingley's ball, sir."

"But I gave you no good reason for you to believe my warning. No explanation. Nothing specific. Certainly not enough to warrant anyone's taking precautions against what he might do."

"Will you help me with this, sir?" She moved to the far end of a long side table that was in the way of where he knew she wanted to place her father's mattress.

"Do not push yourself so hard, Miss Elizabeth. Let Emily or Hannah do this," he said.

"Hannah has travelled since before sunrise, and Emily has worked as hard as I have, if not harder."

He gestured to her hands. "They do not have blisters from mucking out stalls."

Annoyance danced in her eyes. She straightened. "Mr. Darcy, I will not pull them away from their duties to do something I can easily do myself. You are unoccupied at the moment, but if you do not assist me, I will drag this table across the room *alone*."

She would do it; he had no doubt. He bit back a smile and raised the other end of the table. When she lifted her end, he walked backwards to the part of the room furthest from the hearth, where most of the furniture they were not using was now pushed together.

She carefully released her side of the table and brushed off her hands. "Sir, may I ask a favour? Would your driver be willing to take Hannah to my aunt and uncle's home on Gracechurch Street? If my sisters are ill — "

"You said Hannah just arrived today?"

Elizabeth nodded. "She did not even mention my sisters were ill."

"From what your father said, your family must have been ailing for several days. If they sent Hannah, I must assume it was determined they were able to spare her. I doubt anyone would want you to feel guilt for accepting support."

Her brow furrowed, and her gaze sought out Hannah. "I must speak to her about it before your driver leaves, to be sure."

"Go. Emily and I will finish making room for the mattress and help Mr. Bennet to it, then I will send Roberts on his way with the note for my doctor and your list of needs."

"We had best go out to the woods soon after my father is settled." She brushed a wayward curl away from her forehead. "I must return in time to serve the midday meal."

He nodded, and she bustled away towards Hannah.

As upset as she must be after hearing such news, she would not put off her responsibilities, not even for a moment.

What an amazing woman.

Chapter Five

Elizabeth trudged along the path, narrow enough at this point that they had to walk single file. If Mr. Darcy and his footman were not with her, she might consider running to release some of the energy — the pent-up outrage — that was boiling inside her. She looked over her shoulder to remind herself that Mr. Darcy was immediately behind her, while Baxter brought up the rear, leading a stallion that dragged a narrow, sled-like cart. All were quiet, leaving her with her thoughts for the time being.

Before Elizabeth left the house, Hannah had explained Aunt and Uncle Gardiner had hired a nurse so they could send Hannah to help her here. Their generosity warmed her heart. Once Hannah arrived and saw how overwhelmed with patients Elizabeth was, the maid felt it best Elizabeth should find out that her family was ill from the letters she had brought along with her.

Almost exactly as Mr. Darcy had predicted.

Good heavens, why did Mr. Darcy have to be close enough to hear her conversation with her father? How could he not think even worse of her now, after hearing about Lydia's behaviour?

Not that it mattered, really — she and her family were nothing to him — but she was surprised he did not bolt out the door with his driver to London the moment he found out Wickham was among the sick, let alone once he learned Lydia had been secretly meeting with the rascal.

The gentleman made no sense.

That Mr. Darcy had been correct about Wickham bothered her less than she expected it would. *Fancy that.*

It was a good thing there were so many people in the sickroom, or she would have confronted Wickham immediately after hearing her father's news. Maybe she should put his bed further from the fire than the others, or later she could "forget" to heat the water in his washbasin. She sighed. She would never do more than give him a piece of her mind — a very large and pointed piece — but she grinned just thinking about other options.

The path opened, and she moved to the fallen tree, which had caught on another and was suspended at an angle. She turned to face the men. "This can be split in two, to be used in both hearths, do you not think?"

Mr. Darcy nodded. "It is perfect. We should chop it in half before loading it on the cart."

Baxter removed the baskets, already filled with holly, rosemary, ivy, and the herbs Mr. Jones needed for his brews from the cart. She grabbed the empty one. "I will find the mistletoe and return here in a little while."

Mr. Darcy looked at her in such a way that she expected him to say it was unsafe for a lady to walk in the woods without an escort, but he clamped his lips together tightly and said nothing.

As if she was better off being found in the woods with two men?

Earlier he had mentioned that Baxter would act as chaperone, but the world did not work that way and they both knew it. For them to be considered chaperoned, the third person was required to be a woman. If she were seen walking with either of them, separate or together, her reputation would be in tatters. Her only comfort was that she had never seen anyone along this path before. Then again, the path would not be here if nobody else used it.

She sighed. It was her choice to lead this outing, made for the sake of the children now staying at Netherfield.

Nevertheless, she should distance herself from the men while they laboured. If her neighbors saw her walking alone, it would be nothing out of the ordinary — or at least her mother did not hear gossip about it any longer.

The need to hurry along this expedition and return to the house pressed upon her, quickening her footsteps. A few more turns in the path and she was behind Netherfield's apple orchard.

Choosing a tree with a sturdy branch close to the ground, she stepped up and made her way to the higher branches. Leaning her bottom on a thick branch, she stood on a limb and wobbled her way directly underneath where the mistletoe had latched on. Removing a penknife from her pocket, she stretched to cut more than enough for her purposes.

As she dropped the last sprig onto the pile below her, Mr. Darcy moved into view. Folding his arms across his abdomen, he glared up at her.

She wrapped her skirts a little tighter around her legs to make certain nothing that should not be seen was exposed.

"What do you think you are doing?" his deep baritone accused.

These were the same words she had often heard from her mother. The next words would always be *ladies do not* whatever she had done — in this case, *climb trees*.

Annoyed, she took her time wiping the knife on a handkerchief, folding it, and slipping it into her pocket. "I was collecting mistletoe for the boughs the girls requested to decorate the sickrooms."

He closed his eyes for a moment, took a deep breath, and scowled at her again. "Come down so I can speak to you properly."

"Turn around, sir, or else I cannot climb down."

"I cannot aid you if I cannot see you, Miss Elizabeth."

"Mr. Darcy, I estimate that the number of trees I have climbed in my lifetime is probably greater than the sum total of those which you and all your relations put together have even *thought* about climbing. I can assure you, no assistance will be necessary."

It was also in her estimation that if steam could come out of his ears, it would have.

Elizabeth raised her eyebrows impatiently. He turned his back to her.

Carefully making her way down the tree, she jumped from the lowest limb so she was standing next to him when she landed.

He spun to face her and began immediately, "What did you mean by wandering so far away from us? And for leaving the path?"

Her temper flared. How dare he criticize her! He had no right to question what she did or did not do. He was not her father, and he certainly was not her husband.

"If you remember, I *did* inform you I was leaving to find mistletoe, Mr. Darcy. Since I am aware the plant grows well on the upper branches of apple trees, and since it is needed at Netherfield, I drew the logical conclusion that Netherfield's apple orchard would be the most suitable place to find it. When I saw this tree would be easy to climb, I anticipated it would have taken much longer to return to where you were, wait for you to finish, and bring you both back here, than the five minutes it would take me to accomplish the same task alone."

She held her arms out to the sides. "And as you can plainly see, I have done exactly what I intended."

He opened his mouth to speak, but she cut him off.

"However, instead of saving time, as I planned, you stopped your work to come find me. Why? Because you did not trust that I could find my way to a few sprigs of mistletoe, nor did you believe that I could follow a simple path back to where I left you without the guidance of a member of the upper crust. Mr. Darcy, I will have you know that I am so familiar with these woods, I could walk them blindfolded and still find my way — a fact you should remember from when you stayed with Mr. Bingley in the autumn since Miss Bingley never stopped pointing out what a *good walker* I am. Perhaps if I had *better breeding*, I would have been brought up to understand your way of thinking, but no, to quote your hostess once again, I am just *a hoyden, a country nobody with no dowry, no connections to recommend me, and very little in the way of accomplishments*. Does that about summarize the situation, sir?"

Completely worn out at the end of her rant, she paused to catch her breath.

Eventually, he said, "I will not lie and say you are wrong about what Miss Bingley said about you. Since you are using her exact phrasing, I must deduce that you overheard her."

Elizabeth tilted her head to the side and nodded her admission.

It had been difficult not to. When she had stayed at Netherfield to nurse her sister, though she wished to avoid most of the other inhabitants of the estate, for Jane's sake, she did not. It would have been rude to do so. Too often, when Elizabeth approached the room where the others gathered, she had been forced to remain in the corridor until the conversation turned to something other than herself. Never one to avoid confrontation, her only reason for doing so was to avoid causing her host discomfort.

"Miss Elizabeth, surely you understood that Miss Bingley's opinion was not shared by the remainder of those in residence."

"I understood no such thing, sir. Mr. Bingley was the only one who ever defended me."

He widened his eyes. "When you were not present, yes, but only because where Bingley's sister is concerned, it is easier to ignore her babbling." He went on, "Quite clearly, I remember several times you *were* present when Miss Bingley threw a barb ... one time, in particular, we were speaking of ladies' accomplishments — "

"Yes." She raised her chin. "Miss Bingley listed several areas in which she felt I was lacking." She also remembered that he joined in with his own criticism.

"And my answer proved her attempt to ridicule you failed miserably and only brought attention to where *she* fell short."

Anger swelled hot within her breast, a dangerous thing, for it loosened her tongue. "It certainly did not."

He blinked at her. "Miss Elizabeth, until this moment, I thought you purposely misunderstood some of my statements in order to fuel a debate. Are you telling me that you seriously believe that I am not aware of your accomplishments? That I, too, was attacking you during that discussion?"

Elizabeth faltered and took a step back. Something about what he said rang true, for she never did understand Caroline Bingley's reaction to what

Mr. Darcy had said, responding almost as if she had been slapped. She thought Miss Bingley was the one who misunderstood, but ... was it possible he *had* been defending her?

A remarkable concept.

Even more shocking was the fact that a month later, she *wanted* to believe that he had aimed to protect her from Miss Bingley.

To avoid replying, she bent to retrieve the sprigs of mistletoe from the ground and tossed them into her basket. When she rose, he was staring at her, apparently still waiting for an answer. "I ... I am confused, sir."

"But were you offended at the time the conversation took place?" he pressed.

She looked at the ground and nodded.

He took a long breath and expelled it. "I see."

Chapter Six

Growing up, Darcy's mother had often told him that love was something to be cherished. It was her fondest wish that he and his sister would love their marriage partners someday.

At his mother's graveside, even though his father was utterly distraught, he confided that no matter how much pain he experienced at losing her, he would have done nothing differently. Loving her was the wisest thing he had ever done.

If love was such a glorious thing, why then had falling in love with Elizabeth caused *him* so much pain?

After a quick review of all his past dealings with Elizabeth, using this new insight into her thought process as a lens, he now understood he must have affronted her at every turn.

He shuddered to think of how, at gatherings they had both attended, she must have interpreted his inability to keep his eyes from following her every move. At the time, he had scolded himself, thinking she would recognize his attraction, so he tried his best to avoid her. In truth, at the very least, his behaviour must have left her confused. Perhaps even unsettled — or worse.

How could he have been so ignorant of causing her distress?

He glanced over at her, walking beside him.

Knowing she disliked him — for if she thought he had done nothing but criticize her in the past, how could she feel any other way — would it be easier to forget her?

He must decide, and quickly. If he was to speak to her about this, it had to be within the next minute or two, for they would soon come upon Baxter. Once at the house, there would be patients all around them. And tomorrow, when Roberts returned, perhaps he should leave, after all.

His heart faltered. If he left while they were on these terms … chances were that he would never see her again.

No! He could not just go on with his life knowing he had insulted her so badly and leave it at that. It was selfish, but he could not bear to have Elizabeth think ill of him for all eternity.

He swallowed hard and turned to the lady of his heart. "Miss Elizabeth, I would like to make it perfectly clear that I never meant to insult you. It was done most unwittingly."

She kept her gaze directed at the path.

"I hope you accept my sincere apology."

Perspiration broke out across his brow as he waited for her answer.

"I do accept your apology, Mr. Darcy, but only if you will accept mine. I have been thinking … I may have judged you unfairly and, therefore, *expected* to be offended by you, hearing insult where there was none."

"You expected —" He almost choked on the word. "May I ask why?" Wickham must have told her lies about him!

They were nearing where Baxter should be waiting. She stopped and faced him.

"Sir, the reason I did not reproach you earlier for overhearing something that you were not meant to hear was that I had done the same to you once, even before we were introduced."

A dark dread settled in the pit of his stomach. "The assembly ball?" It was the only possibility.

She nodded.

That would explain many things. Recalling his words to Bingley, he thought he might become ill. *She is tolerable, but not handsome enough to tempt me.*

He had barely looked at her before voicing those phrases. A few moments later, when Elizabeth passed him, he realized he had been too hasty in refusing the introduction.

Of all the things she could have overheard! Instead, why could she not have heard him several days later, when he had admired her fine eyes?

He cleared his throat. "Apparently, I must apologize again, Miss Elizabeth. I did not mean what I said; it was only a ploy to convince Bingley to leave me alone. But whether I meant it or not, it should not have been said in public, especially not within the hearing of anybody."

She stared at him for half a minute before responding. "Please do not apologize again, sir, for if you do, I must find an additional deficiency in my behaviour to regret. Then you shall remember something else *I* should forgive, and so forth." She arched an eyebrow. "I am certain we would still be standing here when spring's first flowers bloom."

She smiled teasingly — the first beaming smile she had ever directed at him. His breath caught, and the world became a brighter place.

She continued, "Perhaps we both should simply forgive all previous transgressions of the other and begin again."

It took a moment for the meaning of her words to form in his mind. Once it did, he jumped at the chance. "Agreed."

"Friends?"

She held out her hand.

"Friends." He took her small hand in his and bowed over it, resisting the urge to kiss it.

"After all, what better time for peace and forgiveness than at Christmas?" Reluctantly, he let go of her hand. "And for healing the sick."

She nodded. "And caring for those less fortunate."

Do not forget love, Elizabeth.

~%~

When the trio returned from their outing, Elizabeth spied Mr. and Mrs. Norwood, the vicar from Longbourn church and his wife, at the front door. Unwilling to have them witness that she had gone out alone with two men, she diverted to the kitchen entrance whilst the men went around to the front.

Once admitted, they told of arriving home from a visit to relatives in the south, hearing of the illness at Netherfield, and of their benefactor's affliction. Since they had both contracted chickenpox when they were children, they were there now to lend a hand. Elizabeth welcomed their assistance.

Soon after all the patients and caretakers were fed their mid-day meal, Elizabeth supervised Mr. Darcy and Baxter laying the yule logs in place. Since Netherfield had been unoccupied for several years, there was no piece of last year's log to use to light this one, but they made do. Elizabeth helped Lucy light the one in the women's sickroom and oversaw the oldest boy lighting the other. Mr. Norwood said suitable prayers over each log, and then a perceptive Mrs. Norwood sent Elizabeth to bed.

True to Mrs. Norwood's promise, Elizabeth was awakened by Hannah two hours later.

She peeked into the men's sickroom. Mr. Norwood sat with a few boys, reading aloud. Mr. Darcy filled a cup with water, fluffed a pillow, and then assisted her father to sit up against the wall and take a drink. Good. She had found sitting in an upright position offered relief to the patients who were coughing.

He then moved over to a young boy that she knew still had a fever. The boy seemed asleep. Mr. Darcy took a cloth from the boy's head, soaked it in a bowl of water, and wrung it out before replacing it on the boy's forehead.

Astonishment caused her to step back, out of the room and into the hallway. She leaned against the wall to the side of the opening. Earlier, Mr. Darcy had brought soup to some of the boys at the mid-day meal; it was most shocking to have watched him wink at a tenant farmer's son while dabbing soup off his chin. Now ... how could it be that the great Mr. Darcy was actually *nursing* the sick?

When she regained some equilibrium, she decided to go to the women's sickroom to give herself a little time to recover before witnessing him do anything that might endear him further.

Emily, Hannah, and Mrs. Norwood, along with several others who were feeling well enough, crafted garlands of the greenery she had collected, destined to lay across the mantelpieces of both sickrooms. Baxter was busy hanging a kissing bough from the chandelier at the center of the room. The yule log burned beautifully, warming the room with cheer. All was in order.

After sitting with Mrs. Fletcher — the widow who Mr. Jones feared had pneumonia — until the poor lady fell asleep, Elizabeth entered the corridor.

Deep, rumbling laughter came from the men's sickroom.

She hesitated at the door. Mr. Darcy now sat in a chair between her father and Mr. Jones. Mr. Jones seemed mildly amused with the conversation. Papa displayed a sly smile, barely noticeable from this distance, but an expression Elizabeth knew well. He was about to say something he considered quite witty.

Elizabeth could not make out what her father said next, but the results were a sight to behold. Mr. Darcy laughed, not just a chuckle, but a wholehearted guffaw. Even from across the room, Elizabeth perceived for the first time that the gentleman had dimples when he smiled this widely. In high spirits, he was even more handsome than he had been when apologizing earlier in the day — something she would not have thought possible until a few moments ago.

Mr. Darcy glanced in her direction and met her gaze. Her heart fluttered. His laughter faded but his smile did not. He bowed his head slightly in greeting. She did the same.

Afraid she might make a fool of herself, she entered and moved to speak to Mr. Norwood to check on everyone's progress.

On her way, Mr. Wickham called out to her. Her muscles tensed. She took a deep, calming breath. As she told Mr. Darcy earlier in the day, she *would* care for the sick, even if she would rather slap the man for his attempt to lead her sister astray and cheat the merchants of Meryton.

Mr. Wickham held out his cup. "May I have some water, please, Miss Elizabeth?"

Emily had mentioned his fever had eased last night. It stuck in her craw that he could have — should have — gotten it himself, but instead, he would have her wait on him.

Elizabeth nodded, took his cup, and stepped over to a table where a pitcher stood. When she returned, he took it from her. "Darcy is here?"

What could she possibly say to that? "As you see."

He raised his eyebrows. "I wonder why? I cannot imagine it is out of good will." He took a sip.

Anger flashed within her, partly at herself because, even as late as this morning, she had reacted similarly to Mr. Darcy's arrival. So much had changed in these few hours!

Unwilling to allow Mr. Wickham to pull her into a tête-à-tête, she kept her mouth firmly closed.

Mr. Wickham misunderstood her scowl. "As usual, I see we are in agreement, Miss Elizabeth. Ah, but I am sure he will soon be on his way now that he knows there is nothing to be gained by staying."

"Do not be too hasty, Mr. Wickham. You are wrong if you suppose I *could* truly think like you in any way, ever. In the past, I was deceived by your agreeable manners and open conversation — perhaps too open. In fact, I believe that you acted as if you took us into your confidence so that we would trust you; meanwhile, you were spreading lies."

Mr. Wickham chuckled, widened his eyes, and placed an open hand on his chest. "Lies? Upon my honour —"

"Honour?" She folded her arms across her abdomen and aimed her best glare at him. "Do you have any, even the smallest amount?"

His hand slowly dropped from his chest, and he slumped.

Gratified at the effect her determined look had on him, she continued.

"Mr. Wickham. I am a quick study, and I am much wiser than I was yesterday. As is *all* of my family. Until you are well enough to leave here, I will bring you food and water and any medicine Mr. Jones orders, but do not expect *any* further attentions now or in the future from me or anyone else who goes by the name Bennet."

Planning to make a dramatic exit after such a statement, she took a step back, spun on her heel, and — collided with Mr. Darcy.

His hands on her shoulders steadied her, but he did not move his glower from Mr. Wickham.

Disappointment and elation warred within her.

Here she had thought *her* words and *her* look had caused the change in Mr. Wickham's demeanour, including the colour that had drained from his face, but it had been Mr. Darcy's presence behind her.

And yet, her dissatisfaction was quickly swept away by the next thought: Mr. Darcy had crossed the room to fortify her efforts. Better yet, the fact that he did not release her shoulders while staring at Mr. Wickham proclaimed that she was under his protection.

Mr. Darcy had come into a house full of illness when everyone else stayed away. He had done without servants and had eaten simple fare. He nursed the sick, sent his driver into Town to restock their supplies, and requested a doctor and nurses to come. He had moved furniture, gone to the woods searching for traditional decorations so the ailing would be less distressed about being away from home just before Christmas, and, with Baxter's assistance, he even hauled two heavy yule logs into the house.

He was not the man she had thought he was.

In fact, she could no longer lie to her herself — she had worked hard to convince herself that he was exactly the type of man she would never marry in order to keep her heart from forming an attachment.

However, in just a few hours, and with a few good deeds, he had proved beyond the shadow of a doubt that he was just the opposite of what she had forced herself to believe of him.

Mr. Darcy was everything she had ever dreamed of and more.

Now, he defended her from a man who could have ruined her entire family if his evil intentions had not been discovered. His mannerisms informed the scoundrel — and her — that he laid some sort of claim to her.

All her previous prejudices crumbled and fell away, and a pleasant warmth seeped into every corner of her soul.

Detecting movement to her left, she still could not break her gaze away from Mr. Darcy. Mr. Wickham must have turned to face the other direction, for she suspected Mr. Darcy would not have looked away from him if he had not. When his gaze fell on her, he startled slightly. Releasing her shoulders, he took hold of an elbow and steered her out into the hallway.

"Are you well, Miss Elizabeth?"

She raised her chin to meet his heavenly, dark brown eyes.

"I am well, sir," Elizabeth said out of habit, but in truth, she was not certain how she was. It was as if a delightful enchantment had been cast over her.

~%~

Darcy's heart pounded in his chest. The soft light in Elizabeth's eyes… he could lose himself there forever. A trace of a smile curved her plump lips. She touched them with the tip of her tongue, almost as if in preparation for a kiss. His breath caught. He ached to see her look at him that way every day for the rest of his life.

He blinked, and suddenly everything became clear.

All this time, he had been so busy trying to convince himself that she was far out of his reach, he had never stopped to think about how she might be a suitable match.

Elizabeth was more caring, more giving than any woman he had ever met — except perhaps his mother. The maids present at Netherfield followed her every direction without question, and he could see they had a genuine respect for her. Since she had managed running this estate for the past week almost single-handedly, he could only imagine what she could accomplish with a staff the size of Pemberley's. Additionally, since he had his own fortune, marrying a wealthy lady was unnecessary.

But his family, would they resist?

Elizabeth's forehead furrowed slightly, and she examined his face. "Are *you* well, sir?"

He nodded in answer to her query.

He had no doubt his sister would get along beautifully with Elizabeth. His aunt and uncle would come to accept her soon enough, once they gave her a chance. His other aunt, well, she would never be satisfied with any woman he chose other than her daughter, Anne.

Besides, he was his own man, answerable to no one.

Since she had stood up to him in his foulest moods, as he often had been whilst they were both staying at Netherfield weeks ago, he knew she could handle anything his aunt, or even the ladies of the *ton*, threw at her.

Everything that had happened since he arrived convinced him further that Elizabeth Bennet was everything he wanted, everything he needed in his life.

He slid his hand that held her elbow further down her arm to take her still-bandaged hand in his.

Most importantly, he loved her.

She would make the perfect Mrs. Darcy.

All tension drained from him.

Her brow smoothed.

She was infinitely more than any man could ask for. How could he not…

He stepped back and went down on one knee. "Miss Elizabeth Bennet, will you do me a great honour and make me the happiest of men? Will you become my wife?"

She inhaled sharply, and her eyes widened. Her lips parted momentarily, and then the corners curved upwards. The sparkle in her eyes set his soul at ease. "Yes, Mr. Darcy. I will."

Darcy's heart swelled.

He rose and placed two fingers under her chin, angling her head just so, as he leaned toward her. She closed her eyes in anticipation; thick lashes rested on her creamy cheeks. He pressed his lips lightly to hers.

"I love you." He had not realized he had breathed the words until he saw her eyes open again.

"I love you, too." She blinked at the moisture gathering inside her lashes. "I realized it only a few minutes ago."

His face ached with the breadth of his smile.

Elizabeth glanced upwards and met his gaze again. The most joyful grin he had ever seen spread across her face. "You do know that was much more than is usually expected when a lady is standing under mistletoe, Mr. Darcy."

He looked up at the kissing bough hanging from the ceiling above them. The women had certainly been busy since Elizabeth and he had returned from the woods.

Laughter bubbled from Elizabeth's lips, triggering his own.

Giggles came from the women's sickroom door — the youngest girls and the two maids gathered at the opening.

Blushing, Elizabeth moved away from him. He felt the loss of her in his arms greatly, but in consolation, he was treated to the sight of her eyes sparkling like emeralds.

"I should go to your father —" He turned his head and realized he had never shut the door when he led her into the corridor. Mr. Bennet, Mr. Jones, and Mr. Norwood were staring at them from across the room, through the open doorway.

Had almost everyone in the house witnessed his proposal?

Mr. Bennet crooked a finger, calling Darcy to him.

"I guess you should." She chuckled.

He inhaled Elizabeth's scent, his chest puffing up with pride. The most beautiful woman he had ever known, exquisite in every way, would be his wife. It truly was a Christmas miracle.

She bit her bottom lip, reminding him of where his own had been only moments ago.

One kiss would never be enough, but it had to be. For now.

He hoped it would be a very short engagement.

Chapter Seven

Monday, December 24, 1811

Memories of the years Elizabeth had spent in this bedroom danced around her like the dust motes that glowed brightly in the early afternoon sunlight.

Had she ever slept this late before? She forgave herself the luxury after catching so little sleep the last two weeks. Even though the second week she had a great deal more help, after her betrothed — such a generous man — had ordered every staff member in his London household who had already suffered through chickenpox to return to Netherfield with his driver, she had earned a good rest.

Satisfaction coursed through her. Every one of her patients had gone home before Christmas. All except Mr. Wickham, who had left Netherfield a few days ago, although nobody seemed to know where he was. She hoped he would never be seen or heard from again.

Her father was still not quite himself. Though he was well on the road to a full recovery, she expected it would take some time. Mr. Jones and Mr. Stanley, the physician Mr. Darcy — or Fitzwilliam, as she was now allowed to call him — had called in from London, both felt confident that Elizabeth and her sisters could care for him at home.

Stretching, she sighed. It was such a pleasure to awaken in her own bed again. Especially since, before long, this bed and this room would no longer be hers.

Three weeks and two days hence, all her dreams would come true. She would marry for the deepest love when she became Mrs. Fitzwilliam Darcy.

She smiled at the memory of her family's reunion upon their arrival at home from London yesterday afternoon. Of course, they all had known of her engagement, but when meeting with Fitzwilliam again in person, her mother could not even speak for a full quarter of an hour, then she fussed over her father's health for the rest of the evening.

Today was Christmas Eve, the last she would spend here at Longbourn and her first spent with Fitzwilliam, so she knew for certain it would be special.

This afternoon, they would light the yule log for real, with a sliver saved from last year's log. Mrs. Hill would mix up a bowl of wassail, and she would make treats especially for the carolers who would come from the village. The

Christmas candle would be lit at sundown, and it would burn until the family left for Mr. Norwood's service on Christmas morning. Tomorrow after church, the family would enjoy a feast her mother promised would live on in their memories forever.

Next Christmas would be spent at Pemberley, and even though Fitzwilliam had already invited her entire family to spend it with them, she knew it could never be the same. Still, she looked forward to blending her family's traditions with those of the Darcys to make them their own.

The sound of horses at the front of the house pulled Elizabeth out of bed. A beautiful coach embossed with the Darcy coat of arms was out front.

Her mother burst into the room in a tizzy, her hands fluttering. "Lizzy! Get up and get dressed — quickly!" She pulled open Elizabeth's armoire and began tugging gowns from it. "A servant just arrived with a letter for your father. When Mr. Darcy returned to Netherfield last evening, he found that Mr. Bingley had arrived. Mr. Darcy sent word he would come to visit soon. And he will bring Mr. Bingley, too! Oh dear! What shall we do? How can Mr. Bingley fall in love with Jane all over again if she is covered in pox? Oh dear. But most are gone now — Jane only has two visible on her face. Maybe he will not notice?"

"Even with a hundred spots, Jane would still be beautiful, but I am certain if Mr. Bingley notices them, he will forgive two marks since Mr. Darcy will make sure he knows she has been ill, Mama."

"Yes, he will at that, I am sure. Mr. Darcy is so amiable, so *charming*." She selected a gown and laid it out on the bed. "Put this on and come down as soon as can be, Lizzy. You should be in the parlour waiting when Mr. Darcy arrives. Jenny will be in to assist you with your gown the moment she is finished with Jane."

About to exit, she suddenly turned around. "Oh! And Mr. Darcy also said his sister and their aunt, and uncle — the Earl and Countess of Matlock! — have agreed to attend the wedding. They will come to meet you in two weeks' time, on their way to London. Can you imagine, an earl and countess taking tea in my parlour? Oh dear!" Even before she stepped into the corridor, her mother was yelling, "Jane, are you almost ready? Lizzy needs Jenny's help!"

Her mother was a bit excitable, but Elizabeth would miss her dearly.

A few minutes later, Elizabeth sat in the parlour with Jane. Her father was saving his energy for this evening's activities, and their mother and sisters were suspiciously absent. She was sure she understood her mother's thinking

— Elizabeth would be so preoccupied with Mr. Darcy that Mr. Bingley would be forced to converse with Jane.

When the gentlemen arrived, after greeting Elizabeth, Mr. Bingley immediately crossed the room to sit with Jane. At first, the couple's conversation seemed strained but within a minute or two, their exchange became more natural, and Elizabeth relaxed enough to turn her attention to her betrothed.

Mr. Darcy smiled so widely, she could not help but emulate it. "What is it?"

"I was just thinking — the second best decision I have ever made in my life was to stop at Netherfield."

She tilted her head. "Now I am almost forced to ask, what was your best decision?"

Glancing at Jane and Bingley, who were completely engaged by conversation, he took her hand in his and brought it to his lips.

There was a teasing tone to his voice. "Perhaps it was more a *lack* of decision."

That was not what she expected. "I am all astonishment. When have you ever been impulsive?"

"When I proposed."

"Then I must say I support your being spontaneous in the future, Fitzwilliam."

"I am delighted to hear it." His eyes were sparkling with something she thought she might understand better after they were married. A noise upstairs must have reminded him of their surroundings. He blinked, and it was gone.

He cleared his throat. "I am beginning to read your thoughts in your expression. When we entered, you seemed concerned about your sister, but now all is well."

Elizabeth lowered her voice so the others could not hear her. "I *was* worried about Jane, but they seem to have picked up where they left off. I knew Miss Bingley had not been truthful in her letter."

"She wrote to you?"

"No, she wrote to Jane, a week after you had all gone to London, saying Mr. Bingley was to marry your sister."

"*My* sister?"

Elizabeth nodded.

He looked away, nostrils flaring. When he finally returned his gaze to her, he seemed to have better control over his temper. "Bingley is like a brother to me *and* my sister. He feels the same about her. They would not suit. Besides, she is too young." He shook his head. "When Roberts went to London, I sent three letters other than the one to the doctor. One to Georgiana, informing her I might not be joining them for Christmas —"

Elizabeth gasped. "Even then, you planned to stay at Netherfield to help?"

He grinned slyly. "I could not leave you caring for so many alone."

Every day she learned something new about him ... another reason to love him. "Who were the other two letters for?"

"The second was to Bingley, under the guise of Baxter writing to Bingley's valet."

Elizabeth opened her mouth to speak, but she could form no words.

He chuckled. "A ploy we began a couple of years ago. It seems the seals on my letters to Bingley are always broken before he has a chance to read them."

She caught on. "Only when his sister is in residence?"

A conspiratorial twinkle shone from his eyes. "Yes. And amazingly enough, the same never happens to anybody else with whom I correspond."

"And the third?"

"To my cousin Richard, who is a colonel in the army. He arranged to have Wickham transferred to the regulars. I believe the scoundrel is on his way to the Continent as we speak."

"Oh, so *that* is why he disappeared."

He nodded. "Once I realized how deeply in debt he was, I expected he would abandon his post as soon as he recovered. Assuming Wickham would return to his barracks to retrieve his belongings before bolting, Richard had a man waiting for him there."

"Papa said his debts were paid."

"I could not allow the shopkeepers to suffer." He coloured. "Wickham was given a choice — debtors prison or the regulars."

"He chose the regular army, and *you* paid off his debts." Gratitude swelled in her chest. He was just too good. "And now Mr. Wickham will never bother my sister again."

His smile faded, and he seemed to brace himself. "Or mine."

"*Your* sister?"

He looked down at where their hands were intertwined.

"Poor Miss Darcy."

The tension in his jaw and around his eyes eased. "You are an amazing lady, Elizabeth Bennet."

"And you are a remarkable gentleman, Fitzwilliam Darcy."

He bowed his head. "I have a surprise for you. Would you come into the hall with me?"

"But…" She glanced at Jane, uncomfortable leaving her alone with Mr. Bingley.

"Only for a moment — it is just outside the door, and we shall leave it open."

She could not disappoint him when there was such a plea in his voice. She followed him out into the corridor.

He pulled out a long, red velvet-covered box from his pocket and handed it to her. "I sent to Pemberley for this."

Inside was a gorgeous emerald necklace with a matching ring. He took the ring from the box and slid it onto the third finger of her left hand.

She could barely see through her tears. "They are beautiful, Fitzwilliam."

"They were my mother's. She specifically told me to give these to whomever I chose for a wife as an engagement gift, for a happy marriage filled with love. She insisted they were a good luck charm, given to her by my father. They had been handed down from his grandmother, who had also married the man she had loved with all her heart until the day she died."

Her tears tumbled over her lashes. "I shall cherish them forever. Thank you."

He moved closer, cupped her face in his hands, and brushed away a tear with his thumb. "I hope these are happy tears."

"They could be nothing else."

Something above his head caught her eye. A familiar-looking kissing bough. "Did you bring that here from Netherfield?"

"It is the very one under which we became engaged, my love."

A shiver passed up her spine at his new name for her.

"You have a wonderful sense of the romantic."

He smiled affectionately, displaying his dimples. "You have brought it out in me."

Her eyes were drawn to his mouth. He leaned in and pressed his lips to hers, releasing butterflies in her chest.

"I love you, Fitzwilliam."

"There is no better gift at Christmas than love." He moved to kiss her again, but giggles erupted from the stairwell to her left. She turned and saw at least two different coloured skirts disappear around the corner of the landing.

She tittered. "Apparently we will have an audience every time we kiss under mistletoe."

"I have no quarrel with that, as long as we share *many* other kisses in privacy." His fingers glided across her cheek to her lips. He kissed her, this time with such passion, it took her breath away.

When he eased back, she paused, savouring the experience. Finally opening her eyes, she looked into his and saw pure adoration.

"I predict this will be the first of many Happy Christmases together, Fitzwilliam."

"Of that, I have no doubt, my love."

The End

Other books and audiobooks by Wendi Sotis
Available at Amazon.com

Leading Jane Austen's beloved characters on rambles down unfamiliar lanes.

Wendi Sotis

Promises: Can true love reunite childhood sweethearts Elizabeth and Darcy when resentment, scheming relations, and unhappy circumstances drive them apart?

Dreams and Expectations: Mystery and intrigue unite Darcy and Elizabeth in Hertfordshire, Kent, coastal Broadstairs, and London. How can love flourish when duty forbids it?

All Hallow's Eve: High Priestess Elizabeth balks when Darcy is named her Soulmate, tasked to guard her from Evil. Can love bloom as they work to save mankind's future?

The Keys for Love: Can attraction deepen into love between pompous CEO Darcy and Elizabeth, a "mere" housesitter? A sweet, Austen-Inspired Contemporary Novella.

The Gypsy Blessing: How will Elizabeth's efforts to reshape the events depicted in prophetic drawings alter her destiny with Darcy? Sweet Austen-Inspired Romantic Fantasy

Foundation of Love: The Gypsy Blessing 2: Who do the prophetic photos on Elizabeth's cell come from and why do they pair her with the irritable Will Darcy? An Austen-Inspired Romantic Fantasy

Safekeeping: Is the handsome mysterious man next door part of the danger her subconscious is fighting to keep buried? Romantic Mystery with a clever nod at Austen.

A Lesson Hard Learned: If Darcy returns to Pemberley while Elizabeth is still there recovering from her accident, will he assume the worst of her? An Austen-Inspired Regency

DUE EARLY 2018: *The Pact*: When the heir to an earldom, James Aldridge, discovers his family has made a secret marriage pact without giving him any choice, he assumes Miss Celia Colton, the beautiful debutante he's destined to wed, is as deceitful as her mother and sister, leaving the young lady heartbroken and confused as to his change in behaviour. Regency Romance.

MISTLETOE AT THORNTON LACEY

Barbara Cornthwaite

MISTLETOE AT THORNTON LACEY

"Pug has been very naughty today," said Lady Bertram as she stroked Pug, the fourth dog of that name that Edmund could remember. This was a new dog, for the last pug had expired only a few months before. "She could not be found after breakfast, and Fanny and Susan searched for hours before they discovered her under a bed, chewing on one of Susan's slippers."

"Hours, was it, Fanny?" said Edmund, with raised eyebrows.

"Perhaps not quite that long," said Fanny, smiling in her gentle way.

"And have you had no other news during my fortnight's absence from the family seat?" After so many weeks being greeted by gloomy tidings whenever he came back from Thornton Lacey to visit Mansfield Park—whether about Tom's health or Maria's unfortunate situation—it was cause for gratitude that the only thing that was troubling his mother this day was the behaviour of her puppy.

"Ah, but there is more news than that," said Tom. "We learned only yesterday that Dr. Grant will be permanently in London, and the curate Mr. Kerr will be moving into the manse."

Edmund could feel Fanny's eyes upon him, and his wish to set her mind at rest about him made him answer casually, "Oh?"

"Yes," put in Sir Thomas, "He is to be a canon at Westminster, a rather unexpected development for him, I fancy. And a good thing it is. For Mr. Kerr, of course."

"For everyone, I daresay," said Tom. Then, recollecting that the discussion of that particular sentiment might give pain to some in the family circle, he added, "Certainly the Kerrs will be thankful of a bigger house."

"Yes, indeed," said Edmund. He was a little annoyed that his father, Tom, and Fanny all seemed to think he would be disturbed by any faint reference to Mary Crawford's relatives. He was made of sterner stuff than that, and was no object for pity. "A very satisfactory turn of events for all concerned," he said firmly, and smiled at Fanny to show that all was well. The smile was returned.

"We have much to be grateful for," said Sir Thomas, and though a stranger might have wondered at the seeming arbitrary nature of the statement, Edmund knew what he meant. Julia was settled more advantageously than they had first feared, the Grants were permanently out of the neighbourhood, and Mrs. Norris was gone from the house. Maria was gone, too, of course, and that was something that would never really be satisfactory—there was too much hurt and shame for anyone to be fully reconciled to that change; too much of the dreadful sense of a wasted life.

However, it was some relief that the person who had been the author of so much tribulation was not always before them.

"Will you be dining here tomorrow, Edmund?" said Lady Bertram. "The Merrills come for dinner, you know."

"Yes, I thought I would stay two nights. I should like to see the Merrills again."

"A very good sort of man," said Lady Bertram, "in spite of his antecedents, and I think she was considered a beauty when she was young. And a very good family she came from, too, now that I think of it—the Helmsworths, of Weekfield Hall, you know. I wonder if she disobliged her family by marrying him?"

As no one had any information to give her on this point, the conversation turned to other things. Edmund asked Susan how she did, now that she was turned fifteen, and she answered without any blushes or shyness—how unlike Fanny when she had first come to Mansfield Park! Edmund did not know how it was, but it seemed to him that in the last months Fanny had become more confident than before. She had for years been steady and wise and helpful, but now she seemed also to have more an air of authority. Perhaps it was the contrast with Susan that made her seem so.

* * * *

In the afternoon of the next day, Tom, coming down the stairs, passed Susan, who was looking harassed.

"What's the trouble?"

"It's only that Pug has disappeared again," said Susan, "and Lady Bertram desires me to find her. And this house is so big, and Pug is so small..."

"Cannot Fanny help you look?"

"She is riding with Edmund. I daresay Pug will have re-appeared by then, as she will be hungry in a little while. But Lady Bertram does not care to wait for that."

"Well, I can help, then. I was doing nothing of importance. Where have you looked thus far?"

"Everywhere," said Susan despairingly.

"Out of doors?"

"No, not yet."

"Then let us get our coats and hats and look in the shrubbery. Thank heavens it is no longer raining!"

Within ten minutes the two were looking along the paths and beneath benches and bushes. Tom, in the months since his illness, had been gaining in both strength and maturity, and he had found in Susan a sort of surrogate sister. Susan had been used to brothers, and was able to rise to Tom's teasing as Fanny never would have done. And Tom found in her the only person in the house that he considered to have a sense of humour.

Pug was nowhere to be seen, but both young people knew that Lady Bertram would be anxious and faintly aggrieved if they stopped looking before the dog appeared, so they stayed out of doors, wandering through the kitchen gardens and into the park.

"I think Edmund is in better spirits, don't you?" asked Susan.

"I do," said Tom. "You, who have not known Edmund as long, may not notice, but I can see the restlessness gone from him."

"I wish he had the living at Mansfield. Mr. Kerr is a very good man, I'm sure, but his sermons are a little—well—"

"Dry," finished Tom. "Edmund's are not. The one I heard three weeks ago was his best yet—thoughtful, and somewhat original." He chuckled and said, "If any of my former friends could hear me praising a sermon, they would think it a great joke."

"Were you so very bad, then?"

"I was thoughtless," said Tom. "I was led astray—quite willingly, mind you—by a set of fools and entered into their bad behaviour. I have often thought lately that my injury was a good thing: it stopped me on my ruinous course."

"Yes," said Susan. "I quite see that."

"There are consequences, though. I now have a reputation that I must strive to overcome. I doubt whether..." He paused and frowned.

"Whether what? What is it?"

"I ought not to say," said Tom.

"You may safely trust me," said Susan, and when Tom remained silent added, "Is it about Miss Wright?

He spun and faced her. "How could you know that?"

Susan grinned. "I only guessed. You visit your brother more frequently than there is any need to, and you have no friends there. I can think of no reason why you would be visiting Thornton Lacey so often, except a young lady. And the only young lady I know of is the squire's daughter, Miss Wright."

Tom gave a short laugh. "Yes, and I am a simpleton for thinking of her. Even when I visit Edmund, it is rare that I catch sight of her, except at church. There was only the one dinner-party that the Wrights gave—Edmund was invited, and I was included, too, as I was visiting. I keep hoping that we will be thrown together in some other way."

"And why should you not be? I think it is quite romantic."

"Yes, but I could not pursue her yet, you know. Her family are such good people. You know their house burned down a few years ago, and rather than go into debt to build a new, grand house, they have built a much smaller dwelling—a place that would be below the dignity of many landowners, and yet they are hospitable and cheerful, and only say that they hope to add more to the house when they can. As I say, they are thoroughly good people, and she is the best of them all. Quite an angel, in fact."

Susan giggled, and Tom gave a reluctant smile.

"I sound ridiculous," he said. "But they would not approve of me—what I have been, at least. I cannot speak to her until I have given evidence of having mended my ways."

"You have mended them," said Susan. "You are quite sober and steady now."

"I think I would be hard-pressed to convince anyone of that; it might appear that my quiet life here is only due to my illness. No, I shall have to wait half a year at least before I say anything." He sighed but then added, "However, it is the consequence of my own folly, and I ought not to repine."

"Well that is evidence of maturity," said Susan. "Edmund was saying last night that one of the signs of maturity is that you take your punishment without being angry or casting blame on another."

"Ah, Edmund the moraliser. I cannot help thinking that he will be one of those old men who are always lecturing the young."

"No doubt," said Susan, making a face.

They walked on in silence for another minute and then Tom said, "Well, he is settled and happy in his situation. I suppose the next thing he will do is find a wife. We must be sure he marries to advantage, Susan. A good wife would complete his happiness, and a bad one would cut up his peace forever. He is too good a man to have his soul galled perpetually by an awful woman. The aggravating thing is that I can't think of anyone hereabouts who would be suitable. There is a depressing dearth of young people in the neighbourhood."

"I often think the same about Fanny," said Susan. "She would shine as a wife, but there is no one that comes to Mansfield, and she never travels further than Thornton Lacey."

The same thought struck both of them at that moment. They turned to each other, Tom's mouth slightly agape, and Susan gasped.

"Oh, do you think we could contrive—?"

"Not for us to think of it," said Tom, after a moment's pause. "Really, none of our business."

"No?" said Susan. "I am persuaded that they would do very well together. And so are you. You were thinking so just now."

"If you are contemplating laying some sort of plot to match the two of them, I beg you would forget it," said Tom. "Elaborate plans always misfire, somehow." He paused, ruminating. "Not but what a word might be dropped here and there—in season, of course."

They are not together as much as they might be," said Susan. "Edmund is so much at Thornton Lacey."

"Perhaps we could contrive at that, if the opportunity arose."

At that moment, Pug emerged from a rhododendron, where, it appeared, he had been exploring—and perhaps rolling in—some muddy ground. The subject of a match between Edmund and Fanny was dropped, but not forgotten.

* * * *

The Merrills were punctual to the time for dinner. They were somewhat lately come into the neighbourhood, and were quiet, sensible people. Mr. Merrill had been in trade, but retired to the country with a handsome fortune. Sir Thomas might not have welcomed them to dine in earlier days, but a good deal of his fastidious pride had evaporated with his daughters' scandals, and he was now grateful for the attention showed to Lady Bertram by Mrs. Merrill. She listened patiently to all Lady Bertram's bits of trivial news and mild alarms about Pug, and contrived to make her feel very important.

Mr. Merrill was seated beside Fanny at dinner, and Edmund was pleased to see how easily Fanny conversed with him. She was in very good looks, Edmund thought, and in good spirits, too.

After the gentlemen had their port and rejoined the ladies in the drawing room, Edmund found himself seated next to Mr. Merrill.

"A charming girl, Miss Price," said Merrill. "She listened very intently to all my talk about acquiring goods from China, as if she really wanted to know the details of the trade."

"I assure you, she did," said Edmund. "She has a keen interest in foreign places and undertakings of all sorts. There is no doubt she was truly intrigued."

"Remarkable young lady. And very pretty, too. Lovely soft light eyes she has."

Edmund agreed, and glanced again at Fanny. Yes, she did have soft eyes—not showy, perhaps, but very expressive.

"It is a pity there are not many young people in the neighbourhood," Mr. Merrill went on. "She told me that she has never had a London Season, and how else are you to find a suitable match for her?"

"I do not think she would enjoy the bustle and noise of London," said Edmund. He found that he intensely disliked the idea of finding a match for Fanny, but was given no time to ponder why that might be.

"Yes, it is rather dull here at Mansfield," said Tom, who had been listening to their conversation. "Edmund, I think you should have the family to visit Thornton Lacey for Christmas," said Tom. "It is the time for celebrations and visitings, after all. Last year we had the ball at Christmas. We must not make the ladies here repine for jollier times."

Edmund was slightly puzzled. His mother, he was sure, would not think to compare the ball of last Christmas with any want of gaiety this year. Susan had not even been at Mansfield Park the previous year. And Fanny…well now, Fanny might feel a change. He knew her better than to believe that she missed the attentions that had been paid her by Henry Crawford, but she did miss her brother William, who had been at the ball. Susan might know what Fanny's spirits required, and Tom had been talking to Susan earlier…perhaps that was the reason for this suggestion.

"Do you think Mama would come?" said Edmund.

"But of course!" said Tom, who was not at all sure.

"Very well," said Edmund. "I will speak to Father about it."

As Susan passed by Tom later that evening, he stopped her and said, "I contrived to get an invitation for all of us to go to Thornton Lacey for Christmas."

Susan grinned. "Did you? That was well done!"

"You must persuade my mother to agree to come—she has not slept in any bed but her own for over a decade, I believe."

* * * *

Edmund left after breakfast the next morning; Fanny alone was there to see him off. Sir Thomas and Tom were preparing for a day's shooting, and Susan was sitting with Lady Bertram.

Soft light eyes, thought Edmund as he waved to her. For some reason, the phrase had taken possession of him last night as he had lain on his bed, and so had the memory of the eyes themselves. For some reason, the image that came most often to his remembrance was how she had looked at the ball last Christmas and the joy on her face as she danced with William. Then he had appreciated how nice she looked as if she had been a sister, but now…

The but now occupied his thoughts for the rest of the hour's ride. Edmund had, when he had first taken possession of his house, envisioned himself welcoming a family party to his home, just as he would next week, and in those days he had pictured Mary Crawford at his side. He had long since ceased to wish that she should be mistress of his house, but he was still conscious of an empty place beside him, and the formerly vague disquiet he had felt suddenly put itself into words—he wished he had a wife. He had thought, ever since that horrible day when his heart had been broken, that since Mary was ineligible, he would live the rest of his life as a resigned bachelor. In fact, he had observed to Fanny not long ago that it was impossible that he would ever meet such another woman.

But he knew his own mind now—he did not want a woman like Mary Crawford. Even when he was besotted with her, he had known how superior Fanny was in sense and wisdom. She cared for him, he knew, and he cared for her. In this last visit to Mansfield Park, he had found himself looking to see her reaction to things; and of all the family, her smile was the one that he sought. Perhaps those things were the most important, after all. He was glad that he had a week to think it over before he saw her again.

* * * *

The week was interminably long. He had come back on a Wednesday. On Thursday he wondered if true regard and affection were enough to build a good marriage on, deciding in the affirmative. On Friday he spent his time pondering if perhaps he could, in time, love Fanny in the same way that he had loved—well, at any rate, the way a bridegroom ought to love his bride. By Saturday morning he determined that the answer to that was yes, he certainly could—he was already thinking that no other woman would ever do for him. By Monday he was overcome with nerves—she was too good for him, of course, and she was happy where she was. It seemed only too likely, to his disordered mind, that she would refuse him. And if she said no, then family parties would be very awkward. She was shy, he knew, and it was too much to hope that a declaration of love from him would not shock her very much.

On the other hand, he knew she had affection and admiration for him, and he might be able to persuade her that those things made for a very solid foundation on which to build married love. Some days he felt he could not wait until she arrived to have this conversation with her; other days he thought that he ought to wait and approach the topic with her by degrees, so as not to overwhelm her.

And then he would recall that he was supposed to be working on a sermon, which he now could hear only through Fanny's ears. The verger, trying to discuss with him whether or not an unstable tree in the churchyard ought to be cut down, found him strangely absent-minded.

* * * *

The journey from Mansfield Park to Thornton Lacey was only eight miles, of course, but Pug, whom Lady Bertram did not think could endure existence for a few days without his mistress, enlivened the trip by getting sick, barking at nothing, and escaping once when the door was opened.

Edmund was there to hand the ladies down from the carriage. The parsonage was large—"almost a gentleman's residence," Henry Crawford had once called it, and although the family party had all seen it at least once, most of them had not been there often enough to cease to find charm and novelty in every room.

After the bustle of taking off wraps and directing servants about luggage, Edmund ushered them into the drawing room, where a fire was blazing. He seated his mother near the fire, with a screen carefully placed, and settled Pug on her lap, before looking around for Fanny. She had accepted a cup of coffee from the housekeeper, and was looking contentedly about her. After a week of thinking constantly about Fanny, it was hard work to say nothing to her beyond the ordinary. It seemed too precipitate to speak to her on the very day of her arrival, but he had developed a scheme which would allow him to talk to her on the following day.

Edmund planned to take his family to see the ruined abbey which lay ten miles to the west. It was close enough not to be too far for Tom even in cold weather, but not so close that any of them had seen it before. They would take the carriage, and certainly at some time as they were wandering over the ruins, there would be a chance to talk to Fanny. He even thought that it might be a romantic place to declare his love—or at least broach the topic of marriage.

The trip was proposed immediately after breakfast. It was thought a fine idea by most of the company, only Lady Bertram said she thought she might stay at home, instead, and have Fanny read to her. Edmund was momentarily perturbed, but after thinking rapidly, decided it might work better after all. If he said that he needed to stay at the house and work on his sermon (which was absolute truth), he would probably be just as sure of a few moments alone with Fanny. He knew his mother—she always fell asleep within the first half-hour of anyone's reading to her (or for that matter, sitting silently with her). And when his mother was dozing, he would appear and take Fanny for a short walk around the garden, at which time he would unburden his heart.

At first all went according to plan. Sir Thomas, Tom, and Susan departed, and Lady Bertram was seated cosily with Fanny in the drawing room. Edmund went to his library and sat with his half-finished sermon in front of him for twenty minutes, but his mind was on possible ways to start the conversation with Fanny.

"My dearest Fanny, you have all the attributes that one could desire in a woman." No, no, that sounded dreadful. "The excellence of your mind and your principles, Fanny, have made me desirous of uniting our hearts and our hands…" That was even worse. No, he must begin gently and cautiously.

"My dearest Fanny, we have been good friends these many years, have we not? And yet I wonder if there is a situation that might be yet better for us than friendship." Yes, that struck the right note. Not so ardent as to be alarming, yet getting to the point without being too vague.

He imagined out the rest of his speech, and what Fanny would say, and how he would respond. He went further and planned what he would say to his father and mother, and to Tom and Susan, and then to the people in the parish…

He looked at the clock and found that forty minutes had elapsed. His mother was surely sleeping by now; he would go in and see if Fanny would walk with him. And then he would see if she would marry him.

He opened the door to the drawing room and saw, as he expected, his mother reposing with her head leaning against the back of the chair, lost in sleep. What was not expected was that she was alone; Fanny was nowhere to be seen.

Well, perhaps she was just gone out for a moment—to fetch her embroidery or another book. He waited for a full ten minutes, but she did not reappear. He began to search the house. When he got to the kitchen, he asked the cook, Mrs. Abbot, if she had seen Miss Price.

"Oh, to be sure," she said. "Little John Crooks came with a tale of his mother's spraining an ankle, and wanting a poultice to put on it, and Miss Price wouldn't have you disturbed. 'No,' says she, 'Mr. Bertram is writing a sermon, and must not be troubled. I'll go,' she says. And off she went with him, and I don't know when she'll be back."

"Oh," said Edmund. It was like Fanny, of course, to give aid to anyone who needed it, and his heart warmed again at the thought of her compassionate nature. "Perhaps I should go and find her."

"There's no need of that, sir, beggin' your pardon; I sent Dick with her to see she gets back safe."

Edmund deliberated for a moment. It would not be unreasonable if he went to look in on one his parishioners, and see Fanny home in the process. On the other hand, Dick, the manservant of his establishment, would certainly see Fanny home safely, and walking home with both Richard and Fanny was not what he had in mind. Moreover, he really ought to be working on that sermon, and if Fanny were to return soon, there might still be time for the walk around the garden.

"Very well, Mrs. Abbot," he said. "Apprise me as soon as Miss Price returns, if you please."

It was a full two hours, however, before Fanny returned, and by then Lady Bertram was awake and in a humour to walk sedately around the garden with Fanny. Edmund, seeing them from the window of his library, could almost have ground his teeth in frustration at seeing his place at Fanny's side usurped. His mother would have been quite amazed had she known what annoyance her mild exercise was provoking in his inner being.

* * * *

While Edmund was awaiting Fanny's return, Sir Thomas had found an acquaintance, Sir Richard Phipps, who was also exploring the Abbey with his wife and her sister. Sir Thomas recalled that Sir Richard's estate was only four miles from Thornton Lacey, and the two were soon discussing land enclosure and difficulties with poachers. Tom and Susan, left to themselves, explored the ruins in a leisurely way.

"Well, what do you think?" said Susan. "Has it been of any use to get Fanny and Edmund under the same roof?"

"I think he looks at her a good deal more than he used to. He seems, to me, a little distracted. Probably a good sign, I think, but impossible to know for certain."

"I thought he seemed more attentive to her than usual, but he is always very considerate and it is difficult to know, as you say."

Susan climbed onto a low wall and surveyed the area. "It is a lovely spot," was her verdict, as she took in the scene. "A view of the valley, the stream nearby, and the trees here on this side. Oh! Mistletoe!" She pointed toward the trees, and her eyes twinkled. "I think Edmund needs a little help decorating his house for the festive season, do not you?"

"Oh yes," said Tom, rolling his eyes. "A kissing bough is just what every parsonage needs."

"Don't be satirical! It might prove very useful."

"If you think we will be able to persuade my very stodgy brother that a kissing bough is acceptable in the home of a parson, you very much mistake the matter."

"I shall not need to persuade him," said Susan. "I know just what to do. Here, help me gather some. There is enough ivy and holly around the parsonage to finish off making the bough."

When they returned from their excursion, they invaded the kitchen for their project, for Tom's cajoling ways worked on Mrs. Abbot, who said she liked to see the old traditions kept up, although she wasn't sure Mr. Bertram would think it was quite the thing.

* * * *

Luck was with them. Sir Thomas, who might have voiced some objection to their aims, felt the beginnings of an incipient cold in the head, and declined to join the rest of the family for dinner, preferring a bowl of gruel in his own room.

As the soup was being cleared to make way for the mutton, Susan said to Lady Bertram, "If you please, Ma'am, what is it you were telling me a day or two ago about the way your mama used to decorate the house for Christmas when you were a girl?"

"It was very pretty," said Lady Bertram. "Mama would send the servants to cut holly and ivy, and they would hang it along the stairs and over the mantels. A Christmas fire and a Christmas candle, I remember, we always had. There were pies and mincemeat and games—we would play snapdragon and hoodman blind—and one year the mummers came and gave us a play."

"It sounds enchanting," said Susan. "And did you have mistletoe?"

"Oh yes! There was a kissing bough. It was very pretty, too. I remember, every time someone was kissed under it, they picked off one of the berries, and when they were all gone, there were no more kisses. And there was wassail and giving pennies to those who came to sing…"

"I wish we might decorate the house here at Thornton Lacey," said Susan, looking to Tom for support.

"I don't see why we might not," said Tom. "Mama would like to help me find some ivy and holly, would you not, Ma'am? There is some in the parsonage garden."

"Yes, I imagine I would," said his mother. "It need not trouble you, Edmund. You may study for your sermon. Fanny and I will arrange it all."

Edmund looked at Fanny to judge her thoughts, and it seemed to him that she was a little bewildered. But before he could make any comment on this proposed course of action, Susan said she believed she knew where there was some mistletoe, asked Lady Bertram exactly where she thought would be the best place to display the greenery, and inquired of Fanny if she thought they could acquire silk ribbons to tie up the greenery with.

Edmund was left with nothing to say, and when he walked through his hall the next day and found his mother directing the placement of the kissing bough, he found himself unable to tell her that although he did not mind decorating in moderation, he did have some objection to a kissing bough. At least, he comforted himself, he did not have a gaggle of unmarried servants who would be using it as an excuse for riotous behaviour.

Truth be told, it was a minor irritation compared to his frustration at his inability to get Fanny alone long enough to talk to her. The house, as large as it was for a parsonage, seemed to be bursting with people. He never discovered Fanny in a room by herself; she was always accompanied by his mother or Susan, or even, on one occasion, Sir Thomas.

He must get her out of the house to talk to her, that much was certain. A long walk in the country would be the surest way to be alone with her. Any doubts he'd had about whether he felt the way a prospective bridegroom ought to feel had been put to flight the moment she had entered his home. The only question in his mind now was how quickly he could persuade her that they ought to marry, and if she thought the less of him for having loved another first.

Accordingly, he found her at mid-day and said, "Perhaps, Fanny, you would like to come for a walk with me and see a very pretty spot near the river, since you were not able to see the Abbey yesterday."

"Oh, yes indeed," said Fanny, a smile lighting up her face.

He waited while she went to get her coat and bonnet, anxious that they should be able to leave without another of the family deciding to join them. No one did, however, and he went out the vicarage gate with Fanny on his arm, feeling triumphant that at last he had the opportunity to speak.

As they passed through the village, Edmund pointed out which families lived in which houses, and Fanny admired the neatness of this cottage and the beauty of that tree. They had just gone out of sight of the village, and Edmund had opened his mouth to say, "Dearest Fanny," when a step was heard on the road behind them.

"Hello, Mr. Bertram!"

Edmund stopped himself just in time from groaning aloud. It was the verger, Mr. Pettingill, wanting to know what he had decided about that tree in the churchyard. Mr. Pettingill was respectfully insistent that Mr. Bertram come and look at the tree, which was only a hundred yards from where they were standing. Edmund gave way, and he and Fanny went to inspect the tree, which actually was leaning at a rather alarming angle.

Fanny's opinion, when Edmund asked her for it, was that it looked like it should be cut down. Edmund concurred, and hoped that would end the matter. It did not, for Mr. Pettingill then wanted suggestions on who might be given the task of felling it. He mentioned three or four young men, who all would be glad of the work, but how to decide between them? What with young Smith who was supporting a widowed mother, and Andrews who was planning to be married soon, and Howland who had been ill…

When that difficulty was got over, and Edmund and Fanny resumed their walk, they found that Mr. Pettingill was also walking toward the river, and naturally joined them. Fanny was not bothered by this, of course, for she found Mr. Pettingill's stories about his daughter and her family most interesting, but by the time Mr. Pettingill took his leave of them, Edmund was almost seething with very un-clerical sentiments.

They reached the spot by the river that was considered picturesque by the natives of Thornton Lacey. It was a little way from the road, down a tree-lined path, with large stones on the riverbank that were very convenient for sitting on. After Fanny had admired it as warmly as she could, and said that it must be even more beautiful in summer, Edmund took a deep breath and prepared to say his piece.

He thought afterwards that he ought to have expected the interruption, since Providence seemed determined that he should not have his talk with Fanny. He could not have expected this particular interruption, however: of a flock of panicked sheep who had gotten out of their field and been chased by a noisy dog. The sheep came rushing down the path toward them with the dog at their heels, bleating loudly and knocking over anything in their path. Edmund's first thought was to keep Fanny safe, and he had just helped her to climb on top of one of the larger stones when the sheep came surging around them. The sheep were stopped by the river ahead of them, but were frightened enough that a few were already wading into the river. Edmund knew that if one tried to swim across the river, others would follow; more likely they would try to run along the riverbank, where brambles grew thickly.

"What shall we do?" was Fanny's question.

"I must get that dog quiet and away from the sheep," said Edmund. He wrestled his way out of the mass of sheep and called the dog. The dog, little more than an overgrown pup, wagged his tail, ran in circles, and continued to bark. Good, thought Edmund, at least he is not savage.

"Go home!" Edmund commanded. He might as well have been ordering Pug about for all the heed the dog gave to him. "Well," said Edmund, "if you will not come to me and you will not go home..." He picked up a stone and pretended to throw it at the dog. The dog shied away and looked warily at Edmund. "Go home!" repeated Edmund, and got another stone. This one he actually threw, narrowly missing the dog. The dog retreated still further. At another gesture from Edmund he turned around and trotted back up the path.

"Poor creature!" said Fanny.

"I would not have hit him, you know," said Edmund. "And now we must think what to do with these sorry sheep."

"Will they stay here, do you think? Or will they run again?"

Edmund glanced over the flock, who had begun nosing around the ground, looking for grass. A few of them had found some and were grazing peacefully as if they were in their home pasture.

"They will stay for a little while, as long as nothing else comes to frighten them. Perhaps we can find a boy to stand watch while we find their shepherd."

Edmund helped Fanny off the rock and together they followed the path to the main road, where, as luck would have it, they found two boys who were quite willing to keep an eye on the sheep and chase away any dogs for the princely sum of a penny each. It took a half-hour of calling in at various farms along the road to find the owner of those particular sheep, and Edmund saw with chagrin that clouds were moving in to drop rain on them—they would only miss the shower if they hurried home. As it happened, they came in the door just as the storm broke, and Edmund could do nothing but meditate ruefully on his spoiled plans.

* * * *

The next day was Sunday, and not even so ardent a lover as Edmund thought that he ought to get engaged on a Sunday. He tried to keep his mind on spiritual things, and endeavoured keep himself from brooding. It was a severe test of his self-control.

Monday was Christmas Eve. He tried all day to think of some way of detaching Fanny from the others. He did ask if she wanted to walk around the garden, and she agreed. For some reason, the thought of proposing to her out of doors had taken his fancy, and he found it difficult to imagine himself talking to her in any other place. As soon as their aim was known, however, Lady Bertram decided she and Pug needed an airing as well. By now, he could have recited his piece in his sleep. "Dearest Fanny, we have been good friends these many years ..."

And then, as if from heaven, came the opportunity he had been waiting for.

A note had arrived on Saturday from Sir Richard Phipps, inviting Sir Thomas and Lady Bertram to dine with them on Christmas Eve. Edmund had doubted that his mother would want to go, but it appeared that her sojourn at Thornton Lacey had dissolved some of her languor, and she said it made her feel quite young again to be going into society.

Sir Thomas and Lady Bertram left in good time for the dinner. Susan, who had begun to sneeze during the day, decided to retire to bed. Although sorry she had caught Sir Thomas's cold, Edmund was happy to get another person so neatly out of the way of his talk with Fanny. All that remained of their party was Tom, and if he could only think of a way to get him out of the house, he would have a chance to talk to Fanny.

He must send Tom on some errand—but where could he possibly go at six o'clock on Christmas Eve? Was there any message he could take to anyone? No one in the village, that was certain, because he would not be gone long enough. Well, what about the squire? Perhaps he could send the squire a message saying…saying what?

"Miss Wright!" he said aloud. Miss Wright ought to be introduced to Fanny. He would send Tom with a note to ask the squire to bring Miss Wright to visit in the next day or two. If he knew anything about the squire it was that Tom would not be allowed to leave until he had had some refreshment and probably a little conversation with the family. That would keep him out of the way for more than an hour. Of course, he reflected as he wrote the note, Tom might wonder why he was being sent instead of a servant. Perhaps if he gave the servants a half-holiday, it would be a good excuse.

Accordingly, he dismissed Mrs. Abbot and Dick for the night, and went to find Tom.

"Oh, there you are!" he said when he finally came upon him in the drawing room, sitting by a rollicking fire with a book in his hands.

"Yes, here I am, like the good landowner that I aspire to be, trying to absorb Barton's Principles of Land Management."

"And where is Fanny?"

"I think she is upstairs with Susan."

That was slightly disappointing, but no doubt she would be downstairs soon.

"I wonder if you might do me a favour, Tom, and take this note to Squire Wright. Dick has the evening off, you see, and—" Edmund suddenly realized he had failed to think of an excuse for not taking it to the squire himself.

It made no matter. Tom was out of his chair with alacrity, and almost snatched at the note. "Delighted to do it, Edmund. What is it about?"

"Oh, only to invite Miss Wright to call here in a few days to meet Fanny. And Susan."

"Excellent notion!" said Tom. "I'll take your curricle, if I might."

"By all means. I will …er…be in my library, looking over tomorrow's sermon."

"Yes, the Christmas Day sermon," said Tom. "Hard to be original with that topic, isn't it?" He grinned in a friendly way to show that he meant no impiety, and disappeared on his errand.

Now, thought Edmund, I have only to wait for Fanny.

Conscience propelled him into the library to give a cursory glance at his sermon, and he waited there for ten minutes to be sure that Tom had left the house before emerging again to look for Fanny.

She was not in the drawing room, and when he went upstairs he found Lady Bertram's abigail, who told him that Miss Price was not there, either. In fact, she rather thought Miss Price had gone out.

Edmund came down the stairs again heavily. What must have happened, of course, was that Tom had invited Fanny to go with him to the squire's house. And Fanny, being told that Edmund was working on a sermon, must have decided not to disturb him by telling him she was going.

He stopped at the bottom of the stairs and wondered what he ought to do. The kissing bough was just above him, and it seemed to mock his depressing situation. He was almost frantic enough, he thought, to wait right here until Fanny returned, drag her under the mistletoe, and kiss her passionately, regardless of anyone else who might be there.

Instead he leaned his head against the wall, closed his eyes, and heaved a sigh.

"Edmund? Are you well?"

His eyes flew open at Fanny's voice. There she was, standing in the hallway, looking intently at him.

"You are not gone out?" he managed to say.

"No—that is, I was looking for Pug, who escaped again. I found her, however, curled up on the doorstep at the front of the house." She looked at him with concern and came closer. "You seem distressed. May I help?"

"No, no," he blurted out. "That is—" he tried to marshal his wits into some kind of order. This was the time for his carefully rehearsed speech, but he never thought of it. "Fanny, you must think me a fool."

"Never, Edmund." She came even nearer, and put her hand on his arm. "Never have I thought you a fool."

"I have been, though. I have been blind to a great many things, Fanny. I was blind to the faults of the Crawfords, and I have not seen you in a proper light, either."

"You have always been most kind, Edmund." Her eyes, those beautiful eyes, were full of tenderness.

"And yet kindness is not my goal anymore." He could see her eyes widen at that, and he put his hand over hers, still resting on his arm.

"I wish to make you my wife, Fanny." He stopped and took a deep breath. "I am giving my speech hind-end foremost. I meant to tell you first how much I admire your wisdom, your intelligence and your goodness, and that as we have long been friends, whatever your feelings are toward me, I think you could learn to love…" he stopped again and gripped her hand more tightly. "I am saying it all very badly, but I have been longing to speak to you alone all week, and have now grown so desperate that I am recklessly telling you that I love you and want to make you my wife—hoping that my eagerness will not frighten you into a refusal."

He stopped talking then, and waited for the reply.

Fanny's eyes had stayed wide, but now her cheeks were pink. It gave him encouragement enough to ask, "Do you think you could, Fanny? Learn to love me?"

"Yes," said Fanny quietly, and beginning to smile. "I think I could."

There was a moment of silence while the two of them stood there together, smiling at each other. Then, very deliberately, Edmund reached above him and plucked off one of the white berries of the mistletoe. "I think," he said, "that it is a very good thing when some old traditions are revived."

The kiss he gave her was as tender as it was passionate, and Tom would have been astonished to know how much ardour his correct and proper brother could express in the front hall of his own parsonage.

* * * *

Breakfast the next morning was irregular. Sir Thomas and Lady Bertram were still in bed, having come home very late from their dinner the night before. Susan arose feeling well enough to come down to eat, and arrived at the table just as Edmund and Fanny, who had breakfasted early, departed from it. Susan nibbled at her toast, conscious of a slight depression of spirits.

In spite of all that she and Tom had done to bring Edmund and Fanny together, no progress had been made as far as she could tell.

Tom entered the breakfast-parlour when Susan was half-way through her meal. He was full of hope, mostly due to his excursion the night before. The squire had been friendliness itself, Miss Wright had smiled on him, and Mrs. Wright had even said that she wished her son, at present a scholar at Cambridge, could make his acquaintance. He was full of optimism for his future, and inclined to think that all Edmund and Fanny needed to put them on the correct path to their future was a little nudge.

Edmund and Fanny were walking slowly around the garden together, marvelling not only in their mutual love and affection, but in the fact that they had been able to steal away together without a third party to spoil their conversation.

"I will speak to my father today," said Edmund. "I know he will give consent. You are already such a comfort to him; he will be delighted to have you as a daughter."

Fanny nodded and smiled, but sighed a little, too. "I fear Lady Bertram will not like to give up my company, even to you," she said.

"We must be sure to promote Susan to her in every possible way, as someone who might take your place. She seems to be devoted to my mother, and willing to do anything that is asked of her. It may take a little time, but I believe Susan will make a satisfactory substitute for yourself—in my mother's eyes. No one could ever be a substitute for you in my eyes." The look on Fanny's face as he said this tempted him to kiss her again, but a glance at the house showed him that they were in the direct line of vision of the breakfast-parlour. He contented himself with kissing her hand.

Suddenly Edmund laughed. "I wish Tom could have seen my proposal," he said.

"Do you?" said Fanny, rather startled.

"No, not really. But he does think me such a dull dog—he would have been shocked at my reckless application for your hand. And at the quantities of mistletoe berries that I picked up off the hall floor after you went to bed."

Tom was, at that moment, thinking that Edmund was a very dull dog indeed. Looking at them through the window, he was convinced that anyone could see how much regard they had for one another. If he hadn't known better, he could have thought them already deep in love.

"Look at the pair of them," he said to Susan. "They are perfect for one another, but Edmund is so completely a creature of habit that it has never occurred to him to think of Fanny in any other light than a friendly cousin. I fear nothing will shake him from this obstinate cast of mind."

"You think it hopeless?"

"It may well be." Tom sighed, and then after a moment shook his head. "No, I will not permit it! I will speak to him. At worst he can tell me to mind my own business, and at best it will reveal to him his own heart."

"A bold move," said Susan with approval. "When they return, I will sit with Fanny in the drawing room to be sure you can talk to Edmund privately."

Accordingly, when Edmund and Fanny came in, Susan begged Fanny to sit with her by the fire and tell her what had gone wrong in her needlework, and Tom followed Edmund to the library.

"A charming parsonage you have here," said Tom. "A good living, friendly neighbours, and a church in good repair. You don't seem to want for anything. Except, perhaps, a wife."

"A wife?" said Edmund, flushing slightly.

Tom noticed the change on his face, and it emboldened him to persevere. "I think you ought to realize that your ideal mate is even now under your very roof."

Edmund drew breath to explain how the matter stood, and then through his mind flashed all the boyish pranks Tom had perpetrated on him through the years. The desire to avenge himself for those times gripped him.

"Oh?" said Edmund, working to keep his face serious. "Under my very roof, is she? You mean Susan?"

"Susan! No, you blockhead! Fanny!"

Edmund did his best to feign surprise. "You think I ought to marry Fanny?"

"Of course you should! You ought to have realized it months ago."

"And what makes you believe she would have me?"

"She has great regard for you—anyone could see that. It would not surprise me at all to learn that she lost her heart to you long ago. Only she is so quiet and reserved, you would not be likely to notice. You are a fine fellow, you know, but you are a little too steady and unimaginative. Why—" he laughed shortly—"even if you did consider proposing to Fanny, it would probably take you a whole week to compose a speech for the occasion!"

"You think so, do you?"

"Lord, yes. You are so very predictable."

"Well, you may be right. And then again, you may be wrong. Should you care to come with me and see what Fanny says to your idea?"

"What, now?"

Edmund wanted to laugh at the stunned look on Tom's face, but preserved his gravity.

"Yes, now. Come!" He motioned to his brother and exited the library with purposeful steps. Tom trailed behind, wondering if he ought to urge him to stop and reflect a little, and thinking that perhaps he had not heard him correctly. He had never imagined that Edmund would react to his little speech like this!

Edmund strode into the drawing room, making Susan and Fanny look up in surprise from the needlework they were discussing. He stood before Fanny, trying to look solemn, but unable to keep a faint smile from his face.

"Fanny," he said with no preamble, "would you do me the honour of becoming my wife?"

Susan gasped aloud, and Tom stared with his eyes almost popping out of his head.

Fanny had not the least idea what was happening, but could not say anything less than the truth.

"Yes, I will."

"Thank you," said Edmund. Turning to his brother, he remarked, "I think you will find, Tom, that I am not always perfectly predictable. And now, if you will excuse us, I think there are a few mistletoe berries on the kissing bough that can be redeemed."

The End

Other books by Barbara Cornthwaite
can be found at Amazon.com

Charity Envieth Not: George Knightley is the owner of a considerable estate, a landlord, a magistrate, and a bachelor--a state that his brother John is perpetually prodding him to change. Thankfully, there is no one remotely suitable in his entire circle of acquaintance...or so he thinks. An unwanted interloper, a few romantic mishaps amongst his friends, and the dawning realization that Emma Woodhouse is no longer a child might just change everything.

Lend Me Leave. A rival for the hand of Emma Woodhouse has brought about George Knightley's realization of the true nature of his attachment to her. He is determined to win her in spite of Frank Churchill's charming ways, and he has only to figure out how to make her realize that they were meant for each other. As he joins the ranks of the heart-sore men of Donwell, hope grows ever more faint, but good news sometimes comes at the most unexpected moments.

A Fine Young Lady: When her mother's death plunges her into reduced circumstances, Verity Hollis must leave her life of ease and privilege in London and make her home in the small country village. Her dreams of marriage to a wealthy Christian man with status now seem impossible. With the comfort of her Bible and the amusement of her favorite novels to bolster her spirits, Verity embarks on a life she couldn't have imagined a year ago. Is her faith sufficient to sustain her in her new circumstances? Are her dreams of love, marriage, and family gone? An awkward Baptist minister, an orphaned baby or two, and a village of new friends help her discover what she truly values and the plans the Lord has made for her life

About the Authors

Robin Helm's time revolves around music as she dances (as badly as Mr. Collins), sings (a little better than Mary Bennet), plays (better than Marianne Dashwood – almost as well as Caroline Bingley), and teaches (channeling her inner Elinor). Her books reflect that love, as well as her fascination with the paranormal and science fiction.

Her latest publication is *Understanding Elizabeth*, in which Darcy must decide how much he's willing to pay to have what he wants. Previously published works include *The Guardian Trilogy* (Darcy is Elizabeth's guardian angel), and the *Yours by Design* series (Fitzwilliam Darcy switches places in time with his descendant, Will Darcy).

She lives in South Carolina and adores her one husband (Mr. Knightley), two married daughters (Elizabeth I and Elizabeth II), and three grandchildren.

Readers are loving **Laura Hile's** joyous Regency novels. Her signature style – intertwined plots, cliffhangers, and laugh-out-loud humor – keep them coming back for more.

The comedy Laura comes by as a teacher. There's never a dull moment with teen students!

She recently released *Darcy By Any Other Name*, a comic 'body swap' romance based on Jane Austen's *Pride and Prejudice*.

Laura lives in the Pacific Northwest with her husband and sons. Her fiction is for everyone, even teens.

Wendi Sotis lives on Long Island, NY, with her husband and triplets. While searching for *Pride and Prejudice* from Darcy's point of view, she became thoroughly enamored with Jane Austen Fan Fiction or JAFF. In early 2010, she dreamed an idea for a story and hasn't stopped writing since: *Promises, Dreams and Expectations*; *All Hallows Eve*; *The Keys for Love*; *Safekeeping*; *The Gypsy Blessing*; *Foundation of Love (The Gypsy Blessing 2)*; and *A Lesson Hard Learned*.

Some of her works-in-progress have branched away from JAFF to Regency Romance (*The Pact*, due to be released in 2018) and Contemporary Romantic Mysteries (the *Implicated* series). Wendi will also continue bringing Darcy and Lizzy together again and again in an unusual manner.

Barbara Cornthwaite lives in the middle of Ireland with her husband and children. She taught college English before "retiring" to do something she loves far more; her days are now filled with homeschooling her six children, trying to keep the house tidy (a losing battle), and trying to stay warm in the damp Irish climate (also a losing battle).

She is surrounded by medieval castles, picturesque flocks of sheep, and ancient stone monuments. These things are unappreciated by her children, who are more impressed by traffic jams, skyscrapers, and hot weather.

Barbara is the author of the *George Knightley, Esquire* series, and *A Fine Young Lady*.

Contact Us!

Robin Helm
Amazon Author Page:
>https://www.amazon.com/Robin-Helm/e/B005MLFMTG/

Website: Jane Started It!
>https://crownhillwriters.wordpress.com/robin-helm/

Twitter: @rmhelm
Facebook: Robin Helm or Jane Started It!
Instagram: jrhelm
Goodreads: Robin_M_Helm
Blogging: Jane Started It! https://crownhillwriters.wordpress.com/
http://BeyondAusten.com

Laura Hile
Amazon Author Page:
>https://www.amazon.com/Laura-Hile/e/B003UT6VDS/

Website: Jane Started It!
>https://crownhillwriters.wordpress.com/laura-hile/

Blogging at: Jane Started It! https://crownhillwriters.wordpress.com/
>and https://laurahile.wordpress.com/

Twitter: @LauraHile
Facebook: LauraHileAuthor or Jane Started It!

Wendi Sotis
Amazon Author Page:
>https://www.amazon.com/Wendi-Sotis/e/B005CSBVFS/

Website: http://wendisotis.com
Facebook: Wendi Sotis, Author
Twitter: @WendiSotis
http://BeyondAusten.com

Barbara Cornthwaite
Amazon Author Page:
>https://www.amazon.com/Barbara-Cornthwaite/e/B00J47TTZM/

Website: Jane Started It!
>https://crownhillwriters.wordpress.com/barbara-cornthwaite/

Facebook: Jane Started It!

Made in the USA
Columbia, SC
11 September 2018